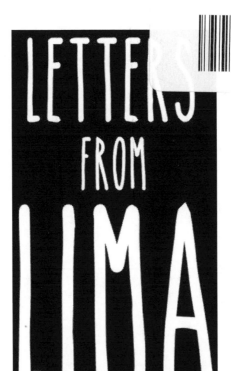

LETTERS FROM LIMA

a novel

SHAUN RANDALL

UBP
UNBINDED PUBLISHING

For media inquiries, appearances, information about permission to
reproduce selections from this book, and large orders:
info@shaun-randall.com

www.shaun-randall.com

Author Shaun Randall

Cover Design and Artwork by Leonardo Flores
Illustrations by Rosa Briceño Perdomo

Editor Jacqueline Pinchuk

ISBN: 978-1-73708242-2
Library of Congress Control Number: 2022919345

LETTERS FROM LIMA
1 234567890

UBP
UNBINDED PUBLISHING

FOR

Lima, all of Perú, and its people.

My reason for going there, Eliet.

Anyone who has ever wondered what life would be like if…

PRELUDE

LIMA

I once believed Heaven
Was perched in the clouds
Much like Lima
But with far less crowds

Civilizing the desert
And watering the sand
On the shoulders of the ancients
Our modernity stands

Part One - Carolina and a Canary

Interlude - Take Your Shot

Part Two - The Dreams We Remember

PART ONE

CAROLINA AND A CANARY

ONE

WHEN IN ROME

Miraflores District

I
t had been one helluva day. Not that day—not yet anyway—but it seemed like every year on that same godforsaken day something would thwart my hopes and dreams. My ex-wife miscarried on that day. Then she left me a year later. The next year I lost my job. DUI the following, and so the litany continued.

I'm not an astrologist, yet it was starting to sink in that the universe was telling me to just crawl under a rock on December 13th. But it was my birthday, and I wanted to go out.

So I went to the bar at Tanta in Larcomar. I descended into the luxury outdoor mall carved into Lima's oceanfront cliffs overlooking the Pacific. As I approached the bar, a resplendent young woman shouted less than resplendently, "Proximity! Mother! Fucker!" into her phone.

I took my usual spot at the bar. It should have been a safe distance from someone who, at first glance, appeared not to know how to take a vacation. At any rate, she was done with the call I'd overheard because everyone in the entire mall had overheard it.

"Sorry, everyone! I was trying to explain to my idiot ex-boyfriend why I'm here in Lima trying to locate my estranged uncle who lives, wait for it, in Lima," the interloper announced with exasperation.

"Who's drinking? Pisco sour please!" She ordered a cóctel as she smiled vividly and cocked her head to the right. She paused briefly before she tossed her dark hair over her shoulder and turned in my direction. "When in Rome, right?! What are you drinking, sailor? Got that Old-Man-and-the-Sea look going. Classic. Love it!"

"How do you know he's a sailor?" asked a young man eager to get into a conversation with the woman who had clearly never met a stranger.

"The rugged gentleman looks like The World's Most Interesting Man if he were going out on a chartered fishing yacht. It's a Hemingway reference. He looks like—never mind." The refined respite from the usual clientele could have been explaining string theory for all this kid knew.

"He wants to ask you which direction a Hemingway is," I blurted out. "El Mago, por favor, un mojito para un amigo," I politely asked the bartender, my friend, Javier, for a drink. El Mago was a magician with his cóctels, among other things.

"You are him!" she said before turning her attention back to the dope in the golf shirt and salmon-colored shorts.

"Hemingway, in addition to being known for his handsome beard, was a writer. He wrote books." She converted her Versace sunglasses into a hair accessory and set her Louis Vitton handbag on a stool next to the bar.

"Books are like websites, but they're printed on paper. Hemingway came to Perú when they filmed a movie—you've heard of those—based on his book *The Old Man and The Sea*. I hear he caught a 700-pound marlin, by the way. Now get lost guppy." She finished dismantling the poor fella.

Javier smirked while he finished making our cóctels. He raised his eyebrows as he looked to the side to make eye contact with me, and I smiled back. *Yes, I think she's wonderful too.* My heart rate elevated slightly as the winsome woman snagged a cardboard coaster from the bar rail, flung it in my direction, and took a thorough sip of her Pisco sour while simultaneously sliding into the stool next to me.

"Allow me to introduce myself. I'm Carolyn Grant," she said.

"Charmed." It was as disinterested as I could pretend to be.

"And you are? Como te llamas? Ernesto?" Carolyn expected me to follow social norms and introduce myself too.

"Collin Allweather. Larcomarvelous to meet you. When was the first time you realized you could get everything you wanted Carolyn Grant?"

She deftly placed her fingers atop my outstretched right hand, gave a gentle squeeze with her thumb, and with a mischievous look and tone of voice asked, "Everything?"

Javi jumped in to introduce himself. "Javier at your service here. Would la señorita y el señor like to peruse the menu? Our piqueos are perfect with your cóctels. Perhaps a Pastel de Pollo or Pastel de Choclo? Please don't forget our Ceviche Clásico is almost mandatory." El Mago performed like never before.

"Javi, you've never once offered me a menu." I pointed out his favoritism.

"Señor Collin, that is because you are an alcoholic only here for the vino and cóctels, and of course, you know the menu so well," Javier said.

"Señorita, I'm kidding of course. He doesn't know the menu at all." El Mago cracked himself and Carolyn up.

"I can see I am outnumbered as usual," I said.

"That is because, as usual, you are here by yourself, Señor Allweather." Javi kept the jokes coming, while also making sure Carolyn knew I was single. For once in my life being alone seemed like it might go in the plus column.

"I found my new favorite bartender!" Carolyn declared.

"Evidently, height is not a requirement for that position," I said.

Javi was used to ignoring my short jokes. "And I found our new favorite guest! How long are you with us in Lima for?"

"Six days," she said.

"Señorita, six days in Lima, or will you be going to Machu Picchu as well?" Javi inquired further.

"Just Lima," Carolyn said.

"If you don't mind me saying, Señorita, that is very unusual. Wouldn't you like to see Perú's wonder of the world?" Javier asked.

Carolyn replied, "I'd love to, but it will have to be another time. I'm here searching for an estranged uncle. Wow, that word sounds awful when it comes out of your mouth."

"Well, if he isn't in contact with your family, he's estranged," I said, being intimately familiar with the experience.

"Yep, still sounds awful. My grandmother left a jewelry box behind when she moved to the States with my grandfather, and she's certain the box will still be at my uncle's house. I tried finding his contact info before I came. Can you believe this guy isn't on the internet?" Carolyn shrugged her shoulders and took a sip of her Pisco Sour.

"Señor Collin isn't on the internet either, but he refuses to tell me why. What do you think is in the box?" Javi asked.

"No idea. My grandmother just said, 'Find your uncle, Tío Dan. Get the box, don't open the box, and bring it back. There's something inside it for your mother,'" Carolyn replied.

"You have an estranged tío here in Perú. Isn't that interesting? Don't you think that is very interesting, Señor Collin?" El Mago asked.

"Your parents have never come to Perú and met your uncle, or anyone else, in the family?" I asked.

"My grandfather, before he passed away, always forbade it. He would say, 'There is absolutely no reason to go there. We left that desert and its dirt behind.' I asked my mom about it, and her guess is maybe my grandfather got cut out of the estate because he moved to the States. Families, right?" Carolyn took in a mouthful of her drink.

"How did you get picked to come down here and find your uncle?" I asked.

"I'm pretty sure my grandmother asked my mom first, but it came down to me or my sister. My grandmother said she can't trust my sister to keep her mouth shut, so here I am," Carolyn replied.

"Loose lips sink ships," I said.

"That's right, sailor! I'm glad someone understands loyalty and trustworthiness." Carolyn patted me on the back.

"Same. I'm sure your sister has some good qualities too," I said.

"No, that's true. She's sweet. Really sweet, if there's something she wants. Sincere and honest too, unless it's not convenient for her. Loyal as well, that is, unless of course she can benefit from betraying you." Her voice alternated between upbeat and disappointed.

"Sounds like you're a big fan," I said.

"She's the kind of sister that will flirt with your boyfriend. Then if the boyfriend cheats on you with her, she'll explain how she did you a favor because your boyfriend didn't really love you, and you were just wasting your time anyway," Carolyn said.

"She's not entirely wrong about that," I said.

"No. But what if it was a spouse instead of someone you were dating?" Carolyn asked.

"Sounds like it's happened before. Did your sister hook up with one of your boyfriends?" I asked.

"The first time was in high school, the day before prom. You know every girl wants to go to prom by themselves. Then again, while I was at law school. So yes, it's happened, and no, we aren't going to talk about Jacquelyn anymore." Carolyn finished her Pisco sour and ordered another.

"Ok, so where are you from?" I asked.

"I'm from Chicago. She's probably fucking my ex Landon now," Carolyn said.

"Chicago! Señor Collin is from Chicago! What a crazy coincidence?! Loca! Is this The Candy Camera!?" Javi excitedly asked while looking over one shoulder and then the other.

"Should I tell him, or do you want to?" Carolyn asked me, while also seemingly uninspired by the revelation that we were both from Chicago.

"I've tried telling him. You give it a try. Javier is proud of his English," I implored Carolyn.

"He should be. It's damn near perfect. Much better than your Spanish, Bubba. Javier, it's Candid Camera." Carolyn explained to Javi by emphasizing the did part of candid.

"Yes, what did I say? Candy Camera, no?" Javier confirmed with glowing confidence.

"I think he is saying it that way on purpose," Carolyn said.

"You're quick," I said.

"Señor Collin, tell her it is very funny. Carolyn, it is a very funny bit. Is this The Candy Camera?" Javi said while looking over his left and then right shoulder before letting out a big laugh.

"Hilarious Javi." I rolled my eyes.

"Hey! I got one. What did the ghost say to the bartender that offered them a food menu? I'll pause briefly in order for you to consider your answers gentlemen. Nothing? Ok. I'm just here for the boos. Get it B-O-O-S!" Carolyn spelled the pun.

"A Halloween joke! What? Am I on The Candy Camera?!" Javier was palms up looking left and right again.

They roared with laughter. They infected each other, and my silence apparently wasn't the cure.

"So what do you do for a living?" Carolyn asked.

"I hate that question," I said.

"Let's pretend for a moment that your disdain for normal questions people ask when they meet isn't relevant." Carolyn opened her big brown eyes even wider and asked, "Now can you muster up the strength for an answer?" Carolyn reminded me I was only allowed to feel socially awkward and not express that feeling out loud with words.

"I work with my hands," I said.

"Ah, I see, a real tradesman."

"Yes! How did you guess?"

"Guess what?" Carolyn asked.

"I am a trader."

"What do you trade?"

"Futures, and stock options."

"No wonder you drink so much," Carolyn said.

"No, that's because Javi overserves me," I said.

"I have done no such thing, Señor Collin," Javier said.

"Hemingway drank a lot," Carolyn said.

"You know an awful lot about Hemingway. Do you know he ended up committing suicide?" I asked and cringed inside realizing I had inadvertently opened Pandora's box.

"Why, Collin? Is talking to me so bad that you're thinking about taking your own life?" Carolyn asked as she checked her phone.

I was trying to wrap my brain around why in the hell I did something so stupid and bring up suicide. Carolyn looked up from her phone and grinned at me, with the exact same look as a cat when it catches a canary.

"What is behind that mischievous grin? Or do I want to know?" I asked, hoping to get away without answering her as to whether I was suicidal or not. Good lord, that would have gone down a rabbit hole.

"Looks like I have more than an hour to kill. My Tinder date just canceled on me for tonight," Carolyn explained.

"That guy is a real dope!" I was trying to be empathetic, but I might have come off a little too excited.

"She, is definitely not a dope. She, had to take her dog to the vet for an emergency." Carolyn corrected both of my idiotic assumptions.

I knew I was on the verge of being viewed as mediocre, so I went big. "I'd let my dog die before I canceled a date with you."

"Real animal lover aren't you?" Carolyn asked.

"Looking for love on Tinder, huh?" I asked.

"You know what they say, you find love when you aren't looking for it, or something like that."

"When you least expect it."

"What?" Carolyn asked.

"You find love when you least expect it. That's what they say," I said.

"I wouldn't say I expect to find love on Tinder—or in a bar in Lima, Perú for that matter," she said.

"Collin, would you like to go out with me tonight?" Carolyn asked the best question ever.

"I thought you'd never ask. And, we are out. And, it is tonight. So if you need some kind of formal response, then yes. I would love to." I over responded, as per usual.

"Collin, I'm sorry, but Carolyn can't go out with you tonight," she said while making a pouty face before continuing, "But, Carolina would love to get into all kinds of trouble with you tonight!" Carolyn's face smiled radiantly, as she explained.

"Where is Carolina? Does she have pets?" I torted.

"Why? Do you have allergies?" Carolyn retorted.

"Collin, Carolyn is what my team members at work call me.

Tonight, I am Carolina. It's my vacation name! Got it, Bubba?" Carolina poked me in the chest and clarified.

"Got it. Next time you see her, let Carolyn know it was great meeting her," I said.

Carolina had just caught her canary.

TWO

DECEMBER 13TH, 2019 EDITION

I couldn't put my finger on it, but something made me want to get to know this dynamo from Chicago. Could someone really have that much self-confidence? It's possible to pretend to have that much confidence—I did it all the time.

Carolyn asked Javier to order some food for us and have it come out poco a poco. I told him to make sure to give Carolyn a proper introduction to Lima cuisine by including the Ceviche Clásico and the Causa Limeña, which is made with chicken salad and avocado pressed between two round cold mashed potato cakes.

"So, you're a trader. Do you want to talk about the market?" Carolyn asked.

"No, not really," I replied and asked, "What would you like to talk about?"

"I'm a politics junkie!" she answered.

Javier kept a keen ear in our conversation and intervened, "Isn't there something besides Collin's work or politics we can talk about?"

"You're right. We're sorry," I apologized.

"He is sorry. We didn't get to talk about politics at all," Carolyn said with a sad face.

"We can talk about religion if you would like to since you are an angel and all." I said ever so sweetly.

"Aww, she's swooning," Carolyn said with a smile.

"She should be drinking," Javi said, as he placed a fresh Pisco Sour in front of Carolyn.

We finished eating, and Carolyn wanted to see what else was around so we wandered out into Larcomar to see what would strike her fancy.

"Seriously, I have to go to Friday's in Lima!" she said, grabbing my arm and darting towards the restaurant with me in tow.

"I promise you. It isn't any better here than in the States," I said while trying to catch up and not trip.

We found our way to the bar, and Carolyn ordered another Pisco Sour. I needed something stronger and ordered Jameson. "Easy on the rocks, and fill it up."

"Is that a Michael Jordan statue?" Carolyn asked pointing across the restaurant.

"Obviously, that is a statue, and I believe that it is, in fact, in the likeness of Michael Jordan," I said.

"We have to take a picture with it!"

"Not happening."

"Come on! My dad played with him, and I always take selfies in front of any and all things MJ to send to my dad. Then I text, 'Here I am with the second-greatest player of all time.' Take the photo with me, and I'll get these drinks." Carolyn sold me.

"Who is the greatest player of all time?" I asked as we posed in front of the statue.

"Number 54, Carolyn Grant, starting point guard, Northwestern Wildcats!" Carolyn responded as she snapped the photo.

As we went back to the bar I said, "Tell me about your grandmother. Are you close with her?"

"Yes! I absolutely adore mi Abuela Rosa! I was basically raised by my grandparents. My dad left when I was 5, and my mom tried but wasn't super domestic. Abuela Rosa was the one who taught me how to read, how to dance, how to sing, how to tie my shoes, and just about everything growing up. Every night she would tuck me into bed, read me a story, and say a prayer with me." Carolyn stirred her drink and smiled.

"She sounds really sweet," I said.

"She's more than sweet. It's hard for me to put into words what she means to me. Here's a picture of her and me when I graduated from Northwestern. I keep it on my screen saver to remind myself everything I have ever accomplished is because of her." Carolyn passed me her phone.

"And she grew up here in Lima?" I asked.

"She grew up in Venezuela. She moved here to work as a chef for my grandfather's family. They got married, moved to the U.S. for him to attend medical school in Chicago, and had mi mamá less than nine months after they arrived. If ya know what I mean!" Carolyn explained and punctuated her sentence with two big winks.

"Nothing like an unplanned pregnancy to really pull a family together," I said.

"Which is another benefit of dating the same sex while on vacation in a foreign country," Carolina re-introduced herself as she got up and went to el baño.

When she came back she said, "Hey, my date from before messaged when I was in the ladies' room. Her dog is doing much better, and she can come out now."

"You declined, right?" I had the impression the night was going pretty well.

"Presumptuous much? No, I invited her to join us." Carolyn obviously had a different opinion.

"Join us, or *join us*?" I tried to stay positive.

"Easy tiger. Keep the snake in the tank," Carolyn replied.

"Got it. Hey, it occurred to me, while you were en el baño, there's a pizzeria named Tío Dan I get take out from sometimes," I said.

"No way! That can't be just a coincidence!" Carolyn said.

"Probably not. It does seem like quite a coincidence that you met a guy at a bar who gets takeout from a pizzeria with the same name as the estranged uncle you're looking for, though," I said.

"I have a feeling that isn't just a coincidence either," Carolyn said as her date arrived, tapped her on the shoulder, and—keeping with the December 13th tradition—interrupted our conversation. Carolyn stood up, and they greeted each other with an embrace and a kiss on each cheek. It was immediately obvious to me there was no way I was going to be able to handle the situation.

After Carolyn introduced us, I said, "I'm gonna head home."

"Really? You're welcome to hang out for a little bit." Carolyn was just being polite.

"I'm going to quit while I'm ahead. But take my number. I'll poke my head into the pizzeria tomorrow and see if I can find out if it's your uncle's place," I said and gave Carolyn my number.

As I stood up to leave, an enraged young man charged in our direction screaming at Carolyn's date. She stood up and started screaming back. When he came within inches of her face she started flailing with both hands at his head. I couldn't understand what they were saying en Español, but it didn't take a genius either to quickly realize Carolyn's date was cheating on her boyfriend. He pushed Carolyn's date backward, and Carolyn caught her.

I stepped in front of him to try to calm him down and said, "Amigo! Tranquilo, tranquilo!"

He punched me square in the eye, and I tumbled backward over a barstool. As soon as I hit the ground he kicked me square in the side of the ribs. I looked up to see his thigh tattoos and bleached blonde hair and knew immediately I'd be in trouble if I stayed on the ground for this footballer to take free kicks. I'd been in this situation at home as a kid many times and knew the only way to survive was to interrupt the attacker's train of thought.

"Señor Juan Carlos esta en el baño!" I shouted.

He stopped mid-kick and asked, "Quien es Señor Juan Carlos?"

I scissor-kicked through his ankles and took him to the ground. Before he knew what happened, I had him neutralized in a sleeper hold.

"Hush, hush now," I whispered in his ear as the blood streaming from the cut on the side of my eye stained his blonde head.

Mall security came rushing in just about the same time I had my attacker put down for his nap. Carolyn's date explained what happened. Carolyn got a towel with some ice in it from the bartender and eased it against my bleeding and swollen eye.

"Are you ok?" she asked.

"Fucking December 13th," I said.

THREE

THE WRONG BAG

After the prior evening's squirmish was sorted out, Carolyn went back to her hotel, and I took a taxi to the hospital to get stitched up. As I finished my second vodka with tomato juice with one hand and poured my first cup of coffee with the other, a text notification popped up.

"What'd you have planned for today?" The message read.

"Other than responding to texts from strangers, not much," I sent back.

"It's Carolyn from last night. There are some ancient ruins right in the middle of the city. I thought I'd check those out." I read her text out loud.

"Huaca Pucllana," I sent back.

Carolyn texted, "Huaca whatever, do you want to tag along? After last night I figure you've earned a shot at the title!"

"Pucllana. I'm in. What time?" I accepted the invitation and my fate as I poured a shot of whisky into my coffee.

Huaca Pucllana Ancient Ruins

An hour later, stitched up eye and all, I was a ball of nerves in front of the entrance to Huaca Pucllana. When Carolyn arrived, I paid the small entrance fee and also for an English-speaking tour guide. It was apparent last night that Carolyn was fully bilingual, but I needed English to easily understand the explanation of the site. Before the tour started, we walked through the little museo that had exhibits showing the history of the site, the customs and daily rituals of those who lived there, and some artifacts from the original Lima culture. Indigenous people who built the massive pyramid and surrounding area around 1500 years before our scheduled tour time.

Our guide had a sacredness in his voice as he described his indigenous ancestors the Wari, Yscha, Chimú, and Lima tribes. The primary deity they worshiped was Mama Killa, Mother Moon. While we traversed our way to the top of the adobe and clay block pyramid, we could see all around Lima. At close range we had the modern residential and hotel towers in Miraflores, the tall office buildings of the financial district San Isidro, and a view to the north towards the Spanish Colonial historical district Centro. Hilly desert ridges surrounded this area along the Pacific Ocean. Once governed by the Inka Empire, the independent and free Republic of Perú, controlled them now. Lima's dense population required departemento buildings sprawling all the way up their sides to the south through San Juan de Miraflores and Chorrillos, with its dramatic oceanfront lookout mount El Morro.

We learned lots about Lima and Peruvian culture together.

"It's so weird. I really know almost nothing about this place where my grandfather's family is from," Carolyn said.

"My grandfather's family is from Ireland, and I don't know much about Ireland," I related.

"I'm just really glad I'm here. I hope I can find Tío Dan, but I also want to find out more about where I come from," she said as the tour guide pointed to a small coca bush beside the path.

He proudly told the group, "Diego Maradona picked and sampled a coca leaf from this exact bush while he toured Huaca Pucllana!"

The group chuckled, and our guide quickly shifted from a naughty grin to a meek expression while explaining, "Peruvian people, we don't use coca that way—for a party or to get high or something—but only for important cultural and spiritual purposes."

Carolyn nudged my arm with her elbow while whispering out of the side of her mouth, "Is this guy for real? And who is Diego Maradona?"

"He is for real. He assumes you had powdered doughnuts for breakfast," I said a millisecond before Carolyn punched me hard directly in the shoulder. I recoiled to the side as the memories of being hit with any solid object within an arm's reach of my mom flashed in my mind. This was a love tap by comparison to the beatings my mother insisted were for my own good. I dismissed the memories as quickly as they came. I hoped my facial expression hadn't shown weakness, and explained, "Diego Maradona was the most successful and famous footballer of his time."

Carolyn's raised eyebrows indicated she was still trying to figure out why we were told about a bush.

"Football is what the entire world, except the United States, calls a game played with a ball using only your feet," I continued.

Carolyn interrupted, "Collin, I played soccer at Northwestern too."

"Diego is famous for many reasons. He was notorious for a voracious appetite for scoring goals, chicks, and blow." I wanted Carolyn to have the whole picture.

"Sounds like a combination of Michael Jordan and Dennis Rodman. Why haven't I heard of this guy?" Carolyn wondered out loud.

"They didn't have replays in sports, and they didn't use social media back then either," I joked.

"I bet he would've been a great wingman in his prime, assuming he could keep up with me," Carolina added.

"I am more than sure he could keep up. This story, about him picking a coca leaf, has to be the least interesting Diego Maradona story of all time. In his prime, he was basically the most interesting man in the world," I said.

"Because he played sports and used drugs? Sounds like everyone I've ever met in a bar in Chicago. Would you consider yourself the world's most interesting man now?" Carolyn asked.

"Definitely not. I heard once that people find you interesting when you are interested in them," I said.

"No wonder I am so fascinated by you," she said.

I had no response to that and only rolled my eyes as Carolyn continued, "Seriously, you're obsessed. You need to get a grip."

I told her, "You get a grip."

Parque Kennedy

We finished the tour, and I recommended we walk over to nearby Parque Kennedy. Things seemed to be going well, and I wanted to extend our date.

"Is this the park with all the cats?" she asked in delighted anticipation.

"It is," I said as we approached the entrance.

"Can you pet them?" Carolyn asked while scanning the fertile green lawns and abundant flower beds for feline friends.

"They're cats. You can pet them, but that is subject to change, with or without notice," I said as Carolyn scampered toward a fluffy, ginger calico that sunned itself on a bench. Carolyn grazed the back of her hand on top of its head, down its curved spine as it elevated its back, and finished with a hand full of tail. Within seconds, dos mas gatos came out of the flower bed behind the bench and hopped up with Carolyn and the ginger feline.

As she stroked them, all three cats purred. She looked up at me with a proud devilish grin and said, "Stick with me, Bubba. I'll show you how to get all the gatitas."

I stretched out my arms with open hands, and in a voice of desperation said to the cats and anyone else who cared to listen, "Love me, please love me!"

The cats recoiled, sprung off the bench, and darted in every direction except into my arms.

We walked around perusing the various art displays from local artists gathered in the park. As we went, Carolyn caressed, cuddled, and named most of the 100 or so cats living in Parque Kennedy.

"I'm getting hungry, is there a good place for lunch we can walk to?" Carolyn asked.

"Lots of them, but I have a better idea," I said.

"What's that?" she asked.

"How about we grab a taxi and check out Tío Dan's?" I asked.

"Two birds, one stone. I like where your head's at Allweather. Is the pizza any good?" she asked.

"Next question," I said.

"Are you saying my uncle's pizza isn't any good?" Carolyn asked.

"There's lots of great pizza places here in Lima, on par with Chicago's best places, but Tío Dan's is not one of them," I said.

"Sad face," she said.

"I wanted to make sure expectations were set appropriately," I said.

"Favorite food you miss the most from Chicago, go!" Carolyn prompted me.

"Portillo's," I said without hesitation.

"What's your order?" she asked.

"Chicago dog, chili cheese dog, beef and cheddar croissant, large crinkle fries with a cup of cheese, and a chocolate cake shake —or a slice of lemon cake when they have it," I rattled off. A day's worth of food I would consume in one coma-inducing sitting.

"We can maybe have babies together one day." Carolyn was evidently proud of me.

"I've been meaning to ask you. No kids with your ex or anything, right?" I asked awkwardly.

"Oh hell no! What about you? Any kids, Collin?" Carolyn asked while laughing loudly.

"No. Almost, once. Never mind. I hope maybe one day," I said.

"That's why I broke it off with my ex. He wanted to get married and start a family, and that is not at all where I am at right now. I'm focused on my career. I see other women balance career and family, but I'd rather be all in on my career," Carolyn said.

"Yeah, I'm not sure I'm willing to sacrifice my time and freedom."

"Then don't have kids, Collin."

"Like I said, maybe one day. Let's get a taxi." I waved my hand into the—hopefully—distant future.

I directed the driver to Pizzería Tío Dan in Barranco. We seated ourselves at one of the red and white checkered tables, and when el mesero approached with menus, Carolyn wasted no time and asked, "Quien es Tío Dan?"

El mesero stared back blankly before Carolyn asked again, "El dueño del restaurante es Tío Dan, no?"

"No sé, Señorita." The young man didn't know who owned el restaurante.

"Tu no sabes. Ya, puedes buscar a alguien que sepa?" Carolyn asked him to find someone who knew.

We both liked pepperoni and mushrooms, so we were quick to decide on what to order while we waited for el mesero to return. He said he asked around, but no one knew who Tío Dan was. No one with that name ever was around. He told us the manager would be in tomorrow during the day, and he might know.

"Back to square one it sounds like," Carolyn said.

"We'll find him." I tried to sound reassuring.

It was a long shot, but I thought things were going well. I asked Carolyn if she wanted to do something later.

"What did you have in mind? I feel like the clock is ticking on finding my uncle," she said.

"You've got four days. Tomorrow we'll come back by here and talk to the manager. I'm sure this's gotta be his place," I reassured Carolyn.

"Gotta be, right? I also want to make sure we're on the same page about what we're doing here as well. I'm having a great time with you, but I don't hook up with guys I've met twice while I'm on vacation," Carolyn communicated.

"Does Carolina?" I smiled.

"That's what I mean. I don't want you to have the wrong impression from last night, even before her psycho boyfriend showed up, I wouldn't have hooked up with that girl on the first date," Carolyn said.

"I'm kidding. I don't have the wrong impression, but I'm having a good time getting to know you," I said.

"Me too. But Collin, see if you can find an eye patch or something. Let's try to cut down on the number of reasons people have to gawk at us," Carolyn said.

"And me looking like a pirate will not add to the list?" I asked.

Carolyn laughed and said, "You would totally look like a pirate. However, that's better than looking like you were in a UFC fight last night."

"I don't look like I was in a UFC fight last night," I said.

"You look like you lost a UFC fight last night," she said.

"But what matters is we know I won the bout," I said.

"Yes, you definitely are working your way up the rankings," Carolyn said with a smile.

Centro District

After lunch, I had gone back to my place to have a few glasses of scotch and a nap. Carolyn had gone back to her hotel to catch up on some work but ended up going out and about to see more of the city. So we decided to meet at the entrance to Circuito Mágico del Agua in the Centro district of Lima. The park sat adjacent to the massive national stadium, surrounded by several museums and lots of incredible Colonial- and Republican-era architecture. The park offered all kinds of different water attractions with lights and music like the fountain at Caesar's Palace in Vegas. We enjoyed a stroll around the park. The grand finale was just after sundown when there was an incredible laser light show projected onto towering sheets of water. The show was truly magical.

After the show, we grabbed a taxi to head back to Miraflores for dinner and drinks. The fresh night air gently blew through the taxi's wide open windows as we slowly crept in the typical Lima traffic snarl. A few blocks into the ride, we were at a dead stop, inhaling noxious fumes behind a large semi-truck.

"What the fuck?!" Carolyn shouted as the wiry arms of a thief shot through the open window to snag Carolyn's handbag. She tugged her purse back like she was fighting for a rebound and pulled the head and torso of the thief into the car as they struggled. He was frenzied, a deep burgundy flush stretched over his bony face and frame. When Carolyn put up a fight it must have startled him. Like a wild animal that was more afraid of us than we were of him as he grappled with Carolyn for her bag.

When he threatened to stab her, I threw—and barely landed—

the worst punch of my life on the side of his face. The glancing blow phased him only for a second, and he lunged back toward Carolyn's abdomen for the bag. I started wailing on the backs of his arms to break his grip. He let go of the bag and went back through the window.

Then the bandit reached back in and opened the door from the inside. He swung around to come into the car for one more all-out attempt for Carolyn's bag, which she now cradled like a football. I charged head first over Carolyn to grab this sonuvabitch and make up for the weak jab that barely scratched him. He let go of the bag and sprinted off like a skin-and-bones jackrabbit darting through cars backed up in four-way traffic.

Carolyn grabbed the door through the open window and slammed it shut as the driver finally began to pull forward. As I fell back to my side, she said postemptively, "Don't even think about it!"

"Roll up your window!" Carolyn shouted as she was already doing the same.

"Are you ok?" I asked as the adrenaline that went unnoticed during the attack now pounded my heart out of my chest.

"I'm ok. Oh my god, you're bleeding!" Carolyn exclaimed while picking up my left hand to look at it.

"I think I caught his teeth. Are you ok physically? You didn't hurt your hands or arms or anything?" I asked.

"I'm a bit numb right now from the adrenaline, but I think I'm fine," Carolyn said taking a quick look down at her arms still clutching her bag. Her body language suggested she wasn't fine, but she had her game face on.

"He picked the wrong car, with the wrong bag, to try and take from the wrong girl," I said trying to process what had just happened.

"The wrong girl, with the right guy next to her. Nice job, Bubba," Carolyn said as she leaned into me.

"That was all you. I don't even know what just happened," I said.

"Fight or flight mode. It's good to know how you'll respond to scary situations in the future. You're two for two," Carolyn said as she slowly released her bag and reached down to take my hand with both of hers.

"Do you want to just go back to your hotel and call it a night?" I asked.

"No, the same thing could've happened in Chicago, and I wouldn't go home," she said.

"She's a trooper," I said.

Miraflores

We slunk down the stairs into Larcomar and went to Mangos. The restaurant sat on top of a cliff overlooking the Pacific Ocean while waves rolled on and off the Lima shoreline. When we arrived, the Maître d' told us that my regular table would be available in about 15 minutes. I assured Carolyn it was worth the wait, and we found a comfortable place in the lounge to peruse the cóctel menu.

Carolyn ordered the Chaufa, a Peruvian Chinese fusion fried rice. I got the club sandwich and ordered two shots of Pisco and a bottle of rosé. I was in my element.

As we ate, she told me about her childhood growing up in downtown Chicago and going to Catholic school. Her undergrad years at Northwestern and how hard she worked to get her law degree from Harvard. After school, she passed the bar on her first try but had gotten involved as a partner for a tech start-up that she was very proud of. When they accepted a fantastic offer to be acquired, Carolyn began working in a senior executive capacity for the company that had acquired them.

It was incredible that she had accomplished so much at such a young age, but as I listened to her, it wasn't surprising at all. The book matched the cover. She was a genuine and authentic person, maximizing her potential and unapologetically enjoying life. I knew I didn't have a chance with a woman of Carolyn's caliber, and I should probably quit while I was ahead. There was something happening between us though. No matter how hard I tried, I couldn't resist the urge to be with her. Like steam emanating from bubbling hot pizza, all the warning signs were visible. It didn't matter. I was willing to blister the roof of my mouth to find out how good it would taste.

Of course, hearts don't heal as fast as burnt skin.

After we ate, I told Carolyn I would hail a taxi to head home and drop her at her hotel on the way.

"I'm not really in a hurry to get into another taxi at the moment, thanks. My hotel is right around the corner anyway. Walk with me?" Carolyn asked.

"I'd love to," I said.

We walked out of Larcomar and along the malecón listening to the sound of the waves crashing into the shore below. We arrived at The Miraflores Park Belmond where Carolyn was staying. Even for me, this would have been quite a spend, but I resisted the urge to ask and just knew Carolyn liked nice things.

As we approached the entrance, Carolyn asked, "Walk me up?"

"Sure. It would be my pleasure," I said.

"Thanks. I hate coming back to a hotel by myself at this hour. Inevitably, some drunk creep gets in the elevator at the same time. Then he just stares at the lit button for your floor in between attempts to check you out in the elevator mirrors," she explained.

"I have quite literally never had that happen to me," I said with a laugh.

"That's because, usually, you are the drunk creep." Carolyn may or may not have been kidding.

We got in the elevator and Carolyn pushed the button for her floor. We stood side by side, and I kept my eyes averted to the ceiling.

"Collin, I was kidding. You can look at what floor I'm on," Carolyn said with her head tilted to the side, batting her eyelashes up and down.

"No, I'm good," I politely responded.

"It's the top one." Carolyn wanted me to know.

We got out of the elevator and made our way down the hotel hallway toward Carolyn's room. We arrived in front of the door, and I thought about attempting to give her a goodnight kiss. But I was there because she was still a little shaken by the attempted robbery, not because she wanted someone to make a move on her.

So there we were, standing in front of her room out of excuses to keep extending our day together.

"Well, this has been one helluva day," I said.

"Yes, it has. I had a nice time with you today, Collin," she responded.

"It was nice. So tomorrow, do you want to tag back up to try Tío Dan's again?" I asked with a touch of hesitation.

"I'd like that," Carolyn answered without the slightest reservation.

"Then it's decided." I smiled.

"Goodnight, Collin." Carolyn gave me an escape.

"Yes, goodnight," I said, trying to take it. I didn't really want to leave, but I slowly turned and walked back down the hall toward the elevator. Carolyn slid the key card in and disappeared into her room.

I didn't hear the door latch, and every fiber of my being wanted to quickly turn back around. I heard the door creak back open, so I turned and blurted out, "Maybe brunch tomorrow? Is that too soon?"

"Not soon enough. I have wine." Carolina responded. All I could see was her face, as her neck was wrapped around the door frame. I casually walked back, and as I neared the door, Carolina's bare arm extended out as she offered her hand. We clasped hands, and I slithered through the narrowly opened door behind her. In her other hand, there was a nice bottle of red wine. I couldn't see what varietal or vintner it was, but one thing was for sure.

"Carolina."

"Yes, Collin."

"There's too much wine in that bottle."

"Would you like a glass?" she asked as she plunged and twisted the corkscrew into the bottle.

"No. It comes in one," I said as I reached for the bottle.

Carolina gave me an admiring smile as the neck of the bottle slid through her grip.

FOUR

THE BRIDGE OF SIGHS

I sipped on my coffee, took a seat on the sofa in Carolyn's suite, and noticed her notebook on the coffee table. I took a look. She had a list of everything she wanted to do while in Lima and a separate column for each day with the subheadings: Desayuno, Almuerzo, Cena, and Bailar. Apparently, she had mapped out all the meals and activities she wanted to accomplish for the week. Tanta and Huaca Pucllana were crossed off. Though not yet crossed off, I was pleased to see that Parque Kennedy, Mangos, and Circuito Mágico del Agua were on the list as well. There was a pen, lying next to the notebook, tempting me like Halloween candy on November 1st, and I decided to be clever. I crossed out all the places she had written and wrote Collin in each sub-category instead.

Barranco District

When Carolyn was ready, we took a taxi to have brunch at Cala, which is the nicest place to eat on the beach in Barranco and is a magnet for the chicest Limeños. While we were waiting to be seated, there was a guy wearing a Harvard baseball hat, and Carolyn struck up a conversation with him. First in English, then in Spanish, and then in a little bit of Mandarin—I think. The conversation dragged on a little bit, and I was hungry.

"Where did you go to college, Collin?" Carolyn inadvertently pushed me over the edge as the host led us to our table.

"I didn't, but it saves me from having to buy all those hats and sweatshirts to tell everyone."

"What? You didn't go to college?"

"I went to Roosevelt University for a few weeks."

"What happened? You seem like a really well-educated person," Carolyn said as we sat down.

"Thanks, I am. I had other priorities. I really wasn't all that interested in the college experience to begin with. It became obvious quickly, at least to me, that I didn't belong there," I explained.

"I loved school!" Carolyn's enthusiasm for something I hated so much reinforced what I already knew.

"Therein lies the difference between us," I said conclusively.

"What difference? That I liked school, and you didn't?" Carolyn asked with a confused look.

"Exactly," I said.

"I don't think that's what you meant. What difference, Collin?" Carolyn persisted, calmly.

"No, that's pretty much what I meant. Can we please order something? I'm starved. Where's the server? You know what we should do? We should open a restaurant where you go in, get the food, take it to your table, and eat," I nervously ranted.

"Those are called buffets. There is one right over there." Carolyn pointed to the brunch buffet.

"Yes, where's the server?" I'd become delirious from hunger and was redirecting my nervous energy from having steered the conversation off a cliff.

"Settle down. They'll get here," Carolyn said calmly.

"So are we doing the buffet or what?" I asked.

"You can get whatever you want. You know Collin, we don't have to do everything the same," Carolyn said pointedly. Her closed mouth forced an irritated smile while her head tilted slightly to the right. It was clear that she wasn't particularly enjoying her brunch experience at this moment.

"The buffet will be the fastest you know. I'm hungry!" I said while remaining in denial about having totally stepped in it.

"You mentioned that," Carolyn said coldly.

"I'm sorry. Are you ok? What's wrong?" I asked.

"Nothing. I'm fine."

I knew she wasn't and took no more than ten seconds to decide to make an attempt at salvaging the morning.

"Look, I'm sorry. If I'm honest, I was a little jealous of you having a conversation in seventeen different languages with that guy from Harvard, and the whole college conversation just brought up a lot of insecurities. I was trying to be funny and make a joke out of the situation, but it didn't land. I really am sorry," I said.

El mesero had impeccable timing, as he approached our table before Carolyn could respond.

"Buenos días señor y señorita. My name is Pablo, and I will be your waiter this day." The long-awaited introduction was excessively pleasant.

"Champagne with orange juice please," Carolyn requested.

"Many apologies, we do not have orange juice," El mesero informed us.

"Grapefruit juice?" Carolyn asked.

"A thousand apologies señorita, we do not have grapefruit juice," Pablo lamented.

"Please bring whatever juice you have," Carolyn gave up.

"La señorita has ordered champagne and piña juice to drink. Is there anything else you would like to drink señor?" el mesero asked.

"Yes, café pasado sin leche o azúcar." I liked my coffee black.

"Señorita, café?" El mesero checked with Carolyn.

"Yes, do you have coconut milk?" she asked.

"No, señorita," el mesero said, as his shoulders slumped.

"Do you have almond milk?" Carolyn asked in a final attempt to order all the things el restaurante did not have.

"No, señorita," Pablo was at a loss.

"Fine. Café con leche please. Do you have Splenda?" Carolyn asked hopefully.

"Sí, señorita. I'll be right back with your coffees, and Splenda for la señorita," el mesero said as he began to turn away.

"Ya momentito, mil disculpas señor." Carolyn mercifully stopped el mesero from walking away, so we could order.

"Can grumpy just go get started on the buffet?" Carolyn asked permission for me to eat, or maybe she just wanted a break from me for a few minutes.

"Of course, señorita. Buen provecho señor," el mesero said as he bowed slightly and motioned in the direction of the buffet.

When I came back from the buffet, Carolyn wasn't at the table but had left a tiny handwritten note. Around the edges of an empty Splenda packet, she'd written 'Buffet—back in a minute, which should be enough time for you to worry about me accepting your apology. XCareOlinaXO'

Carolyn returned to the table and abruptly dropped her plate on the table. I began chewing my food much slower, and she had my full attention.

"I don't know how successful you are or aren't. Though my impression is that you're doing just fine. You're going to have to drop the insecurities with me. I met you less than 48 hours ago, and we're now hanging out for—what—the fourth time? Get it? More importantly, you need to know I don't give a shit how much money you have, what you do for a living, where you went to college, or how many soccer trophies you won growing up. That's right fuckboy, I'm the mashed potatoes and the gravy!" Carolyn put me in my place immediately upon returning to the table. Interestingly enough, this wasn't the same as being put down.

"Champagne?" I asked, as I had already lifted the uncorked bottle, and begun a supple pour into Carolyn's glass. I clearly understood that we were moving on.

"I thought you'd never ask," Carolyn said with a smile.

"See, that's the difference between the two of us," I said with a straight face. Carolyn sprayed her first sip of champagne across the table, trying to hold her laughter in.

"This champagne isn't nearly as dry as I expected," I said as I patted my face dry with a napkin.

"It's definitely not as dry as your sense of humor, and you deserved that," Carolyn said while continuing to laugh.

"This really is fantastic, having brunch beside the ocean,"

Carolyn proclaimed. Carolyn had that gift. She didn't walk through life with a contrived disposition of everything being fantastic all the time. If something wasn't fantastic, she would address it, and get back to enjoying herself right away. I was envious of that.

I'd been enjoying our time together so far but certainly had no expectations for our chance meeting to actually work out. In that moment at brunch, with the sound of the ocean waves crashing onto the rocky shore and the sunlight raining down through the tall windows onto our table, I had to acknowledge I wanted to have expectations of what might be.

Carolyn's voice retrieved me from my daydream. "Seriously, though, nice job bringing us down here to eat. Coming from Chicago in the wintertime, I can't get over the smell of the ocean and watching the waves. I'm starting to see the allure of Lima for you."

"It's gotten to the point I'm really only able to eat if I can hear and see the waves," I said with a contrived tone of concern in my voice.

Carolyn asked, "What do you do when you eat at home?"

"Push the button on the remote to open the roll-ups and slide open the doors to the terrace," I said with a shit-eating grin.

"Can not wait to see where you live Collin."

AFTER BRUNCH, we grabbed a taxi beachside to go back to Pizzería Tío Dan. Carolyn asked for the manager, who came out after a short wait. She asked if the owner was Tío Dan, and the manager said that he wasn't. He seemed to be a little nervous as he explained the owner had named the place after someone, but he didn't know who or anything about them. Carolyn asked him to get in touch with the owner and see if he could find out who Tío Dan was. She tried to leave her number for the owner to call, but the manager initially didn't want to take it. Carolyn explained she thought she was Tío Dan's great-niece, and she was trying to get him back in touch with her family in the US. Eventually, he took her number and said he would give it to the owner.

As we walked out Carolyn said, "I can tell that is going right in the garbage can."

"Restaurant people act weird when you go into their restaurant and aren't there to eat. I think he's just being protective. He doesn't know us. He knows who Tío Dan is for sure," I reassured Carolyn.

"I really hope you're right, or I'm screwed."

"You're not screwed. Do you know the general whereabouts of the estate?"

"Yes, it's down in Lurín."

"Great, if we don't hear back today, we'll drive down there and start asking around at stores and restaurants. Someone'll know who he is." I was genuinely confident there wouldn't be a problem.

"The clock is tick-tock ticking," Carolyn said.

"So do you want to hang out today, or what's on your agenda?" I asked.

"Yeah, let's walk around Barranco. I hear it's interesting," Carolyn said.

"You heard correctly. Do you mind if we swing by my place, so I can change clothes?" I asked.

"I totally forgot you hadn't been home yet, of course," Carolyn answered.

We walked over to my place and took the elevator up.

Carolyn checked me out in the mirror and said, "Don't worry, I'm not going to look at which floor you're on."

"It's the top one," I said.

When we entered my condo, and before heading back to shower and change, I said, "Head straight down the hall, and you'll see the kitchen and living room. Grab something out of the fridge to drink, and make yourself at home."

I came out, and Carolyn told me I had a nice place in a rather uninspired tone of voice. She must have missed the stunning view of the Pacific. To my chagrin, she had two bottles of water ready for us and asked if I minded if she left her bag here while we walked around. I didn't, and we ventured out into the bohemian chic neighborhood. I took her to see the small central plaza, and we poked our heads into several art galleries and boutiques along the way. The myriad of painted murals, gardens, haunting trees, and a mix of restored and abandoned broken-down, colonial-era buildings, gave Barranco a certain mood. It called to us like a kitten in a dark alley.

"You hungry?" Carolyn asked a couple of hours into our excursion.

"Perpetually. How hungry are you?" I replied.

"Famished actually."

"Perfect, let's go to Budare."

"What's Budare?"

"It's a Venezuelan restaurant. It's not on your list," I answered.

"Why are we going to a Venezuelan restaurant in Perú?" Carolyn asked.

"I want some Venezuelan food, and we aren't in Venezuela. Didn't you say your grandmother is Venezuelan?" I asked.

"Yes, she is. I've had more than my share of arepas. Wait, how do you know what restaurants are on my list?" Carolyn asked.

"You left your notebook on the coffee table. You really did your homework before you came. You said you were hungry right?" I asked.

"Famished," Carolyn said again.

"Then it's time you had a pepito from Budare." I had a solution.

"I don't remember that one growing up, What's a pepito?" Carolyn asked.

"It's a sandwich you eat with your entire face and possibly a fork and a knife," I said.

"Sounds exciting!"

"It's a full-body sandwich experience. This sandwich was voted most likely to scare Guy Fieri."

"If it scares Guy Fieri, how am I supposed to eat it?"

"Not sure, but I usually take a shower and a nap afterward."

"I might order something else if that's ok." Carolyn was informing more than asking me.

"Suit yourself. I plan to order a few Hallacas to take back to the condo as well. It's December, which is the only time they make them, and they're absolutely one of my favorite things to eat." I shared my real motivation for going to a Venezuelan restaurant.

"Those are the tamales made especially for Christmas time right? Mi Abuela Rosa used to make dozens and dozens of those every year for the holidays. She would tell me, 'I make them just so I can see the look on your face when you eat them.' I can't wait to see her face when I bring her jewelry box to her," Carolyn said with a daydreamy expression on her face.

After lunch, we walked back through the central plaza and down to el Puente de los Suspiros. This was my favorite location in Barranco and all of Lima. The bridge crossed over a deep ravine that led down to the ocean. Ravine translated to barranco en Español, so I assumed the town derived its name from this ravine, lined with old colonial-style buildings filled with restaurants, shops, and some residences. Vendors peddled handmade jewelry, and there were lots of sculptures, more murals, and poems written on the walls. To all who make their way up or down the hillside plunging into the Pacific Ocean, art, culture, fashion, food, and drink vibrate good energy.

"It's local legend when crossing the bridge, you have to hold your breath and make a wish. If you make it all the way across, your wish will come true," I said as we walked down the concrete steps from the central plaza toward the bridge.

I took her hand, and we approached the bridge. We drew in deep breaths and set out onto the creaky wooden suspension bridge. Our heads rotated slightly to the left, keeping one eye on the spectacular ocean view and one eye toward oncoming foot traffic as we crossed. We successfully made it to the other side and let our breath out at the same time. Our hands let go when Carolyn turned to give me a high five.

"I wished that I'll find Tío Dan and mi Abuela Rosa's jewelry box," Carolyn said.

"You can't tell your wish. That's bad luck!" I said and closely guarded mine. We walked up the steps and out of the ravine. For the few blocks left on the way home, I'd been wishing that my wish was to hold Carolyn's hand the rest of the way, but what I hoped for wasn't that simple.

As we arrived at my building, one of my neighbor's regular drivers was out front standing beside his black Chevy Tahoe, so I asked if he was free at the moment and could take Carolyn back to the Miraflores Park Belmond. He agreed. We went up to grab Carolyn's bag before sending her on her way.

"Get a nap if you can," I said as Carolyn grabbed her bag off the kitchen counter.

"You read my mind, but why are you saying it?" Carolyn asked.

"Javi took the night off and is coming out tonight. I don't want to be presumptuous, but I'm hoping Carolina would join us."

"She would love to! I wouldn't miss it either. Where and what time?" Carolyn asked.

"Ayahuasca. It's a colonial mansion that's been converted into a hip restobar. It's right around the corner from here. 8:30 pm for dinner and leave Carolyn at the hotel," I said with a smile.

"I'll see you then!" Carolyn said enthusiastically. She paused, and then she raised up on her tiptoes and kissed me half on the cheek and half on the mouth.

Twenty minutes later she called.

"I have good news and bad news," she began.

"Lay it on me." I was already mentally prepared for her to cancel.

"Tío Dan called! You were right Collin. We found him! Fun fact, as we were told, he doesn't own the restaurant, but the owner's mom worked at the estate for the family. Tío Dan was a father figure to him, so he named the place after him." Carolyn explained.

"Such a small world," I said.

"Tiny little world. Anyway, he isn't sure where the jewelry box is but seems to remember what mi Abuela Rosa is talking about. He said he'll try to find it. He wants me to come to the estate tonight, so he can meet me. Isn't this fantastic?! I was really starting to worry I wasn't going to be able to get the jewelry box for mi abuela," Carolyn excitedly gave me the update.

"The bad news?" I asked.

"I have to cancel our plans tonight," she said.

"Totally understand. I'm so happy you found him!" I said.

"We found him, Collin! Thank you so much. I have more good news," Carolyn started.

"Oh yeah, what's that?" I asked.

"If I can get the box tonight, we'll be able to spend as much time together as we want the rest of my trip," Carolyn said.

"I'm looking forward to it," I said before we ended the call. I really was. Maybe we would have just enough time to get something more permanent going between us. That of course would depend on just exactly how much time she wanted to spend together though. My enthusiasm was guarded.

FIVE

YOU CAN DANCE IF YOU WANT TO

In spite of the disappointment that Carolyn wasn't there, Javi and I were having a good time enjoying a light and leisurely tour of the piqueos menu, and an inverted pace ramping our drinking up. Javi took off to el baño, and I refilled our glasses, as was our custom when one or the other excused himself for extra-curricular activities. The restobar Ayahuasca had several different bars, sitting areas, and little places to dance. It was well-appointed with incredible colonial-era art and furniture. I couldn't help but feel like the Spanish aristocracy must have felt, in Lima, in the 19th Century.

Javi came back to the table and slid next to me on the sofa. My open palm was lying next to my thigh awaiting Javi's fist to transfer his little bag of magic. I took the bag and my bad intentions to el baño.

While I was in the boys' room powdering my nose, Carolyn showed up unexpectedly and found Javi at our table.

"Collin, look it's Carolina!" Javi shouted before I was anywhere near close to the table on my way back.

"He looks like he has seen a ghost," Carolyn said with a chuckle as she stood to greet me.

After a quick kiss on the cheek, I slid on to the sofa to make the exchange with Javi, who proceeded to fumble the football. We hit heads as we both lunged under the table to grab it. Carolyn had taken a seat in a large plush colonial-style chair adjacent to the table, grinning at the two of us attempt to regain composure and act normal.

"Carolina! What are you doing here? Collin said you were going to your tío's. Come sit down! Can I get you something to drink?" Javi welcomed her.

"What are you guys drinking?" she asked.

"This is Glenlivet 18. This is Casa Amigo Reposado, and this is Portón Mosto Verde. Scotch, tequila, and Pisco, los Tres Amigos." Javi finished the description, as Carolyn stared blankly at the bottles.

"Are there mixers on the way?" Carolyn asked with nervous laughter.

"We use glasses and ice for mixers," I said.

"There is no way in hell you guys will drink all that tonight," Carolyn said.

"Of course not, mi amor. It will be after midnight when we finish." Javi explained the technicality.

"I don't normally drink straight liquor," Carolyn said.

"Pisco is not liquor," Javi explained.

"I don't normally drink straight Pisco," Carolyn answered.

"Let's get you a Pisco Sour, just like you like," Javi offered.

"When in Rome," Carolyn replied.

"So glad you're here, but what happened with your uncle?" I asked.

"He flaked out. About an hour after I called you, he called back and said he was having trouble locating the jewelry box. He said he and his son were having some business meetings, and tonight wasn't a good night for me to come to the estate. So he asked to meet tomorrow for dinner," Carolyn explained.

"Seems weird that he didn't know he had business meetings when he spoke to you the first time," I said.

"Totally. He was awkward and nervous about the whole thing. Something happened between the two calls," Carolyn said.

"Did you press him on it?" I asked.

"Have we just met? Of course, but what can I do? He said he needed more time to find the box, and to save me the trouble of the trip to the estate, he'd meet me up here in Barranco for dinner tomorrow night. He obviously wants to keep me away from the estate for whatever reason. I bet my mom was right, and that is why he and my grandfather cut each other out of their lives. His wife probably told him it was better if I didn't see the estate." Carolyn explained.

"Now I want to see this place," I said.

"Right? Before I came down, I could not have cared less about it. Now I'm desperate to go. I figure once we've met, he'll be open to me coming by," Carolyn said.

Javi excused himself to el baño. The conversation between Carolyn and I stumbled and fell awkwardly into silence. I was stunned it had taken so long for that to happen. Javi came back and smacked the side of my thigh with the back of his closed fist. I didn't want to take it and didn't reach down. Javi dropped the little snowball next to me, and I had no choice but to pick it up. I needed El Mago to get Carolyn warmed up a little bit for me. I grabbed the bottle of Pisco, left my friends behind, and made my way out to the small area between our table and the bar where I could safely dance. I raised the bottle and shouted, "Quien quiere tomar Pisco!?!?"

"When the girls approach he says, 'hola me llamo es Pisco,'" Javier gave away my trade secret to Carolyn, while I was still within earshot.

I turned and said, "It works every time," and gave Carolyn a wink. I had successfully enticed a few people onto the dance floor with me. Javi knew his job as a great wingman and kept chatting with Carolyn.

I was now dancing with a lovely señorita who was a far more skilled dancer than I. Carolyn squirmed in her chair, and I sensed that the slightest amount of jealousy grew little by little with each turn about that I and the young señorita took. I made sure we kept making passes by the table, so I could keep tabs on Javi's conversation with Carolyn.

"Carolina, don't worry about me. You can dance if you want to," Javi said. Apparently she was not yet in the mood as they continued to chat.

"Javi, how old is Collin?" I overheard her ask as I cruised behind her chair. "He's 42," Javi responded while I made sure we lingered for a moment behind her.

"I'm 29. Do you think that'll be a problem?" Carolyn asked.

"I can't see why it would be. You seem to have enough substance and sophistication for Señor Collin to enjoy your company." El Mago didn't miss a beat as the tiny dancer held me closer, and we moved away from the table.

"Oye! Amiga, me voy a bailar con este muchacho ahora," Carolyn said as she placed herself in front of my now former dance partner.

"I thought you were going to sit there and talk to Javier about me all night. Glad you decided to join me on the dance floor," I said to Carolyn.

"So weird," Carolyn said.

"What?"

"That you suck this bad at dancing. Don't get me wrong. It's hilarious!"

"Thanks. I aim to please."

"Any chance after we're done dancing, you could ask Javi to hook me up with that cola sack you two went scrambling for under the table?" Carolyn asked.

"I have no idea what you're talking about." I couldn't believe Javi and I had blown our cover. I couldn't believe Carolyn wanted in on the action. Generally, I like to keep my debauchery to myself.

"Come on, Bubba. Don't be a drag. I'm not stupid. I can tell when boys are being boys," she said.

"The mice thought the cat was going to be away," I responded.

"Come on. If I'm going to keep up drinking with you guys, I could use a little pick me up," Carolyn pleaded her case.

"You need what?" I asked in an attempt to appear more confused than I was.

"This isn't Blues Clues! Flake, blow, sniff, sneeze, snow, booger sugar, white devil, nose candy, vitamin C, toot, the white, La

37

Cocaina!" she spelled it out and unfurled a pretty decent Al Pacino as Scarface impression for the final flourish.

"Oh, you mean a little pick me up. Nobody calls it toot anymore," I said before raising my index finger to my lips, indicating she needed to keep her voice down.

"Will you ask him?" Carolyn implored.

"You can just ask him yourself, you know." Against my better judgment, I acknowledged the availability of party favors.

"No, I think it's best if you ask him, so he doesn't feel like I've been spying on him," Carolyn said.

"But you're ok with me feeling like you're spying?" I asked, laughing.

"I had to pick, and based on the scene you've been making, I figured your embarrassment threshold wasn't particularly low." Carolyn explained her sound decision-making process.

"Here's the thing. Javi is particular about who he shares with for two reasons. He doesn't want it to be public knowledge; discretion is extremely important to him. Also, he doesn't like to give it to females. He feels really guilty about that. Like he's leading them down a dark path," I sincerely explained Javi's hang-ups.

"But he's good with giving it to guys?" Carolyn asked with irritation.

"Yes, he's sexist in that way. Which by the way, I denounce sexism in all its forms in no uncertain terms," I said, trying not to laugh and to steer clear of the further appearance of misogyny.

"So, then you'll go ahead and hook a *girl* up?" Carolyn asked.

"If you're comfortable with me lying to my friend and being dishonest yourself, then sure." I have a tendency to be ornery with the people I like the most.

"How about this? Whichever one of us can pick up the hottest chica here decides whether we tell Javi or not?" Carolina flashed a grin.

"It's impossible for you to win that bet," I said.

"How so?" Carolyn asked.

"You can't pick yourself up," I said with a smile.

"Smooth, but you can't pick me up either, Collin. You don't

have nearly as much game as you think you do." Carolyn shot me down immediately and apparently had no idea just how little game I gave myself credit for.

"Ok, looks like we're at an impasse then," I said to regain my leverage.

"Fine. How about you don't be a dick, and we have some fun tonight?" she asked.

"Do those things have to be mutually exclusive?" I wondered out loud and pushed away slightly from her.

"They may, or they may not," she said as she pulled my waist closer to hers.

"We understand each other then. Excuse yourself to el baño, and check your bra strap on your left shoulder," I said.

Carolina immediately reached up and pulled out the bag of cola I had ever so discreetly deposited.

"How in the fuck did you do that? I didn't feel a thing," Carolina asked.

"Unfortunately, I get that a lot. There was a sequence to the instructions you were given. Seriously, this isn't Chicago. This stuff is way more taboo here in Perú," I quietly admonished Carolyn for drawing unnecessary attention to the situation.

"How in the hell did you do that?" she asked again.

"We were dancing, close." I stated the obvious.

"So what was all that bullshit about Javi, if you could just give it to me all along?" Carolyn asked.

"That was me being a dick and us having some fun tonight. Not being mutually exclusive," I said as I winked at her.

"Ugh, you win," Carolyn said before she turned and went for the ladies' room.

I was in my element. A few drinks, a few trips to el baño, and suddenly the grinding depression and gnawing anxiety from years of mistakes were nowhere to be found. Unlike the rest of our time together so far, I didn't have to fake my confidence.

When she returned from el baño, Carolina grabbed the bottle of tequila from the table where Javi was talking to a few locals and re-joined me on the dance floor.

"Cierras los ojos y abre la boca," Carolina instructed me before she poured a vacation-sized shot of tequila down my throat. She followed up by swallowing a good-sized shot of her own. As she closed her mouth, a stream of tequila ran down the side of her face and neck before eventually cascading over her collarbone.

"Oops, I spilled a little bit," Carolina said with a giggle as she shrugged her shoulders. She returned the bottle to the table and then came back to the dance floor.

"Quien quiere tomar la Carolina?!" She stole my line and shouted to find out who wanted to drink the most exclusive top-shelf spirit in the bar.

I raised my hand and smiled back at her. It was happening. The music kept getting louder, and the pulsating tribal beat aroused primal instincts. We kept drinking the Pisco and tequila, while Javi seemed content to revel in the scotch. We danced until the sweat went from beading on our foreheads to streaming down our bodies. The windows and doors were all open, so the evening breeze could blow in and out of Ayahuasca. The moon was full and bright outside. You could smell the ancient mystics who danced on this ground before the colonial mansion was built here, brewing their potions. As the aromas and spirits wafted in, we breathed heavily cheek to cheek on the dance floor.

Carolina and I breathed in anything and everything we could as fast as we could. With each deep inhalation, feeling more alive and invigorated. The candles around us seemed to dance with us. Our pulses raced the mystical spirits spiraling around the room. They won the race and possessed us. They took us around the corner, down the stairs, and into a unisex bathroom together.

"Have you ever been this high before?" Carolina asked as she laid out a line of the White Devil on the back of her hand.

"We can get higher," I said as I inhaled the back of her hand clean.

"Is the door locked?" Carolina asked as she turned around in front of me and faced me in the mirror.

I leaned forward and whispered, "Yes. Only the ghosts can get in."

Her head fell softly forward and rolled slowly to the left and then back to the right, as she arched her back. "That's good. Ghosts are welcome. I have something I want to show you, but you can only see it with your eyes closed in the dark," Carolina said as one of her hands reached behind her, and the other slid down the wall to turn off the light. Leaving only a candle and our bodies to flicker in the darkness.

SIX

A BAD, OR AT LEAST SLIGHTLY CONCERNING, OMEN

When I woke up, I called Carolyn to make sure she made it back to her hotel safely. I assumed so, but my memory was blurred towards the end of the night. Javi had texted, 'Home safe, McDonald's was good, love you brother,' and that meant that he was more worried about himself than us. So that was a good sign. Carolyn didn't answer, so I texted her, 'Epic night, going back to sleep,' and tossed the phone over to the other side of the bed.

I woke up again around 2 pm and reached for my phone. Carolyn had texted, 'Epic night, just waking up,' about fifteen minutes before I'd woken up the second time. I called her back.

"Hey there, rock star," Carolyn said in a raspy voice.

"Hey," I said.

"Can you come with me for dinner tonight with mi Tío Dan?" Carolyn asked.

"For sure. I'm hoping to eat something sooner though. I'm going to order something from Rappi. You should just come over, bring everything you need, and get ready for dinner here." I'd have to summon my strength, but it'd be worth it.

"What's Rappi? Do they make wraps?" Carolyn asked.

"Rappi is all those motorcycles you see defying death, weaving in and out of traffic, carrying the orange cube food warmers with the white mustache logo. It's Lima's version of Grubhub," I said.

"Ok, but I want pizza. Thin crust. I can't do anything too heavy after last night," Carolyn said.

"Yep, I have the perfect place. I feel like you were given proper warning," I said.

"You did. I knew when I arrived, and there were three bottles for two people, that it was a bad, or at least slightly concerning, omen," Carolyn said with a laugh.

"But no, seriously. That was a great time. I haven't partied like that in years, nor will I again for several more years," Carolyn continued while still laughing.

Carolyn came over, and we polished off the familiar-sized Primavera pizza from La Linterna, a local place with as good a thin-crust pizza as I've found anywhere in the world. After we ate, I gave Carolyn the grand tour. When we came back down from the rooftop terrace, I opened a bottle of cold rosé, and we relaxed on the terrace off the living room.

"Do you think if you move back to Chicago, we would end up dating more seriously?" Carolyn asked.

"I wouldn't hold your breath on that," I told her.

"That's mean!" Carolyn shouted.

"No. I mean I don't think I'll be going back to Chicago," I said.

"No? Why is that?" Carolyn asked.

"I may not stay in Lima the rest of my life, but the chances of me ever moving back to Chicago are minute," I explained further.

"Why not? I love Chicago," she said.

"I do too, but I lost myself in the city life. I had to get out of there before it was too late." I stared out over the tide as a thousand bad memories washed over me.

"Don't you miss your family?" Carolyn asked.

"No," I said.

"I bet they miss you," she said.

"I'd really rather not go into it. Please don't take that the wrong way. I'll just say this. When the people who are supposed to love you no matter what can't do that, it really fucks with every other part of your life. I'm here to insulate myself from that." I knew I'd said too much and expected Carolyn to change her mind about having me go to dinner with her and take off. But she didn't.

She stayed.

We sipped rosé and took in the view. There were a dozen or so black vultures gliding back and forth across the blue sky. Los Gallinazos de Cabeza Negro were the most readily visible of all the wildlife in, and surrounding Lima. We watched as they filled the air with majesty. They would purposefully swoop downward and then effortlessly drift back to higher elevation. They angled gracefully through the air as they engaged in their pre-hunt ritual dances. The birds were cultural icons in Lima.

As long as there had been humans in Lima, there had been los Gallinazos de Cabeza Negro, and in Barranco they were honored with large statues in the park near el Puente de los Suspiros. Apparently Carolyn, however, was just noticing them for the first time.

"My god they're huge!" Carolyn exclaimed, describing their meter-and-a-half-long wingspans.

"They look like some sordid sorcerer's harbingers of death, obsequious soldiers ready and waiting to do the bidding of their dark master." Carolyn certainly had a way with words.

I laughed and tried to remove the supernatural overtone of the conversation. "I think they're beautiful, like flying black stallions!"

Carolyn wasn't having any of that and replied, "Yes, black stallions in an aerial death march. They're fucking creepy Collin!"

Just then, one of those beautiful creatures made a crash landing. It ferociously flapped its long black wings with white tips to slow its momentum onto the terrace rail. Then another joined side by side. A few moments later, yet another gallinazo landed and formed a row. One after another more than a dozen swooped down, slowing gravity with their powerful wings and resting on the rail. Their featherless, black heads would occasionally rotate to one side or the other, all while their sturdy bodies remained perfectly aligned shoulder to shoulder. We counted 18 of them, from beginning to end of their formidable row.

The sun began to descend toward the ocean. Bright yellow, orange, and pink swaths of color filled the sky, transforming into deep blues and purples as the sun got ready to go out for the evening. Soon, all those beautiful colors would be swallowed by the dark of night.

"No, this isn't ominous at all, Bubba. Seriously, ominous. A bad omen. Is this a daily occurrence?" Carolyn asked.

"You're exaggerating. Slightly concerning omen, possibly. Occasionally, two or three will land on the rooftop terrace rail and stand guard over the ocean, but there have never been this many. Normally they like to gather in the larger trees down by the ravine around sunset time. They must be here to welcome our new favorite guest," I joked to try and ease Carolyn's growing alarm.

"Wonderful." Carolyn interpreted my attempt at humor as an obvious denial of reality.

"We need to get you ready for dinner. Let's get a nice warm bath going for you. You can relax and think about where you would like to eat tonight. How does that sound?" I asked.

"Better than having a staring contest with Dr. Death's volt of vultures you're so fond of. Tío Dan made reservations at Central. Didn't I tell you?" Carolyn asked before turning to take her glass to the kitchen for more rosé.

"You might have. I'll get the water started," I said as I walked down the hall to the master suite, and los gallinazos stayed, silently enjoying the cool evening air.

I slid open the large glass door that enclosed the charcoal-colored stone shower and bathing area. Along the back wall was a large stone pool, with four separate nickel-plated, wide waterfall faucets. Two long, stone benches graced the sides of the stairs to the top of the pool. Large tug-of-war style ropes hung from the bare concrete ceiling five meters above so you could steady yourself as you climbed the stairs.

I didn't have the biggest or best penthouse in Lima, but my bathroom was on par with a luxury spa. I had little hope or expectation of impressing Carolyn in general, but I thought if it was going to happen, this would probably be the moment.

"There's an extra robe in the closet. The water is about ready," I announced to Carolyn who had made her way into the bedroom.

"Casa Allweather," Carolyn said as she pointed to the writing on the robe above her heart. "You have monogrammed robes, Collin?" Carolyn asked while snickering at me and entering the bathroom.

"Strictly for inventory purposes," I said.

Steam billowed out of the slightly open glass door. Carolyn slid her robe off her shoulders and tossed it on the vanity. As the steam billowed around her, Carolina turned her head over her left shoulder and motioned softly with her hand. Each finger supplely folded into her hand individually from pinky to index finger like falling dominoes. She took hold of the rope with one hand above the other, climbed the steps, and disappeared into the steam. I froze momentarily before removing my shirt, unbuckling my belt, and letting my pants fall to the floor. As I reached the top of the stairs, Carolyn's hand emerged from the water gently bobbing below her collarbone to point to my boxer briefs, and she said, "Those too."

AFTER OUR BATH together and a cat nap, we got ready to go to cena with Tío Dan at Central. Perennially it is one of the highest-rated restaurants in the world, a must for all international fine diners. Even having lived so close, I hadn't been there yet, though. In my mind, it was a special occasion type of restaurant, and I hadn't had any of those. Tonight was indeed a special occasion.

As we were heading to the door I asked, "Did you want to say goodbye to los gallinazos before we leave?"

"You mean good riddance," Carolyn said as her phone rang.

"Hey, mom! Just heading out to dinner to meet Tío Dan. What's up?" Carolyn asked.

Her body became still, and the life fell out of her expression as she listened to her mom on the other end of the call. Carolyn gathered herself enough to pace down the hall into the living room where she stared out over the dark ocean and spoke with her mom. Whatever they were discussing was important enough that Carolyn was either unaware or unconcerned with the row of black vultures that still perched on the terrace rail blending into the dark evening sky. She turned toward me, and I could hear the end of her conversation.

"Ok, let me find out what flights are available. I'll text you. Tell abuela te quiero for me. Love you," Carolyn told her mother before lowering the phone from her ear, and a tear streamed down her cheek.

"What happened?" I asked.

"Mi Abuela Rosa had a massive stroke. She's in the ICU, and they don't think she's going to make it. I need to get on a flight back tonight," Carolyn said as her voice cracked, and more tears welled up in the corners of her eyes. She'd already begun looking for flights on her phone.

"I am so sorry. Whatever you need, just let me know," I said trying to be as supportive as possible during this utterly horrifying moment.

"Thank you, Collin. 10:52 pm, boom, booked it." The alacrity that Carolyn demonstrated in finding and booking a flight wasn't surprising, but the reality that she was leaving was a gut punch.

"What about the jewelry box?" I asked with a lump in my throat.

"I think it's superfluous at this point, don't you? Abuela Rosa is fighting for her life, Collin. Family—the actual people in it—are more important than old family heirlooms. I need to call Tío Dan to cancel," Carolyn said as more tears cascaded down both cheeks.

She dialed his number. "He's not picking up," Carolyn said staring off in another direction trying to gather her composure.

"Text him maybe?" I suggested.

"He's like, almost 80 years old, Collin. I don't think he texts." Carolyn continued to hold the phone to her ear.

"Tío Dan, hola, soy Carolyn. Abuela Rosa tuvo un derrame cerebral, está casi muerta y en el hospital. Me voy a Chicago inmediatamente. Me llamaste cuando escuchaste este mensaje." Carolyn hung up the phone.

"I need to get a taxi and get back to the hotel to get packed and head to the airport. I'm so sorry this has to end so suddenly. I really have been having a great time with you, Collin. Not even joking, we should have known something bad would happen when those birds

47

showed up," Carolyn said hurriedly as she headed down the hall to gather her belongings.

Not just one bad thing was happening. Carolyn was losing her grandmother, and I was losing the best thing that had happened in my life in so many years. As hard as I tried, I couldn't help but think of what I was losing. I kept telling myself not to be so myopic and to focus on how I could support Carolyn in this incredibly difficult moment. I waited for her by the door.

"I'll take you to the hotel and then to the airport after you pack up at the hotel." I offered my help despite feeling completely helpless.

"You're so nice, but you don't need to do that. I'll get a taxi," Carolyn said.

"I insist. It's the right thing to do and really no trouble for me. It will be more efficient and comfortable for you. I really would like to help. And to be direct, I would like to at least spend a little more time with you in the car trying to figure out a way to say goodbye while we drive." I took my best shot to convince her to accept the ride.

"Ok, Collin, you're the best." Carolyn, to my purely internalized delight, accepted the ride, and at least for a second, I felt a little better.

The elevator took us down to the garage, and when the doors opened, I stepped out briskly to take the lead to the car. I opened the passenger side door for Carolyn to get in and waited to close the door behind her.

"This Jeep is so you. Strong and intimidating on the outside and super luxe on the inside." Carolyn hopped in my black Jeep Wrangler High Altitude.

I walked around to the driver's side, freaking out by what she meant by that, and responded as I was getting in. "Carjackings are a thing here. It's comfortable but keeps a low profile."

"They are in Chicago too," Carolyn said as she slung her overnight bag into the back seat.

"I remember. Do you really think of me as super luxe on the inside?" I asked as I fastened my seat belt.

"Yes, is that surprising?" Carolyn seemed surprised I was surprised.

"No, I guess. I don't know. Never mind. I can't take a compliment," I admitted the obvious.

"You remember where the hotel is, right?" Carolyn asked.

"I'll never forget."

I could feel her turn and smile at me. I kept my eyes on the road and nodded affirmatively one time. Tears welled up in my eyes. If I looked at her, I knew I would cry. Then she would cry, and I was supposed to be supportive in that moment. So not only was there no turning back, there was also no turning to the side.

We discussed logistics on the way to her hotel. I would ask security to allow me to leave the Jeep up front in the loading zone, while Carolyn went to her room packed up, and checked out. I would order some food to go, so Carolyn could eat something on the way to the airport. Attending to the necessities kept my mind from wandering too far down a dark path. For Carolyn, that path was the peril that her grandmother was in. For me, that was the thought that I might never see Carolyn again. We hadn't had any discussions about our future, and now just wasn't the time.

As I waited in the lobby for the food and for Carolyn, there were no necessities for me to attend to, and my mind led me down that dark path. I wanted to tell her how I was feeling. I wanted to ask how she was feeling. I wanted to tell her that her grandmother would be ok. I wanted to believe that. I wanted to believe that she didn't have her career and life in Chicago and would be free to come back here. I wanted to believe that maybe I would move back to Chicago, and we could date and keep getting to know each other. I wanted to believe I wasn't a crazy person for thinking about all these things if she wasn't feeling at least a little bit the same way. I wanted.

This just wasn't the time or place for this kind of conversation. Carolyn was in a precarious place emotionally. I knew all she could think about was getting home to say goodbye to her grandmother, while at the same time hoping she would pull through. I wasn't going to say anything. We'd had a great time, and if more was to come of it, then it would come. I just didn't know where or when, if ever.

Carolyn came through the lobby with a member of the hotel staff transporting her luggage. Another member of the hotel staff came from around the front desk with flowers for Carolyn's grandmother. Word had spread quickly that the hotel's new, favorite guest was on the verge of losing her grandmother, and the entire staff was incredibly attentive. The doorman came and took the luggage to the car. The hotel manager came and presented Carolyn with his business card. He offered a twenty percent discount for her next stay when she could come back to finish her vacation in Lima. This was without a doubt my favorite part—that I wasn't the only person in Lima hoping for Carolyn to return.

When the food came, I asked what was owed. The staff told us there would be no charge. Carolyn was like a movie star, drawing everyone in with her charisma. At the same time, the staff treated her like a foreign dignitary, attending to her with the utmost respect as if every move had some sort of geopolitical importance.

Hotel staff loaded her luggage, and we were ready to go. I didn't normally carry much efectivo but fortunately had just enough to tip each of the staff members who had helped us. We pulled away and headed to el aeropuerto. Carolyn put the windows down to enjoy the scent of the ocean in the night air as we passed by Larcomar, where we first met.

"It really was Larcomarvelous meeting you Collin!" Carolyn said with a laugh.

"Damnit! Why didn't I think of that one? I really have to Larcomarvel at your creativity." I said sarcastically with a roll of my eyes.

"I could really go for a Larcomartini right about now."

"You're Larcomarked for greatness Carolyn."

"Collin, you've lost your Larcomarbles."

We volleyed back and forth like this for a few more minutes. At the end, we agreed we needed to send our conversation to the Larcomarketing department. We were still laughing when we arrived at the departure terminal of Jorge Chavez International

Airport. I pulled up to the curb, got out to unload Carolyn's bags, and turned to tell her goodbye.

"She's going to make it," I said to reassure Carolyn.

"We don't know that," Carolyn said.

"We don't, but she will make it long enough for you to see her again. I can feel it." I was lying. I couldn't feel anything except the pangs in my heart that Carolyn was leaving. The pang that something that could've been so great seemed to be over before it started. One of the most remarkable people I had ever met was going to be in—and right back out—of my life.

"I hope you're right. Listen, I've gotta go, but I just want to say I know we both want to say something. Since we don't know exactly what, and if we do say something, it will be the wrong thing and mess everything up. Let's just know that and not say anything, ok?" Carolyn was providing a solution, and for me, some hope that she was having the same feelings as I was.

"Agreed. Please let me know when I may speak again."

"Wait, all I had to do this whole time to get you to shut up was ask?"

"Don't you always get what you ask for?"

"Always." Carolyn embraced me one last time.

"Always." I held on for way too long but not long enough.

INTERLUDE
TAKE YOUR SHOT

SEVEN

ASKING FOR A FRIEND

Barranco

Javier was posted up at the bar at El Gringo, our regular starting place in Barranco on his nights off. The bartenders affectionately referred to us as 'El Mago y El Gringo.' Javi had just begun sipping on the biggest glass of whiskey I had ever seen.

"When I'm at the bar, and you're on the other side, my drinks don't look like that," I complained to El Mago.

"The drink size is in proportion to la propina you give me. You cheap mother fucker."

"La propina size is in an inverse proportion to the tab size. You greedy mother fucker."

Just then Javier's hand tapped the side of my thigh. I reached down to find his closed fist and accepted the sack of snow.

"That's not how it works." Javi continued the conversation as his now empty hand reached for his drink, and my full hand slid into my pocket before awkwardly making its way back onto the bar top.

"Where is our new friend? What's she up to today?" Javi asked.

"She left. Her grandmother had a stroke and is near death. I took her to the airport late last night," I said.

"Is she going to make it? Do you think she'll make it?" Javi asked.

"I'm not sure. I don't have a lot to go on, but I can tell you from the way Carolyn reacted, that she doesn't," I said.

"That's sad. I remember when all four of my grandparents died. It was very sad each time. You don't get used to it. Every time was just as bad as the first time," Javi said while running his hand through his hair.

"You were close to them?" I asked.

"Oh yes, very close."

"I've always wondered what that would be like."

"Señor Collin, what did the ghost say to the bartender after he offered them a menu?" Javi asked.

"I'm just here for the boos, Javi. Seriously, just the booze, El Mago. I don't want to think about Carolyn, Carolina, or her jokes."

"Just the booze, Bubba?" Javi impersonated Carolyn's puppy dog face.

"No, you're right. I'm going to el baño. If it's not too much trouble, get me one of those whiskeys like the one you have," I said.

"Con mucho gusto, amigo," Javi said.

"Gracias, mi hermano," I thanked Javi for all the things he was doing and being in that moment.

I left for el baño and made my way into an empty stall. I untied the small plastic bag and contemplated the level of fiesta I was planning to reach esta noche. I knew I would be drinking heavily to ease the sting of Carolyn's departure, and earlier in el día, I had closed all my open trading positions. I didn't have to worry about getting up on time en la mañana for work.

"Fuck it," I said out loud, pulling out a credit card and dipping the corner into the finely ground powder. El Mago had it prepped just the way I liked it. I retrieved a good size bump from the bag, first for the left side and then again for the right. Followed by a deep breath in through both nostrils and then another round. Four big bumps to get the party started, and I was feeling better already.

I returned to el bar, sat down, and tapped Javier on his thigh to pass back the magic powder to the magician.

"Why haven't you gotten married? Jennifer is a great girl," I asked Javier about his longtime girlfriend. Her given name was Yanaquyllur, a Quechua name that means little black star. She wanted something more modern, and she loved Jennifer Aniston, Garner, and Lopez in alphabetical order. So Jennifer it was.

"I have my mom to look after, my sister and her kids. I love Jennifer, but I also love my independence. And you know, the nightlife. What we are doing here isn't exactly the life of a family man you know," Javier said.

"I get it. You know I get it, but I'm sitting here thinking there's got to be more. And maybe being married, having kids and a family, is the thing. I don't know. Maybe it's worth trading independence for fulfillment, and I worry the longer we wait, the less likely we are to actually make it happen," I said.

"Would you say that you meet more single people who are happy or married people who are happy?" Javier asked.

"Probably about the same I guess," I said.

"Sí, Señor Collin. You can be happy or miserable whether you are single or married," Javi said.

"You're right. I've always said, if you're not happy being single, then you definitely shouldn't get married. That won't be the answer," I said.

"See, you already know."

"Yeah. Do you want kids one day, Javi?"

"Not right now. Maybe someday."

"We are getting older, Javi. Does Jennifer want kids?"

"She does."

"Javi, you'd be a great dad."

"You would be too, Señor Collin."

"I'll practice and babysit your cóctel while you hit el baño." I was ready for another ski trip to go play in the snow, but Javi needed to go first.

"You read my mind, Bubba," Javi said.

"Are you mean because you have to shop for clothes in the kid's section?" I asked.

That's how it went the rest of the night. Order a drink, chit-chat a bit, take turns in the washroom, and go outside for cigarettes. By the time the bars in Barranco were closing, we grabbed a taxi and went back to my place. The scotch was better, and the countertops were ideal to set up rock star-sized lines of la blanca. We walked in, and Javi who had been over many times made himself at home on a bar stool at the kitchen counter. I poured Johnny Walker Blue, while Javi ripped the first big line.

"Grancha!" Javi shouted as he shook his head after the snort.

"When in Rome." I took the rolled-up c-note.

"Hey Collin, are los gallinazos always sitting out there like that? I've never noticed them before." Javi pointed through the glass doors in the living room to the terrace.

"No, but they showed up yesterday and spooked the shit out of Carolyn. She said they were bad omens, harbingers of death, and some other superstitious shit," I said.

"Maybe they are waiting for her to come back. I'm not superstitious, just a little bit stitious." Javi cracked both of us up.

"Maybe I'll go sit next to them and wait for her to come back too. It's bad luck to believe in bad luck, you know," I said.

Redirecting our attention back to the task at hand, I asked Javi, "Is that everything laid out on the counter?"

"Who wants to know?"

"I'm asking for a friend."

"Ah, in that case, tell your friend, yes that's it." El Mago let me know the curtain would soon be coming down on this evening's performance.

"Ok, I'll let them know." I bent over and took a pass from right to left over one of Javi's generously portioned rails.

"That reminds me of this chica from Tanta who was trying to get information on you last week," Javi said with a chuckle.

"I told her, if you want to find out about mi hermano, you're my brother you know. Anyways, hermano, I told her, if you really are interested in este churro, you have to find out for yourself," Javi slurred through his story.

"Exactamente!" I exclaimed as Javi and I made an awkward attempt at a high five.

"I said that to her."

"What did she say?"

"She said she was asking for a friend."

"I wish her and her friend were here now. Why don't we have any girls here, Javi? Are you El Mago or no?" I teased him.

"I don't see a hat, but you want me to produce not one, but two rabbits. Señor Collin, I thought Carolina was going to be joining us this evening en el bar, and obviously she would take charge of finding new friends. I guess you scared her out of the country," Javi said.

"I distinctly remember saying that I didn't want to talk about Carolyn," I reminded him.

"How badly does someone have to want to get away from you they flee the country?" Javi went for the kill shot.

"Not that badly if they live in another country, and their grandmother is dying in the hospital. Puto." I refused to concede that round to Javi.

"See, you have no reason to be depressed, Señor Collin." Javi topped off our glasses with Johnny Blue and poured two shots of Jameson.

"She left because she had to. She will come back. But you, of course, could visit Chicago and go see her." Javi was ever the optimist.

"No, fuck that. If she wants to see me, she can come back here," I drunkenly grumbled.

"Take your shot and stop feeling sorry for yourself," Javi said.

"Fair enough," I replied.

"Do something about it, or don't do anything about it. But don't make yourself miserable wondering which direction you should go." Javi had the words of wisdom.

"You're right."

"What? Is this Candy Camera? Señor Collin says I am right!"

"El Mago,"

"Yes, Señor Collin?"

"Cállate the fuck arriba."

"Señor Collin, that doesn't exactly translate." Javi smirked at my spanglish.

"This is my simple approach to life. The present is a gift. Open it and enjoy, mi amigo," Javi enlightened me.

"Did you get that from a fortune cookie?" I asked.

"No, but I think Confucius may have been the first to say it," Javier said.

"Speaking of fortune cookies, I've got some leftover Chifa en la nevera if you're hungry Maggi." I offered Javier my leftovers.

"I'm good right now," he said.

"Saving space for McDonald's on the way home?" I asked.

The next couple of weeks were pretty much Groundhog Day. Javi and I hung out four to five nights a week, either at Tanta when he was working or on one of his nights off. The other nights I just got drunk at home by myself. Each night ended later and later in the morning. I hadn't been getting my usual exercise from surfing and was gaining weight.

I was trading badly and losing money. I'd allowed my fear of loss, fear of missing out, and the worst fear of all—my fear of fucking up—to creep into my trading world. A world I had created and constructed to be impenetrable. Those fears, of course, just mounted bad trade after bad trade, which led to the truly worst fear of all. That I'm inadequate and unworthy of love. Trading was so much easier when I wasn't concerned about getting my emotional needs met. This was an absolute nightmare.

In two short weeks, I had lost over $100k, and my solution was just to sit outside on one of the terraces chain-smoking, drinking scotch or Pisco, and talking to my new friends: los gallinazos. I'd even given them names based on their distinct personality traits: Richard, Dick, Richard, Dick, Richard, Dick, Richard, Dick, Richard, Dick, Richard, Dick, Richard, Dick, Richard, Dick, Dick, and Señor Richard Head.

Miraflores

I was drunk and sulking at the bar Tanta when Javi finally had enough of my downward spiral.

"Señor Collin, do you plan on wallowing in self-pity for the rest of your life?" Javier asked.

"Not in the mood."

"Neither am I. I was asking for a friend."

"You have friends? That's nice," I slurred.

"Collin, I have the best friend."

"You have a best friend. That's nice," I slurred again.

"Oye! Look at me. Collin, this is ridiculous. Have you called her?" Javi asked.

"Who is her? Is she around? Can she come out tonight? I'm asking for a friend." I waved my hands around in my drunken haze.

"She is Carolyn. She's not around, and she won't be if you don't reach out and call her. You know, try," Javi scolded me.

"You want me to call Carolyn? Should I call her right now?" I asked dramatically.

"No, you should call her two weeks ago. What are you afraid of?" Javi asked.

"That she will have figured out she's too good for me. Since you ask," I said soberly.

"I'm too good for you. That hasn't stopped you from stalking me." Javi attempted to disrupt my pattern of self-doubt. It didn't work, and I continued staring at the ice melting into my whisky.

"Señor Collin, you don't want to be a member of any club that would have you," Javi tried again.

"You're right."

"So what makes this any different?"

"I can't explain it."

"No explanation needed. Call her, or you can't come drink here anymore. That's your choice. Do what you know you should and overcome your fear, or go be miserable somewhere else," Javi said as he slid the credit card from my open tab toward me across the bar top.

El Mago stared at me, as he waited for my reply, and said, "I'm asking for a friend."

EIGHT

CALLS, TEXTS, AND THE LETTERS

Barranco - Chicago

Javier was of course right. It was time to give Carolyn a call. Her grandmother had passed away shortly after Carolyn got home to Chicago. Carolyn had gone straight from the airport to the hospital to give herself the best chance to say goodbye, but her grandmother never regained consciousness. I knew that had been hard on her and wanted to give her a little time and space to work through her loss. We shot back and forth a couple of texts here and there, but that obviously was not going to go anywhere. If I wanted to get her back to Lima for a visit, I was going to have to step it up a bit.

I couldn't believe how nervous I was. Talking on the phone was never my thing to begin with. Something between mild irritation and paralyzing fear gripped me every time I had to make a call. If the call was for business, to catch up with a friend, or order takeout, it didn't matter why, I hated talking on the phone. The list of things I could do to put off a phone call was infinite, but I dialed her number anyway.

"Holy shit, Collin, you do have my number!" Carolyn answered.

"Obviously. I've texted you several times." This was exactly why

I didn't call people. The same person making a sarcastic comment about me not calling, apparently thought their phone was special and only receives calls. I've often wondered what it would be like to be that important.

"I know! It's just so good to hear from you!" Carolyn alleviated any concerns over call frequency.

"It's good to be heard from," I said with a smidge of nervous laughter trying to cover the fact that I totally froze and couldn't think of a thing to say. Despite having thought about this call for weeks and planning out exactly every word I should say, none of those words were readily available.

"What are you up to?" I asked.

"I'm in Clearwater, Florida," Carolyn answered.

"What are you doing in Clearwater?" I asked.

"You know, another presentation, another convention, another client. All of the above. It's a Chicago-based client who likes to schedule conferences down here during the winter. I don't hate them for that," Carolyn answered.

She continued, "I'm actually looking for the client now. I'm not sure who, but one of us is lost."

"If I was in Clearwater, and I couldn't find you, I would check the beach first. Not there, check the hotel bar. Not there, go back to the beach assuming we just missed each other. After I went swimming, go back to the bar and get a vodka soda with lemon— not lime—and strike up a conversation with the bartender," I nervously rambled.

"Hilarious, Collin. I'm in work mode. Good bit though. I've got to run right now. I'll give you a call tomorrow when I'm on the way to the airport if you're around," Carolyn said.

"I'm around. I don't think I like work mode as much," I said with a little disappointment in my voice.

"Carolyn pays for Carolina's vacations," Carolyn said.

"Heard. Talk to you tomorrow. If I don't pick up, I'll call you right back," I let Carolyn know.

"Trading tomorrow?" Carolyn inquired.

"Yep," I confirmed.

"Sounds good. Talk soon. Bye." Carolyn ended the call.

The call was rather anticlimactic without much trauma and little payoff, like most phone calls, but the next day Carolyn called.

"Carolina!" I enthusiastically greeted her.

"Work mode Collin!" Carolyn said with a laugh.

"You're in that mode a lot," I said.

"What are you up to? Not in the middle of making a million-dollar trade, I take it?" Carolyn asked.

"No, definitely not. I don't have a good read on the market right this minute, and my number one rule for trading is that if you don't see an edge, don't make a trade. So I'm free to talk, and taking my eyes away from the screen is probably a good idea." I soft-served the fact that the market was handing me my ass, and I was on a terrible losing streak that had set me back $150k in three weeks. After every trade I placed, I had to immediately go throw up.

"And, you wanted to talk to me," Carolyn said.

"Well, yes, I was expecting your call." The tension mounted in my gut.

"I'm saying, you called me last night and wanted to talk to me. I'm returning your call. What's up?" Carolyn expertly delivered the slow play over the phone.

"Not much. Just wanted to see how you were doing. We chatted last night, albeit briefly." My stomach bile began to reach the top of my throat.

"Be that as it may, it seemed like you wanted to talk more," Carolyn responded. Something seemed to have changed since she was in Lima, but other than her grandmother dying, I wasn't sure what was going on.

"I wanted to see if I could entice you to come back to Lima sometime soon." I wrenched back the gathering momentum in my stomach.

"I have considered it, albeit briefly, but, Collin, you know I can't take more time off from work this soon," Carolyn said.

"Be that as it may, you know you could use a break from the cold. Come on Carolina!" The sweat began to bead on my forehead.

"You have every opportunity to come to Chicago if you want, while it is considerably more difficult for me to come back to Lima.

Besides, I'm in Florida taking a break from the cold now, albeit briefly," Carolyn said.

"Be that as it may, you have two reasons to come back to Lima, and I only have one to go to Chicago," I bargained as I white-knuckled the sides of my chair.

"I'll consider it. I definitely would like to meet Tío Dan, and get mi Abuela Rosa's jewelry box. Two reasons. Did I tell you? I couldn't have you never called. Mi abuela regained consciousness momentarily in the hospital and told me to 'Ask him for the letters,'" she said.

I asked Carolyn to hold, muted the call, and barely made it to the bathroom in time to launch all my expectations into the toilet bowl.

"I'm back. Sorry about that," I said.

"No worries. Anyway, I was saying. If you wanted you could definitely come visit me in Chicago. My sister Jacquelyn wants to meet you, which is definitely a bad idea on so many levels," Carolyn continued.

"I'll come visit you in Chicago sometime, but it definitely won't be during the winter time. The weather here is good now. Maybe this coming summer, when the weather is bad here but great in Chicago, would be a good time to come." I tried to reign my expectations back in.

"It's good to know your interest in seeing me is contingent upon the weather improving from where you'd be leaving to where you'd be going." Carolyn sounded a little impatient.

"A little needy aren't we?"

"I'm not being needy, just making an observation."

"Albeit a needy one."

"Be that as it may, I'd like to believe that you could muster up the courage to visit even if it was cold."

"Fair enough. I'll book my ticket and let you know." Giving in didn't feel like giving in, given the fact that vomit chunks were still clinging to the side of my face and all over my shirt.

"Wait, what? Seriously?" Carolyn asked and seemed to be excited.

"Yes, I really want to see you. I mean bad." I dropped the

pretense of being cool and used my shirt sleeve to wipe the puke stream off the side of my face.

"Awww, Bubba! Ok, let me know asap, so I can make sure I don't book any work travel," Carolyn said.

"Will do." I ended the call, and when I leaned back in relief, the office chair slid out from under me and slammed me on the floor.

I scrambled back up and booked my flight right then.

THE NEXT DAY I texted Carolyn to let her know when I would be coming. "What's good? Booked to arrive this Friday, January 17th at 8 pm."

"Amazing! So excited! Can't wait to see you!" Carolyn texted back with the requisite number of heart-incorporated emojis.

My heart jumped inside my chest. Part of me couldn't believe this was actually happening. That I was going to see Carolyn, and she was genuinely happy about it. I attributed it to the fact that I am a much better texter than phone talker. It is incredible how little cartoon faces, as ubiquitous as they've become, can trigger so much serotonin in an adult human.

The universe had other plans in mind when it sent a nasty snowstorm to Chicago that Friday. My flight was canceled. I texted Carolyn with the bad news. "Flight canceled because of the storm. Looking like maybe Sunday I can get re-booked."

"Dang. I was afraid that was going to happen. This storm sucks," Carolyn texted back. Followed by, "Can you push it to the following weekend? I'm really busy this week, and without the weekend, it will be hard for me to make any time for you. I can take this coming Friday off, and then Monday and Tuesday that week. How does that sound?"

"It sounds like forever, but that totally makes sense. I will see what I can come up with and let you know. Stay warm. Effing Chicago winters!" I texted back.

The next day, Carolyn called and without exchanging pleasantries said, "Please tell me you haven't re-booked your flight."

"Not yet. What's up?"

"I have bad news and good news. Please don't kill me!"

"I can't kill you from Perú. Or can I?" I used a mysterious voice trying to be humorous, while I nervously waited for the bad news part.

She ignored my futile attempt and began, "I have to travel for the next three weeks solid, and I don't want you to come up here. That's the bad news part."

As pressure began to turn circles in my stomach, I interjected, "That's the worst news."

"But! I talked with our CEO, and as soon as I come back, I'm going to take a month off. It's been too much lately. I haven't even really grieved for mi Abuela Rosa properly, and I'm haunted by her telling me to ask Tío Dan for the letters. Anyway, I'm going to come back to Lima as soon as I get done with this next work marathon. Since you didn't fly here, my flight there will be carbon neutral so that's a win too." Carolyn delivered the good news.

"You're shitting me, right? You had me at carbon neutral!" I said loudly as the office chair and its wheels betrayed me yet again. The bastard sent me flying backward as it slammed into the desk with a loud crash.

"Nope! Not shitting you. What was that?" Carolyn asked.

"What was what?" I said while wincing. "I'm just trying not to sound too excited, but I'm really excited!" I said as I stood up.

"I am too, Collin," she said back.

"I'll let Javi know right away. He'll be totally beside himself." I was already planning ahead.

"No, let's surprise him!" Carolyn said.

"I love that idea!" I agreed.

"So on Saturday night, I'm going to go to my Tío Dan's for dinner, but I get into Lima on Friday. We can go to Tanta and surprise Javi that first night," Carolyn planned out loud.

"That's great. I better get my big boy pants on," I said.

"Ha! You'll be ready, and maybe we take the partying down a notch, just saying. Hey, Collin, I haven't booked a hotel room yet," Carolyn began.

"Casa Allweather has vacancy!" I blurted out.

"I'm sure, but the rates are exorbitant," Carolyn said.

"There's a discount rate for preferred guests named Carolina. Seriously, please plan to stay with me." I didn't think I was going out on a limb.

"That's not where I was going with that. I was going to ask if you thought it made sense to book the same hotel I had last time or something closer to the estate. Let's not get too far ahead of ourselves, cowboy." Carolyn clarified and sawed off the branch.

"Collin, I'm interested in you. I'd be lying if I said I wasn't. But —" she began.

"But what?" I didn't really want to know.

Carolyn told me anyways. "Remember what I said after we were attacked in the taxi? It's fight or flight. When Abuela Rosa passed away, you took weeks to call me. I thought you were a fighter, but you flew. I haven't forgotten that. I'm not sure I will ever forget that. Hate to tell you this, but we're back to square one."

The next three weeks seemed like an eternity.

NINE

FIGHT OR FLIGHT

I had initially been taken back by Carolyn relegating me to square one, but as I thought about it, I realized we'd never made it to square two. I had no idea what the hell square two was or how to get there, anyway. When we first met, there was no thinking involved, just a spontaneous connection. That had played in my favor. Now I faced fighting off a negative thought, at least every half hour, about Carolyn's upcoming trip being a disaster.

What I needed was a plan. Any successful endeavor requires a plan. As I pulled into the parking lot at Jorge Chavez International airport, I still didn't have one. I did bring flowers and a sign that had Carolyn written on it, with Carolina crossed out above it. She seemed to like that. She took the flowers, hugged them, and then squeezed me tight.

"Ok, Collin, you're off to a good start!" she said.

On the way to Tanta in Larcomar, we devised our plan to surprise Javi, and Carolyn shared everything that was going on in her mind: Abuela Rosa's passing, meeting her Tío Dan, and her grandmother's dying words to ask him for the letters.

"It's entirely possible there won't really be anything that important in the letters," Carolyn said.

"That seems unlikely to me. Your grandmother probably

wouldn't have used the last few moments of her life to share something that wasn't of extreme importance," I said.

"My gut tells me you're right. Here's the other thing. Part of me is here so I can get the jewelry box and ask about the letters solely because that's what Abuela Rosa wanted, and I would do anything for her. But the other part is compelled to find out who my family is. Where do they come from, and what will all that tell me about myself?"

When Carolyn finished her thought, I instinctively placed the back of my hand on top of her thigh, and she took my hand.

"I wanted to find out more about you too," I said.

"Be careful what you ask for, Collin!"

"It's too late for that."

Miraflores

Carolyn and I approached the bar from separate sides, and when I could see that she had Javi's attention, I slid in successfully unnoticed.

"Carolina! Increíble! I can't believe you're here! Señor Collin must be so happy!" Javier said while coming out from behind the bar to greet Carolyn.

"He doesn't know I'm here," Carolyn said as I hopped just a few paces behind Javi.

"Ah, perfect. I love a good surprise," Javi replied as I inched closer.

"Do you now? I'm not sure I plan on seeing him," Carolyn said.

"What are you saying? I thought you two had been talking? Did something happen?" Javier asked.

"No, it's just that I really need to get what I came for the first time and get back home. Mi Abuela Rosa passed away right after I made it home last time. I need to get her jewelry box to bring back to her, to say goodbye, and let her go," Carolyn answered.

"But Señor Collin would love to see you. Don't you want to see your Bubba?" Javi asked.

"Ugh! What a stupid nickname. No, not really," Carolyn said.

I almost laughed out loud and blew my cover.

"I know he would want to see you," Javi persisted.

"So I'm supposed to arrange my schedule to make sure Collin gets what he wants? Did we just meet?" Carolyn asked with an agitated laugh.

"No, of course not. I mean to say, Collin would go out of his way to make time to see you. You know he really missed you after you left, and honestly, he really hasn't been himself since." Javier was desperate now.

"Just exactly who have I been?" I asked as I swung around and startled Javi.

"You mother… What am I on the Candy Camera?" Javi started laughing.

We had a group hug. Carolyn and I grabbed stools as Javi went back around the bar.

"What are we drinking? Wait, I have just the perfect thing!" Javi said as we settled into the bar.

El Mago went to work, placing two beautifully garnished cóctels in front of us. "Voila! Pisco Sour para la señorita, y un mojito para el señor!" Javi said glowingly as he remembered our drinks when Carolyn and I met for the first time.

Carolyn wasn't drinking hers, so I asked, "Everything alright with your cóctel?"

"Yeah, I'm trying to put on a brave face, but the flight was pretty rough and my stomach isn't feeling great. Probably just lagged out from the flight," Carolyn explained.

I could tell she wasn't quite herself, and she just picked at the food. Otherwise, it was a fun night of reminiscing the highlights from Carolyn's first trip to Lima and establishing our chemistry once again. We made plans for the next day to visit Pachacamac and Punta Hermosa before dinner at Tío Dan's in the evening. Carolyn said she just wanted "to play it by ear," after visiting her Tío Dan and meeting her family, but we discussed going to Machu Picchu and some of the other places Carolyn wanted to see in Perú.

"So are you at the same hotel?" I asked.

"I, actually, was thinking that if the invitation was still open, I could stay with you." Carolyn had reconsidered her lodging.

I didn't know why but didn't care why either. "Yes! That's great!"

We hung out at the bar while Javi got everything closed up, so the three of us could walk out together.

"Where should we head to? Do either of you have any place in mind?" Javier asked.

"Javi, amigo, mi hermano, I think we are heading home." I tried to let him down easy.

"Come on! Let's go somewhere for just one drink!" Javi was pleading.

"Not me, I want to get a good night's sleep. It's ok to have fun and be a responsible adult too you know," Carolyn said while laughing.

"When I grow up, I want to be like Abuela Carolyn," I said, with a great deal of aspiration in my voice.

"You have no chance. When I grow up I want to be a ballerina," Carolyn said. Then after a short pause, during which she could see my wheels turning to say something smart, she warned, "Don't you dare say it!"

"When I grow up, I want to be taller." Javier broke us all up and completed the list of things we could all never be when we grew up.

Javi headed for McDonald's, and Carolyn and I went back to my place.

Barranco

When Carolyn woke up that morning, I was in the kitchen making café pasado, and the fresh aroma lured her from the bedroom into la cocina.

"Buenos días!" Carolyn greeted me with a stretch and a smile.

"Buenos días!" I poured coconut milk into her coffee cup with a Splenda packet laying next to it.

"Wow, coconut milk, Collin! You're really going all out," Carolyn said in a raspy morning voice.

"Anticipating our guests' desires is our specialty at Casa Allweather." I took a bow.

"Thanks! What's the breakfast menu like at Casa Allweather?" Carolyn smiled as she took her coffee.

"How does an omelet with tomatoes, onion, spinach, mushrooms, and cheese sound? I've got granola and fresh fruit as well," I said.

"Sounds amazing!" she said.

"Perfect. There's an omelet pan in the cupboard on the left side of the stovetop, cooking utensils in the drawer on the right, and everything else you need is in the refrigerator. Let me know when it's ready," I said.

"You're joking. You're not serious right now. Collin!" Carolyn's voice slowly rose, as I casually sipped my coffee.

"I don't even know how to make omelets." Carolyn continued her resistance to the idea of making breakfast for us.

"And yet, you do have access to the internet on your phone," I said.

"Collin!" She shouted before changing her tone and body language into something between a coquettish damsel in distress and the cutest puppy in the pet store window. Then she convinced me to make breakfast with just one word, "Buuuuuuubbaaaaaaaaaa."

We ate breakfast and discussed the plan for the day.

"I got us an Airbnb down in Punta Hermosa. We can check out Pachacamac this morning, hit the beach afterward, and save time by staying local to Lurín to shower and clean up before we head to your Tío Dan's." I submitted my plan for Carolyn's approval.

"Great idea. Love it! What do I need to bring?" Carolyn asked.

"Whatever you want to wear tonight, obviously, and good shoes for a long walk in the dirt. Oh, and beach attire," I answered.

"You could have said hiking boots and saved a few words on your shoe description." Carolyn chuckled. "Tío Dan wants us to stay with him on the estate for a couple of days, so I'm going to take a suitcase with me. You can give me stuff to pack or just bring your own bag if that's easier. But I'd like you to stay down there with me." Carolyn had committed me for a longer stay with her uncle than I'd originally planned for.

"I'll bring a bag too then." I chose to just go with the flow, even though I hated the idea of staying at a stranger's house. I didn't want to end up back at square one again.

The Pan-American Highway

We loaded up the Jeep and were on our way within the hour. We went south, out of Barranco through Chorrillos, to catch the Pan-American highway down to Pachacamac. It was Carolyn's first taste of what 'the other Lima,' as the locals say, looked like. She hadn't yet encountered the parts of Lima that displayed an emerging economy nation that at times brought to mind taboo phrases like 'slums' or 'third world country.'

Viewing the countless piles of rubble and garbage mixed in with the densely populated apartment buildings, that in many cases were crumbling or lacked windows and roofs in the middle of the desert sand, felt like being trapped in a cold shower. All was not well in the 'City of Kings.'

There was little to no discussion as the stark reality of the two Limas was setting in, but I felt Carolyn's uneasiness and frustration. At least I thought that was why she was so pensive.

"You ok?" I asked.

"I'm ok. It's easy to forget that places like this, like the South and West sides of Chicago, exist," Carolyn said.

"It's tough to see for sure," I said.

"Can you imagine living in these conditions and having a child?" Carolyn asked.

"I'm not sure I could imagine either part of that scenario," I replied.

Carolyn turned and shot me an annoyed but anxious look, whatever that could mean.

Pachacamac Ancient Ruins

Carolyn remained pensive as we made our way through the site up to the highest temple mount. From there, the incredible panoramic views of the Pacific and the Lurín River Valley revealed an active polo field and an inactive, or at least we hoped, bullfighting arena. While Carolyn stared into the valley looking for her Tío Dan's estate. I read the sign describing the two temples.

"The original temple was built for Pacha Kamaq and housed The Great Oracle, who tribes from all over would come to consult," I began to explain.

"I could use one of those," Carolyn said.

"When the Inka conquered the site, they built The Temple of the Sun for their god Inti. They made a mass human sacrifice to appease Pacha Kamaq, who had been worshiped at the site for well over a thousand years, and incorporated him into their religion." I continued.

"Interesting," she said.

"They were wise enough to tolerate other religions, while also sacrificing human life to find favor with the gods," I said.

"At least one or two of the gods," she replied.

"Collin, who would you be? The shaman making the sacrifice, the king, or one of the powerless praying onlookers?" she asked.

"Shaman—except for the killing part—so I guess that would make me an onlooker," I replied.

"Better than being the sacrifice I guess," she said.

"There's a reason most of us blend into the crowd. And you? Shaman, queen, or onlooker?" I asked.

"King." The desert sun reflected off Carolyn's sanguine expression.

Punta Hermosa

On the way to the Airbnb, Carolyn asked, "Hey, have you thought about lunch?"

"There are lots of places by the beach. We can grab something," I said.

"Let's stop by a store and grab stuff to have a little picnic on the beach," she said.

"Not a bad idea at all," I replied.

We entered la bodega like two dusty cowboys entering a western saloon. Carolyn grabbed a small basket and started filling it with stuff to make sandwiches.

"Hey! These Lays chips are made with 'Papas Peruanas.' I guess they don't import their potatoes," Carolyn remarked.

"No, they are borderline arrogant about the potatoes here," I confirmed.

"And exactly why is that? Aren't potatoes just potatoes everywhere?" Carolyn asked.

"They have like 4000 different kinds of indigenous potatoes here. Anyway, you'll know when you taste them," I replied.

"They better be the best potatoes in the world now that you've built them up," Carolyn said and laughed.

"They are. They have the best roasted chicken in the world too." I committed to the claim.

"You may find this odd, but I really love dipping potato chips in ranch dressing," Carolyn said.

"Not odd at all. We might be soul mates. Ranch dressing makes everything better," I said.

"Finally, we have something we can enjoy together." Carolyn amused herself.

"There is one eensy, teensy, weensy, problem. They don't have ranch dressing here," I informed her.

"Really? If you don't mind, let's stop at another store then," Carolyn requested.

"I do mind. Because that other store would require a flight," I said.

"What?" Carolyn asked.

"They don't have ranch dressing here in Lima." I broke Carolyn's heart, as mine had been when I first went grocery shopping in Lima.

"You have to be kidding me?" Carolyn shook her head.

"Wish I was. I mean, I'm sure it exists—I would surmise that the US Ambassador has it imported for their office—but you won't find it in stores," I said.

"What is that white sauce I see them putting on tables in the restaurants?" Carolyn asked as she held out hope.

"It's a mayonnaise-styled dressing. It's good, but it's not even remotely close to ranch dressing." I only had bad news.

"Oh my god, Collin!"

"What?"

"How long have you gone without ranch dressing?" Carolyn asked, as though I might die a virgin.

"I can't remember. I've blocked it out. Frankly, you're bringing up repressed trauma right now."

"It's important we talk about it."

"The next time I see a bottle of ranch dressing, I'm going to unscrew the cap, raise the neck of the bottle to my mouth, squeeze the bottle with both hands, and guzzle to my heart's content," I said.

"What if it's a glass bottle?" Carolyn asked me.

"Well, then I'm just going to have to exercise a little extra patience. I've waited this long. I guess it'd be ok if it took an extra minute or so to finish the bottle."

Carolyn had walked around to the other side of the shelf, shifted her attention to the other available condiments, and asked, "Why do all the condiments here come in pouches, as opposed to bottles? Also, what is Ají?"

"Why do kangaroos carry their young in pouches and reptiles lay eggs? It's a creamy spicy mustard. I don't want to make a firm commitment, but after ranch dressing, that may be the world's greatest condiment," I replied.

"Why do female praying mantises eat the male after mating? Will Ají go well with these chips made with Papas Peruanas?" Carolyn asked.

"Not ranch dressing well, but I think you'll find it quite enjoyable if you like a little spice in your sauce. It's perfect for the sandwiches," I said, as Carolyn grabbed the Ají, and we went to the counter to pay.

"What do you want to drink? What's Inca Kola? It looks like Mountain Dew." Carolyn inquired about the neon green soda in the cooler beside the bodega counter.

"It tastes like bubblegum. People here love it. Try some at room temperature like the locals drink it, and let me know what you think," I said.

"I think I'm going to pass. What do you want to drink?"

"Agua con gas, por favor, and Gatorades. Do you want to grab a bottle of wine or some brewskis?"

"No, um, you can if you want, but I'm not really in the mood," Carolyn said as she grabbed the soda water and Gatorade.

"Since when is being in the mood a prerequisite for wine or beer? You sure?" I asked.

"I'm pretty sure." She sounded annoyed.

I was annoyed that I hadn't had a drink in more than 12 hours.

We went to the Airbnb, showered, and changed into beach attire. I smeared Ají on the sliced bread, and Carolyn layered the cheese and jamón. We packed up our picnic and headed out. I flagged down a mototaxi to get through the beach traffic quicker.

"I've always wanted to ride in one of these!" Carolyn said.

"Be careful what you ask for," I said as the driver pulled up.

"Cinco," the driver said after Carolyn told her where we were going.

"Tres." Carolyn countered like she'd been taking moto taxis her whole life.

"Cuatro," the driver said as she flung open the door for us to hop in.

We slid across the rickshaw-style bench seat, and the driver hit the throttle, taking off like a bottle rocket on the Fourth of July. She made the first turn so fast I crushed Carolyn as the inertia of my large frame pulled me into her. We'd just gathered ourselves when the driver didn't see, or chose not to slow down for, a speed bump that sent our heads bouncing off the roof. As we drove down a two-lane street with thick weekend beach traffic, our driver constantly blared her horn and forced her way between cars.

"Collin, I don't have life insurance. What is this madwoman trying to accomplish?" Carolyn shouted over the loud revving engine.

"We're going to change lanes or die trying!" The roaring engine drowned out my response as she passed a car slowed by traffic. It sounded like we clipped their side view mirror, but our driver didn't stop to find out.

"Collin, if we die before we get to the beach, I just want to let you know I really admire your courage to pick up and move to a new country, but I think it may be time to consider moving back to Chicago!" Carolyn screamed in desperation.

"Courage? It's not like I'm risking my life!" I shouted.

"You're risking your life every time you get in one of these moto thingies!" Carolyn shouted through her laughter.

Our lives were spared, and we hopped out of the mototaxi as quickly as possible. Carolyn paid the driver the cuatro soles fare, and I began doing deep breathing exercises. Carolyn came to calm me down, put one hand on my arm, and took my hand with the other like we were in a Lamaze class.

WE FOUND a good spot in the sand and put down two large towels with a beach umbrella in between them. Carolyn brought a portable speaker with us.

"What kind of music do we want to listen to?" Carolyn asked.

"Whatever you want to play DJ." She had one of her playlists going at the condo while we ate breakfast, and it was apparent she had great taste in music.

"I believe I have the perfect playlist for the occasion." The Girl From Ipanema began to play, and she slid her phone into my backpack.

We laid back and relaxed with minimal chitchat. After about thirty minutes, I decided to get in the water to have a little swim. Carolyn wanted no part of the dark, brownish-green and cold water, so she volunteered to stay behind and keep an eye on our stuff. After about fifteen minutes, I came back to air dry, and Papa Don't Preach played on the speaker. We continued to enjoy Carolyn's eclectic, yet carefully curated playlist, and breathed in the salty-sweet ocean air.

"Hey Collin, there's something I need to talk about with you," Carolyn began.

"Ok." I didn't particularly care for the way she said the words "something" or "need."

"I don't know for sure for sure, but I think I'm pregnant," she said.

"How not sure are you?" I asked, trying to assess what exactly we were dealing with.

"I haven't had my period since before I came to Lima last time. With my grandmother dying and everything going on with work, I really didn't think about it until a couple of days before my flight back. The first test I took at home came back positive, and so were the next two tests I took," Carolyn explained.

"So you're pretty sure," I said.

"Yes, I'm almost 100% sure. False positives are rare. Three false positives would be like winning the Powerball," she said.

"How are you feeling about it? What do you want to do?" I asked.

"I don't know, Collin. This isn't supposed to be happening to me. Why is this happening to me?" Carolyn broke down into tears, and I pulled her into my arms.

"I'm scared too, but I'm here for you. We'll get through this together," I said to comfort Carolyn, but it just made her cry more.

She gathered her composure and began "Collin, it's complicated."

"I know, but we'll figure it out."

"Collin, I'm not sure if you're the father."

"So that's why you were hesitant to stay with me when you came down. You're seeing someone in Chicago," I said as I released my embrace.

"I'm not seeing anyone."

"Then what, I don't get it. Why aren't you sure?"

"After mi Abuela Rosa passed away, I hooked up with Landon."

"Landon? Who the fuck is Landon?" I asked raising my voice.

"Landon. My ex. You know!" Carolyn shouted before starting to cry again.

"Oh, Landon. At the risk of being insensitive, how did that happen?" I asked.

"It just happened! He was there for me when Abuela Rosa passed. I didn't have anyone else to turn to. A fucking phone call would have been nice Collin!" Carolyn screamed at me.

I sat quietly for a moment and collected my thoughts before I asked, "Are you guys together again?"

"No, we were never back together. It was one time. I told him it was a mistake, and he needed to find someone else," Carolyn answered.

"Carolyn, who do you think is the father?" I asked.

"You, Collin, I think you're the father. I should have had my period by the time I was with him," Carolyn said.

"Then I want to be the father, if that's what you decide," I said.

"Really? Then I want you to be the father too, Bubba," Carolyn said with a sniffle and a smile.

"And you want to keep it?" I asked.

"I hate that you're asking me that question. I don't know. All I can think about is Abuela Rosa keeping her pregnancy, marrying my grandfather, and moving to the United States. She left her life and career behind so she could have my mother. Who had me," Carolyn explained.

"That was a different time. More importantly, it was a different person. All of our decisions have to be made based on our lives. We can look to others for wisdom and experience, but we have to do what is best for ourselves," I said.

"It sounds like you don't want to keep it," Carolyn said.

"I don't know what I want. We'll figure it out. I'll support whatever you decide and help with the decision in any way I can. Just because it's your decision, I won't abdicate my responsibility to share that burden." I pulled Carolyn into my arms again.

"Thank you, Collin," she said and burrowed in.

"Fight or flight," I said.

"We fight, Bubba."

PART TWO

THE DREAMS WE REMEMBER

TEN

EL GRAN SUEÑO

Lurín District

W
e went back to the Airbnb to get ready for Tío Dan's.
After our conversation on the beach, Carolyn was back
to being Carolyn again. She said she was really excited,
and also really nervous, to meet her Tío Dan and see the estate
where her grandfather grew up and met her Abuela Rosa. Tío Dan
had invited all of the extended family, and family friends to la fiesta
at the estate. He wanted to welcome Carolyn to Perú. He also used
the occasion to rename the restaurant at the entrance to the estate,
Cocina Rosa, in honor of Carolyn's abuela.

I managed to put on a collared shirt and sports coat to dress up
a bit for the occasion. I loaded up the Jeep and returned the key for
the Airbnb. When I returned, Carolyn was dressed to the hilt in a
long, flowing sapphire dress with printed white flowers. There was a
slit up to the middle of her right thigh, and the square neckline with
off-the-shoulder short sleeves framed her collarbone and confident
long neck. Carolyn achieved the perfect balance of summer sexy
and classic modesty for a family gathering.

"That dress looks amazing on you." I had to tell her.

"What? This old thing? It's nothing fancy," she demurred before flashing a smile that revealed the truth: she possessed the One Ring To Rule Them All.

It was going to be a momentous occasion, and I grew suspicious that our lives would never be the same. Meeting Tío Dan and the rest of the family at El Gran Sueño that evening would change everything.

Tío Dan sent Carolyn a map that she used to navigate our way to the estate via a few kilometers of dirt roads from the main road. We arrived at the entrance. There was a stone archway over the gigantic open wooden doors decorated with pink and white balloons that spelled out 'Bienvenidos Carolyn.' When I rolled down my window, the attendant immediately realized who we were and slid his clipboard under his left arm, so he could reach in and shake hands. He directed us to pull into the parking lot and make a slight left turn into the loading zone in front of el restaurante.

I pulled up, and we got out. The attendant asked for the keys, took our vehicle to the private garage, and moved our luggage into the main house, so it would be ready for us after la fiesta. Carolyn stood on the sidewalk with the biggest and brightest smile I'd ever seen. There was a large, painted portrait of her Abuela Rosa and thousands of flowers to greet all as they arrived to the newly named Cocina Rosa.

"I think I'm going to cry, Collin!" Carolyn said to me as I came from around the jeep and joined her at her side to go in.

"Increíble," I said slowly. We hadn't even gone inside yet, and we could feel a megaton bomb's worth of love ready to detonate for Carolyn's arrival.

A young woman, in a beautiful long white dress embroidered with flowers in traditional bright Peruvian colors, presented herself beside the portrait. She motioned excitedly for us to come in. The whole staff was giddy with excitement. This was a homecoming three generations in the making.

We entered el restaurante into the large outdoor seating area. Towering massive timbers supported a roof covering that was close to ten meters high in the air. There were two bars, a large round stage in the center, and a large grassy area with a circular clay pit for horse demonstrations. Dinner and a show. There were plants and flowers growing everywhere in different barrels. Large pottery, natural soil beds, and flower boxes created borders for all of the different areas. It felt more like a wellness resort than a family gathering.

Two rows of staff lined either side as we walked in. Damas wore white dresses with brightly colored flowers and caballeros wore white, collared, long-sleeve shirts with polished black shoes, pressed black pants, black belts with shiny silver buckles, and well-fitted black vests. They erupted in applause as we walked through and showered us with flower petals. As we passed each person, they would pause their applause to touch Carolyn lovingly on the shoulder or forearm and say, 'Bienvenidos' or 'Bendiciones' to either welcome or bless her.

This was seemingly the most important moment in their lives, to meet and greet Carolyn Grant at the El Gran Sueño estate. The dramatic reception seemed like a bit much for welcoming your niece, but I wasn't familiar with the customs of wealthy estate owners. So, I withheld my skepticism.

As we made our way through the reception, there was a handsome, elderly man wearing ranchero boots, black pants, a light blue, button-up shirt, and a big-brimmed, tan cowboy hat. He was fit, especially for his age, and his strong jaw and chiseled cheekbones framed a bushy, mostly salt—with a little pepper— mustache. As we approached, he handed his walking cane and hat to el caballero beside him, stretched out his arms, and, with laughter like Santa Claus, said, "Carolyn!"

"Tío Dan!" The two embraced, and tears of joy streamed down their faces.

"Mi preciosa! Me alegro mucho!" Tío Dan was overjoyed as he pulled back from the embrace and admired his precious Carolyn.

"Wow! No puedo creer que nos conocemos aquí finalmente!" Carolyn couldn't believe the moment had finally arrived.

"Tío Dan, este es mi amigo, Collin Allweather." Carolyn introduced me.

"Mucho gusto, Collin!" Tío Dan said while shaking my hand.

"Carolyn, Collin, este es mi amigo mejor, puedes llamarlo Tío

Patricio." Tío Dan introduced the man to whom he had handed his hat and cane.

"Carolyn, tengo un regalo para ti que es muy importante y tiene mucho significado," Tío Dan said as he motioned for one of the staff to bring the small floral-painted wooden jewelry box to Carolyn.

"Mi abuela's jewelry box!" Carolyn shrieked.

"Abrelo! Abrelo!" Tío Dan encouraged her to open it.

"Este relicario era de tu Abuela Rosa cuando ella vivía aquí en Perú," Tío Dan said as Carolyn opened the box containing a locket that belonged to Carolyn's grandmother.

"Que hermoso! Muchas gracias!" Carolyn thanked him as she opened the beautiful heart-shaped locket.

"Mis abuelos!" Carolyn exclaimed when she looked at the photo inside the locket of her grandmother and grandfather when they were younger.

Just then, a man somewhere between mine and Tío Dan's age walked up to join us with presumably his wife and their young adult twin daughters.

"Daniel! Perfecto!" Tío Dan said excitedly.

"Carolyn, Collin, this is my son Daniel, his wife Carla, and their two daughters: Rosa and Isabella. Named for your abuela and her sister." Tío Dan made the introduction in English for my benefit.

"My other Tío Dan!" Carolyn said, caught up in the excitement.

"Primo Dan to be exact, I believe," I interjected to point out they were cousins.

"Really, Collin?" Carolyn asked as though I made it rain in Lima for the first time ever on this special occasion.

"Actually, he is as correct as he is handsome. We are your primos, and we are so happy to have finally met you!" Carla came to my rescue with what. If I didn't know better, I would have considered it a flirtatious comment. Carolyn didn't squirm one bit or show any signs of jealousy.

I wasn't sure if she was just that confident or, other than our predicament, didn't really have strong feelings for me. Maybe when one alpha female tests another, they know what's happening, and the rest of us just hope to keep them both pleased.

"Let's get you two something to drink," Carla stated as she motioned for el mesero to come over.

"Champagne? This is a celebration. No?" Carla asked.

"You know me so soon!" Carolyn said, forgetting herself for a moment as she curtsied and acknowledged she'd met an adequate and friendly rival.

She caught herself and declined. "But, um, no thank you. I'm not drinking today."

"I see," Carla said before leaning in and whispering loud enough so both of us could hear. "I hope it's his. Fantastic bone structure. And that scar at the end of his eyebrow. Que rico."

Carla quickly pivoted away before either of us could say anything and spoke directly and rapidly to el mesero, instructing him how to bring the champagne. It became immediately obvious she was in charge of operating the estate.

Carolyn would be the guest of honor and the most important person at El Gran Sueño that night, but that would be at the behest of its matriarch, Carla. The staff hinged on her every word and responded with the utmost respect and urgency to every instruction. It was the kind of respect that was earned. They might only be related by marriage, but there was an uncanny similarity between Carolyn and Carla.

Carla had Tíos Dan and Patricio seated on a long, beautifully upholstered, colonial-style sofa bench with her daughters, Rosa and Isabella. Daniel sat in a rather large, and extravagantly hand-carved, wooden chair next to them. Carolyn and I remained standing as we watched el mesero pour the champagne into the eight glasses. Another mesero, who apparently had nerves of steel, held the tray perfectly stationary as though suspended in mid-air by some mysterious force.

We were terrified. Not because of the probability of the laws of physics resuming and the tray tipping, but because Carolyn had to come up with a reason for not drinking her champagne. In front of everyone. As the guest of honor.

After the bubbles settled, we each received a glass.

"Saludos a Carolyn!" Carla exclaimed as we all raised our glasses.

"Saludos a mi papá!" Daniel declared.

"Saludos a nuestra angel Rosa!" Tío Dan completed the toast. We all said 'Saludos' with great gusto, and seven of us imbibed our first sip of champagne.

"Off we go!" Carla said as she took Carolyn's arm gracefully to lead us off to meet each and every one of the family and friends gathered to celebrate.

"Just carry the glass around with you, and appear to be taking a dainty sip every so often," Carla discreetly advised Carolyn.

She introduced us to each party, as though she'd known us for most of our lives. In the same manner, she conveyed to Carolyn and me how meaningful each and every one of the guests were to her and her family. It was the finest example of social grace and charm I'd ever witnessed in my life, and it reinforced I was out of my league here at El Gran Sueño with Carolyn and Carla.

After all the introductions had been made, Carla brought us to a table where Tíos Dan and Patricio sat with primos Daniel, Rosa, and Isabella, and directed us to the large buffet with lots of Peruvian favorites to choose from. I filled up on arroz con pato, táquenos, chicharrón pescado, and pollo asado. Carolyn enjoyed a few bites of everything but made sure to save room for dessert. We were told by young Rosa and Isabella that Tío Patricio's homemade chocolate cake was so good we would sell our souls for a second serving.

As Carolyn scraped the last smidge of frosting off her second plate of cake, Tío Dan invited us to take a walk around the gardens surrounding the backside of el restaurante and adjacent inn. Tío Dan preened like a peacock as he informed us they grew all of their own produce and herbs for el restaurante. Much of the meat and poultry were also raised at El Gran Sueño.

We walked through a rose garden, a Japanese-styled bonsai garden, and a cactus garden filled with unique and strange-looking cacti, including the largest one I'd ever seen.

"I like to spend time here in the cactus garden because it is the only place at El Gran Sueño where I'm not the oldest living thing. Some of the cacti are more than a hundred years old," Tío Dan said as we approached an archway with an open black iron gate and two golf carts waiting for us on the other side.

"I want to show you to the main house to get you settled in," Tío Dan said as he motioned for us to get in one of the carts.

"Sounds good, Tío!" Carolyn said as she sat on the driver's side of the cart, and I walked around the cart to get in on the other side.

"This place is quite remarkable. It really is El Gran Sueño," I said as Carolyn pulled away, and we followed Tío Dan and his driver.

"It's beyond words for me right now," Carolyn responded.

"It's hard for me to imagine why your grandfather wanted to leave all this to go to the U.S.," I said.

"No, my grandfather liked books and buildings and being inside of them. There would be way too much family interrupting his alone time. He always had a certain heaviness that surrounded him, and the rest of us, as you can see, are so outgoing. It was like he was from a different family or something. It was weird," Carolyn explained.

"Collin, I feel this strange sort of calling to this place, a need to find out more. Who are these people?" Carolyn wondered out loud.

We were shown into the grand house. We sat down in the parlor, and Tío Dan requested three glasses of Pisco be brought for us. As we talked, Carolyn continued to heed Carla's advice with her make-believe, baby sips every so often.

"Tío Dan, I have to ask you something. Before mi abuela passed away she told me to ask you about some letters. I'm not really sure what that means, but I'm hoping you might know. Do you know what she's talking about?" Carolyn politely, but eagerly, inquired.

"Yes, she sent several letters here to the family and her sister Isabella the first couple of years she lived in Chicago. She did love to write. I remember that," Tío Dan answered.

"Do you know where they are?" Carolyn asked.

"Yes, her sister Isabella took them as keepsakes when she moved to Lake Titicaca with her husband many many years ago." Tío Dan waved his hands for dramatic effect.

"Do you know why she would want me to ask you for them?" Carolyn asked.

"I have no idea why she would want that," Tío Dan said slowly with a confused look on his face, before anxiously scratching his thighs and forehead with both hands.

"Can Isabella send the letters here or scan and email them?" Carolyn asked.

Tío Dan chuckled and explained. "No, that isn't possible. She lives on an island in the middle of nowhere and has no electricity in her home. But you could visit her. I'm sure she would be happy to let you read them or maybe take them with you. I know she would love to meet you as well."

"I'm sorry, she doesn't have electricity? Is that what you said? She didn't pay her bill, or they're doing work to her house? I'm not following you?" Carolyn expressed her confusion.

Tío Dan laughed again and clarified, "Where she lives is a different world, like you have never seen. She's an artist and a seer. She's at one with nature at all times. Regardless of the letters, you really should go."

"I would definitely love to meet her, but we weren't planning to go to Lake Titicaca. Just the name of it makes it sound really far away," Carolyn responded.

"As fate would have it, your primo Namash, who is Isabella's grandson, was just visiting this last week. He's in Paracas now and will be making the journey to Lake Titicaca to visit his Abuela Isabella the day after tomorrow. If you want to go, you should have him take you. I'll send word for him to expect you. Lake Titicaca is on the way to Machu Picchu, if you were planning to go there. Tell Namash, Tío Dan said for him to be your guide, and he'll gladly take you," Tío Dan explained.

"Sounds great. Machu Picchu is definitely on the list. Do you have his number?" Carolyn asked.

"No. Namash doesn't use a cell phone," Tío Dan said.

"Then how exactly are we going to get in touch with him?" A rather bewildered Carolyn asked.

"Paracas is a tiny town, and Namash is beloved there for his art and mystic healing abilities. He has one of his art galleries there to sell his and Abuela Isabella's paintings and sculptures. I'll send word for him to expect you. If he's not in the gallery, ask around, and it won't take you long to find him. Besides, that will be more fun than —how do you kids say it—texting him." Tío Dan explained.

"I have to meet this guy," I said in disbelief that anyone could get by without a cell phone.

"Right! How the hell does he communicate, make plans, or get around?" Carolyn wondered out loud.

"Namash lives in the moment. He's a relic of a different time but in a young man's body," Tío Dan explained.

He continued, "Forgive me, I'm a relic from a different time in an old man's body, and I need to go to retire to my bedroom for the evening. We'll have to forgo the full tour of the house until tomorrow, but I'll show you two where you're staying. After that, if you would like, feel free to explore around the house on your own, or you can go back to la fiesta which will last until the last guest falls over."

"Thank you. I know Collin is ready for more drinks at la fiesta," Carolyn said while poking me in the belly with her index finger.

"Will you be sharing a bedroom, or do you need separate rooms?" Tío Dan asked us.

"Sharing is fine." "Separate rooms."

We answered simultaneously while looking at each other and then Tío Dan.

"Ahhhhh, ha ha ha! I'll take that to mean that one room will do the trick. You know, I'm old and old fashioned, and, in fact, I'm so old I remember when it wasn't so scandalous for boys and girls to like each other. Don't worry, the staff is very discreet." Tío Dan, through his laughter, managed to make an awkward situation for the three of us only awkward for Carolyn and me. Which of course, we deserved.

He continued since neither of us responded, "It's ok Collin, I don't know Carolyn's father, so I can't tell him. You can share a room."

Tío Dan took us upstairs to a series of guest rooms and said we could pick out whichever one we wanted. Our luggage waited at the top of the stairs. He recommended the room at the end of the hall, as it was the largest suite with a spacious and recently renovated bathroom. We took his recommendation and our luggage to the room before heading back to la fiesta.

"You really have a lot of the same features as your Tío Dan. Same facial expressions and mannerisms, when you speak. It's uncanny," I said to Carolyn as we rode back to Cocina Rosa in the golf cart.

"Really? Do you think so? I don't see it," Carolyn said.

"I think it's difficult to see the resemblance we share with family members because we just see ourselves as, well, ourselves," I said.

When we arrived back at el restaurante, la fiesta was still thriving. La musica had gotten louder, and dancing family and friends filled the large circular stage. The volume of the music, the rapidity of the conversations, and the dozen or so Piscos I'd imbibed made nearly everything being said incomprehensible to my intermediate, check that, advanced beginner level Español. I did fully understand el mesero when he would ask, "Pisco otra vez?" We'd have many such conversations throughout the night.

By the time la fiesta wound down and Carolyn and I headed back to the house, I was done for. Carolyn laughed at me wobbling into the house, and we snickered while trying to keep our voices down as she helped me up the stairs. I fell into bed, and Carolyn removed my shoes and pulled my jeans off. My sports coat must have been left at el restaurante, and I passed out in my shirt, socks, and underpants.

I passed out hard and woke up hard. My pulse pumped to the beats of the drummers in my head, leading to the next day's hangover, as the inevitable pain marched forward. Carolyn had gotten up in the middle of the night, and I woke up when she sat on the bed to put her shoes on.

"What's going on? Everything ok?" I asked as I came to suddenly.

"All good. I'm just having trouble sleeping and want to go for a walk. Go back to sleep drunky, and I'll try my best not to wake you again when I come back," Carolyn whispered.

She seemed aggravated, and I hoped it wasn't by my overindulgence. Carolyn was probably disappointed the letters weren't readily available to her at Tío Dan's like she hoped they would be. She'd traveled a long way, twice already, to bring back her grandmother's jewelry box. Now we'd have to set out on a new expedition.

It was also obvious how much joy she'd experienced getting to meet her family here in Perú, and I'm sure she still had the excitement of that running through her veins. There was the other thing too. Her head must've been spinning—almost as much as the ceiling was when I would crack open my eyes. I couldn't have slept either.

When I woke up the next morning, Carolyn wasn't there. I could smell freshly brewed coffee, bacon, and huevos. I followed their scent down to the parlor where Carolyn, Tío Dan, Tío Patricio, Carla, and Daniel were all enjoying café pasado. I hadn't slept in particularly late, but when I arrived, I felt like I was late for the first day at a new job. They were all dressed as though they were going to church, and I came down in the same jeans and shirt from the night before. Carolyn patted the space on the sofa next to her with one hand and offered me a cup of coffee with the other.

"We were just talking about you. I told them you wouldn't be too far behind me," Carolyn said with a smile, pretending that my arrival was anything but awkward.

"And I told her I wouldn't leave you unattended in the bedroom for even a minute. There's a long history of men fraternizing with the help in this house." Carla held a dead serious look on her face, just long enough for me to feel like it was a million years before she and everyone else burst out in laughter.

"Bubba, you wouldn't dream of such a thing, would you?" Carolyn asked while still laughing.

"As a matter of fact, I dreamed of something eerily similar last night," I said with a grin.

"I knew I liked him!" Tío Dan shouted.

We had a nice desayuno, and afterward, Carolyn and I packed for Paracas. She was excited to meet Namash and eager to get to her Tía Isabella's to find out why Abuela Rosa's letters were so important to her. Part of me wanted to go back to Barranco where I had better things to do, like recoup the losses in my trading account and earn a living; however, I also knew if Carolyn was pregnant, if it was mine, and if she decided to keep the pregnancy, we had better find out sooner rather than later if we were going to be able to work as a couple or not. The truth is, I was terrified and didn't know what else to do.

As we closed our suitcases, Carolyn looked at me with a smile and said, "Fight or flight. Outside of your last 7 Piscos last night, you're doing great so far Collin. Thank you."

We went downstairs and sat with Tío Dan in the parlor for a few minutes before we left.

"Tío, why did you and your brother stop talking?" Carolyn asked.

"I wish I could tell you. We had a disagreement before he left, and that was it. He never looked back, and he never wanted to hear from us ever again," Tío Dan explained.

"So weird. He definitely carried the grudge his whole life. I wish I knew why," Carolyn said.

"Me too. As you know, Rosa would write, but he put a stop to that too. I have wanted to ask. How is Samuel?" Tío Dan asked.

"Tío Dan, I'm sorry, I thought you must have known, mi abuelo está muerto." Carolyn said solemnly.

Tears welled up in Tío Dan's eyes and quickly began to stream down his cheeks into his mustache, and as he choked back over 50 years of pain, he said, "You two need to get on the road. I need to excuse myself and mourn mi hermano."

He and Carolyn embraced for several moments. I shook his hand, and we said goodbye.

We could hear Tío Dan weeping as we walked to my Jeep. I said to Carolyn, "There's something he's not telling us."

"Oh, do you think so Inspector Obvious?" Thankfully Carolyn still had her sense of humor.

ELEVEN

PACHAMAMA

The Pan-American Highway

C arolyn and I really didn't know each other all that well yet, but I had a feeling road tripping together would change that. Aside from handling our situation responsibly, I was hesitant to take the next step with Carolyn. I wasn't afraid of what I might learn about her; I was afraid of what she might learn about me.

People tend to fall into one of two categories when traveling. Those like me, constantly wound in a ball with anxiety. Will we be on time? Are we going to miss out on something essential to the experience? What little mishaps could possibly ruin the day? The other group has little concern for any of those things. They just bemusedly go about enjoying themselves without a care in the world. No fear of missing a departure, losing a passport, or the remaining battery length of their cell phone.

I suspected Carolyn belonged to a small, third category of people who are easy to travel with for both types of travelers. She was able to bemusedly go about enjoying herself without a care in the world, while also not ever losing anything or being late.

Technology and a thorough plan were her friends, but she wasn't beholden to them.

About 15 minutes into our drive, Carolyn turned to me and said in a dead serious tone of voice, "It's always important to enjoy the journey as much as the destination, except when you are on the Pan-American Highway going from Lima to Paracas. In that case, Paracas needs to be way better than the way there."

"The desert really is such an unusual place. Isn't it?" I responded.

"Especially when you make it habitable for humans. It's like Tatooine with mid-century architecture," Carolyn commented.

"It's like a postmodern apocalypse."

"It's like Mars—but not as cold—and the sand isn't red."

"Do we know that the sand is red on Mars?"

"It's the red planet. So yeah, the sand is red," Carolyn replied before asking, "Did they film Mad Max here?"

We assumed they had and continued to chit-chat as the road whirred beneath us. Painted-white stone walls lined the highway with the names of Presidential candidates painted in bright red or blue. Which had to be far more effective than lawn signs that the competition could just pull out of the ground. That said, the signs lasted longer than the Presidents themselves.

On the ocean side of the Pan-American Highway, there were little beachfront communities sporadically placed along the coastline. Every so often, we'd think we'd come across a little tree nursery for palms, until the big glass boxes—modern luxury homes—revealed they were trying to build suburbs in the middle of the desert.

The jagged Andes Mountains carved their way through the sky in the distance to the east. The topography of the lowlands and foothills leading towards them made it seem like we were driving through a painting. Vast agricultural fields lined the highway, most likely growing potatoes, corn, or quinoa. Industrial factories would pop up along the way, as well, from time to time. Truth be told, we were enjoying our journey to Paracas, despite our cynical sarcasm as we'd gotten on the road.

We were getting closer to Paracas when Carolyn discovered the town of Pisco on the map and begrudgingly said, "I can't believe I will not be having a glass of Pisco in Pisco. Almost criminal."

Paracas

The bright, multi-colored sign modeled after the internationally renowned Cancun sign greeted us immediately as we pulled off the highway. Paracas was small. If we had to go door to door asking for Namash, we could locate him inside of a day. Based on Tío Dan's description of his popularity, we set the over-under at five for the number of people we'd have to ask. Carolyn had the under. The bet was covering dinner that night, so there wasn't a lot of financial risk involved. I was willing to lose the bet as quickly as possible, if it meant not having to wander the streets looking for Carolyn's cousin all night.

The art gallery Tío Dan sent us to was closed. So we walked along el malecón where all the fishing boats bobbed in the bay as we went. We popped into a bar called Sol de Paracas and asked the bartender. Sure enough, they knew where to find Namash.

"He was just here having a Pisco. You're his primos? Me too! Loco! Me llamo Javier!" The bartender enthusiastically introduced himself.

"We must be on The Candy Camera," Carolyn whispered to me through the side of her mouth.

"We're not. There's only one El Mago. This is not the real Slim Shady," I replied.

"Cusqueña por favor." I ordered a Peruvian beer as a courtesy to the bartender, so we could leave a propina for his help. And because I really wanted—check that, needed—a beer.

He popped the top and offered a glass. Carolyn slid the bottle over to me and declined politely on my behalf. She most certainly knew that beer, like the bottle of wine we shared almost a lifetime ago in her hotel room, already came in a glass. The bartender told us Namash had gone to Waikiki, el restobar around the corner—not the beach near Honolulu. I took a few swigs of beer, and I left 20 soles on the bar for la cerveza and his help. We followed the directions around the corner to Waikiki, and one of the staff welcomed us. Carolyn asked if Namash was there, and moments later they came back to take us to his table.

Namash had the aura of a rock star. Mostly because rock stars tried to look like enlightened faith healers and gurus. Or, maybe gurus tried to look like rock stars. Either way, Namash had the one thing that rock stars and gurus had in common: pure magnetism. His cousin Carolyn had it too, so in the ongoing nature versus nurture debate, chalk this one up to nature.

Namash was well-tanned with long, black hair and electric, green eyes that radiated kindness. When he smiled, bright white teeth beamed out from behind full lips and a dark beard. Although exuberant, his smile also offered solace, making me believe he knew something I didn't. The secret to life was in his back pocket, and he could take it out and share it any time he wanted. When he spoke, his voice soothed and exhilarated the senses all at once. In his presence, I was alive. I was blessed. He not only knew the path to happiness and fulfillment, but I bet he could lead us there too.

"You must be mi prima, Carolyn. You're curious. That's very disco." Namash clasped both of Carolyn's hands and stared deeply into her eyes.

He released Carolyn's hands and turned towards me. Before either of us could say a word, he pulled me in for a hug. With his head next to mine, he said in a whisper, "You're hoping I give you the secret to life, but I can't. I don't know it. And, Collin, you already do."

Namash then clasped one of Carolyn's hands and one of mine while both of us were still mesmerized, and he spoke in a soft, sacred tone, "Carolyn and Collin, it's so nice to meet you both. As you know my name is Namash. I hear from Tío Dan you would like to visit Abuela Isabella on Lake Titicaca. He has asked I guide you there and mentioned you would like to visit Machu Picchu as well. It would be my pleasure to do so with just one condition. When we practice the ceremonial rituals of our ancestors, when I ask you to disrobe, you do so without question. Will you agree to that?"

After just enough time had elapsed for us to inhale all the air out of the room— but before we could let it out in order to respond—

Namash burst out in laughter and said, "I'm fucking with you primos!"

"Welcome! Let's sit down and get to know one another," Namash said as he released our hands and clasped his together in front of his chest to bow slightly forward.

Namash led the way to his table, which was low to the ground inside a teepee with cushions and pillows for us to sit on the floor. The whole restaurant was hippie chic and felt like a cross between a surf lodge and campsite from The Burning Man Festival that was moved indoors. Namash ordered several items off the menu for us to share.

Carolyn confirmed she was eager to meet Namash's Abuela Isabella and listed a few places she wanted to visit in southern Perú on the way there.

"While we're here in Paracas, I highly recommend a boat ride out to las Islas Ballestas tomorrow morning. Tomorrow night we can stay in Huacachina," Namash said.

"I'm going to text our friend Javier to let him know. He's been trying to get me to go to Huacachina, so he could show me the first bar he worked at after getting out of the army. He's got a friend that does dune buggy tours there, and he said we could go whenever," I said.

"Excellent! Always great to have a local connection," Namash replied.

The food arrived along with three glasses of Pisco, and la mesera said with a look of affection, "Let me know if there is anything else I can bring you Namashi."

"Namashi, what else do you recommend we see on the way that I haven't mentioned?" Carolyn asked in a longing tone of voice, mimicking the admiring server.

"Nazca—" Namash began.

Carolyn interrupted and asked, "Nazca is where all the cool drawings that were made by aliens or something are, right?"

"If you believe such things are possible, then yes. It's not every day you get to see the fingerprints of the ancients, alien or human," Namash said.

Namash raised his glass of Pisco and said, "Por Pachamama."

He then poured the first bit of his Pisco on the floor next to the table and invited us to do the same. He explained, "Pachamama is Mother Nature, La Madre Tierra. We offer the first sip to her to say thank you for all she has provided for us."

"Por Pachamama," Carolyn said as she dumped her whole glass on the floor without Namash noticing.

Carolyn and Namash discussed Latin American art while I remained quiet and mostly nodded. I stayed quiet but with less head nodding when Carolyn brought the conversation around to politics. She was curious how the political parties worked in Perú and what the prevailing political philosophies were. Namash was knowledgeable about all 10 major political parties, and the conversation was a lot like taking a Peruvian civics class. Namash, like myself, came off as apolitical.

Namash, apparently, figured since we'd talked politics, we might as well give religion a shot too. He asked Carolyn if, as he assumed, she was raised catholic.

"I'm a lapsed Catholic with a secular humanist compass," she said.

Then Namash turned to me and asked, "What about you my brother? I can tell by the pensive expression on your face you have made a deep and thorough examination of the world's religious expressions. Tell us your story."

"I'm Hinddhudist," I said.

"Hinddhudist?" Carolyn asked.

"Hinddhudist! Bro, that's great! You roll all the spiritual teachings into one philosophy. It's like a cross between Hinduism and Buddhism," Namash explained to Carolyn while laughing.

"Oh kay," Carolyn drew out the syllables while rolling her eyes. "What guides you spiritually, Namash?" Carolyn asked. The good vibes radiating from her cousin must have compelled the question.

"I let my spirit guide me spiritually," Namash said with a wry grin.

He continued, "I have the teachings of my ancestors, and I practice those rituals. Our spirits and gods are symbols for the things we fear or aspire to. I can explain more, but I think as we spend time together, you'll understand better than me just telling you."

"Sounds fascinating, deeply fascinating," Carolyn responded.

When we wrapped up the dinner and conversation. Carolyn pointed out in our excitement to get to Paracas and meet Namash, we'd overlooked booking a place to stay. Thankfully, Namash had us covered because as it turned out, Tío Dan had failed to mention he owned a hotel in Paracas, and Namash was staying there.

"He didn't tell you about the hotel? That is so Tío Dan!" Namash said with uproarious laughter.

"No he did not," Carolyn confirmed in a tone of voice that was less than amused at her uncle's sense of humor.

"He's like you. He's very disco," Namash said while continuing to laugh.

We walked into el hotel lobby and approached the front desk where Namash directed a staff member to take us to our room.

"I must apologize in advance. Your room will be fairly basic and not likely on the same level of the accommodations you've grown accustomed to. It certainly isn't El Gran Sueño. Unfortunately, the best suite is already occupied by a very important guest," Namash said with a grin.

"Namash, you're that guest aren't you?" Carolyn asked.

"Very disco," Namash replied with a joyful smile.

"So, I guess we'll meet you down here in the morning to go to the boat dock?" Carolyn asked Namash.

"No, I'll be already out and about by the time you get going. I'm an early riser," Namash replied.

"How should we find you to meet up?" Carolyn asked.

"Ah, yes. Let me give you my number so you can text me when you're headed out," Namash said.

"You have a cell phone?" Carolyn was stunned.

"Of course," Namash said with a confused look.

"That muh…" Carolyn began to say.

"Tío Dan told us you didn't have a cell phone," I quickly interjected as a smile came across my face. We'd been had.

"And you believed him? Ha! Que cómico!" Namash burst out laughing.

"Yeah, hilarious. That muh—" Carolyn began to say again.

Namash cut her off, "What's that you say in America? Don't hate the player, hate the game? Or something like that."

"That jugador has got jokes all right." Carolyn crossed her arms.

"Prima, it's called a prank. I'd trust Tío Dan with my life," Namash reassured.

"He told us that Abuela Isabella doesn't have electricity. Please tell me that is a prank too," Carolyn said.

"Ha! Not a prank. She doesn't use electricity," Namash confirmed.

The next morning, we laid in bed until Carolyn ran to the bathroom to throw up. After we took desayuno en el hotel, Carolyn texted Namash we were on our way to the dock. Along the way, on the beach wall of el malecón, we encountered a local who had apparently domesticated a pelican. I snapped photos of Carolyn with the gigantic bird, while the bare-chested man tossed fish into its gullet.

"See, Collin, this is a friendly bird. Unlike the Wicked Witch of the West's flying death monkeys from the Wizard of Oz you let sit on your terrace." Carolyn wasn't letting go of the birds in Barranco.

"Just keep following the Yellow Brick Road."

"After we get to Oz, will you pull back the curtain to show me the wizard, while I click my heels three times?"

Namash was waiting for us with a boat, and we cast off toward las Islas Ballestas. As the islands came into sight, sea lions joined us, looking for their breakfast and having a nice, morning swim. They seemed to be smiling, as they went about their business being sea lions.

Las islas were perilously jagged rock islands that had been carved out by the ocean from hundreds of thousands, if not millions, of years of waves crashing back and forth across their treacherous surfaces. The water took on a beautiful deep crystal blue color as it engulfed the burgundy-red rock bases plunging to the depths of the ocean. Mysterious tunnels and archways created enchanting passageways that pierced through the incredible rock formations.

The solid rock archipelago held no habitability for humans but swarmed with wildlife. Glorious pink flamingos, countless packs of seals and sea lions, and plenty of Carolyn's favorite—Humboldt Penguins—waddled around the rocky cliffs, plopping on their bellies as they dove into the ocean. After we finished circling the islands and headed back to Paracas, Namash summed it up well when he said, "Pachamama has given us many remarkable places here in Perú, but none are more endearing to your heart than las Islas Ballestas. It's a magical place.

TWELVE

PAST, PRESENT, AND FUTURE

S wirling sand laced the highway to Huacachina. The top was off of the Jeep, and the afternoon desert sun was cooking us. DJ Carolina had the music blasting over the sound of the wind and the rubber tires running over the road. There was a palpable exhilaration in the air. The kind of feeling you have when you don't know exactly what, but something exciting, is going to happen.

In the distance, we began to see the foothills of the muscular Andes mountains. The panoramic view of the desert was vast and spectacular. Just the way it was on the way to Paracas, it felt as though we were driving through a massive mural of southern Perú. Carolyn seized the moment.

"Namash, I need you to take my picture cruising through the desert," Carolyn shouted to her cousin over the wind and music as she unbuckled her seat belt and turned to hand him her cell phone.

"I'll tell you when I'm ready," Carolyn continued to shout directions after she turned back around and unhooked her bra underneath her tank top from the front passenger seat.

"You ready? When I say go, just start snapping fotos," Carolyn directed, as she stood up and pulled her bra out from the tank top.

"Listo!" Namash shouted up to Carolyn in the front seat to let her know he was ready.

"Three, two, one, disco!" Carolina shouted the countdown, and then she pulled off her tank top and spread her arms wide into a 'V'. She had her tank in one hand, bra in the other, and both hands flashing peace signs.

"Yasssssssssssss! Are you getting this Namash?" Carolina knew she was magnificent, charging towards the Andes chest first into the bright sun, beaming with an exuberant smile.

"I'm getting it! Video now! Put your chin down, shake your hair out, and then show your face to the sky! Yes! Yes! Yes! That's it! Love it!" Namash cheered Carolina on and managed to become a professional videographer in the back seat.

I had no idea what the handful of cars and trucks passing in oncoming traffic thought, but just once in my life, I'd like to be that spontaneously cool. Just one time. Of course, I'd already tried many times. Of those, perhaps the most spectacular failure was an attempt at a friend's wedding in the Florida Keys to lead the group skinny dipping. Nobody followed. On top of that, there was no ladder out of the water back over the sea wall, so my only route back to land was a moss-covered boat ramp made from a mixture of coral and concrete. As I slipped and fell my way up the ramp, my hands, arms, feet, and legs were lacerated in about a thousand places. The streaming blood was at least a distraction from the retraction of my shriveled masculinity.

At any rate, Carolyn really was born with it.

Huacachina Desert Oasis

The desert oasis of Huacachina was on the outskirts of Ica, known for its vast Pisco and wine vineyards. Several places offer tours of vineyards and distilleries with bodegas offering tastings of the local treasure. Since we weren't going to be doing any Pisco tastings, there was no need to stop as we drove through town.

Javi and his girlfriend, Jennifer, greeted us when we arrived. Jennifer was just a little taller than Javi and had jet-black hair cut shoulder length. She was wearing denim shorts and a tank over a bikini top.

"Jennifer wants to head to the pool and relax while the rest of us hit the dunes," Javi said.

"Oh my god, a pool sounds amazing right now! I'm going with Jennifer!" Carolyn said as it just occurred to me that a dune buggy ride wasn't in the cards for her right now.

"Sure. Yeah. We can hit the pool," I said as the excitement drained out of Javi's body.

"No! You boys go play in the dirt," Carolyn said.

"Are you sure?" I asked.

"Yes, she's sure!" Javi grabbed my arm and marched us toward his friend's beat-up, white van.

Javi's friend slid the door open and we hopped in.

"A month ago you were afraid to call Carolyn on the phone, and now you want to follow her around like a puppy dog," Javi said as we headed through the local town on a winding road lined with bodegas and barefoot children playing in the dirt.

"Javi, are you sure you're tall enough to go on the dune buggy?" I asked as Namash rolled with laughter in the row behind us.

After we reached the launch point into the desert dunes, we got out of the van and hopped in the buggy. Javi's friend gave us some basic instructions, "Please wear your seat belts, and if we flip over, don't die. I'm not insured for that."

He did come around to check our belts, then hopped in the driver seat, and took off like an Usain Bolt of lightning. The adrenaline kicked in immediately as we flew up and over the dunes. Each hellacious turn felt like our bodies were belted in, but our guts were going to fly out of the vehicle. We would pop up to the top of a dune—the Andes in one direction and the sun descending over the horizon in the other—before instantly losing sight of both as we dropped 30 meters down the face of the dune in less than a second.

This was faster and more thrilling than any roller coaster I'd ever been on. I was at once terrified and exhilarated. My face hurt from laughing so hard. There was no choice. Relent to the skill of the driver, the design of the vehicle, and enjoy the ride. Anytime he slowed the buggy to navigate the sand, all I could think was, 'Faster, faster, again, again. Do it again!'

The driver found a good place on top of a ridge for us to catch our breaths and watch the sun set. From our vantage point, it was impossible to know where exactly in the world we were. The past, present, and future of the vast Peruvian desert were being blown over billowing dunes. The sun was setting in the west, as it's known to do, but other than that, there was nothing but wilderness. The whole experience was breathtaking.

Night had descended, and the driver turned the headlights on for us to buggy back down into Huacachina. The dark water of the oasis reflected the lamp posts placed along el malecón to light the path for evening strollers, as well as the lights from the hotels, restaurants, and bars that surrounded the small desert oasis.

Carolyn and Jennifer were ready to go to dinner when we came back and waited for the rest of us to shower up and change quickly. When we were all ready, Javi took the lead and walked us around the oasis to the place where he had his first bartending job after he'd served in the Peruvian Army.

"Señor Collin, Namash, Carolyn, it would be my pleasure to introduce you to el restobar Huacafuckingchina!" Javier proclaimed with his arms wide open. He was beaming with pride.

This three-level restobar was the epicenter of la fiesta. Young Peruanos and Peruanas had come here to let their inhibitions get lost and wander in the desert, and they were thirsty.

La musica was pumping, and Carolyn was ready for it. She and her cousin Namash danced their way up the stairs as they followed Javi to the two tables he had reserved for us on el balcón, overlooking el malecón and the Huacachina Oasis. Jennifer was reserved, as though she was saving her energy for more important things. It would've been easy to confuse the atmosphere for Bourbon Street in The Big Easy. Though you would need to substitute Pisco shots for beads, and the DJ's beats bouncing off the beautiful waterfront for the marching jazz bands in the gritty streets of the French Quarter. The crowd was eating, drinking, and being merry.

After we ate, Carolyn placed her hand on my knee and said, "Tell me that deciding to go to Tanta that first night I came to Lima wasn't the best decision of your life?"

"You're resulting."

"What does that mean?"

"You're attributing the quality of the result to the quality of the decision. It's an expression poker players use."

"Would you like to gamble? Do you feel lucky tonight, Collin?" Carolyn spoke slowly, as her chin now rested on my shoulder.

"The odds appear to be stacked in my favor," I answered blithely and tried to ignore my heart rate elevating in proportion to the stakes Carolyn was raising.

"Do you have to make sure the odds are stacked in your favor before you make every decision?" Carolyn said as her chin lifted off my shoulder, and the tip of her nose grazed my neck just below my ear lobe.

"No, I make plenty of bad decisions," I answered while chills ran up my spine.

"You want to make a bad decision right now, don't you?" Carolyn whispered seductively, and she slid her hand from my knee up my thigh.

"I want some of my available bloodstream to return to my head, so that I am capable of making a decision." I confessed what she already knew: she had complete control of my anatomy and its individual components at this point.

"Let's get out of here and go back to the room. Yeah?" Carolyn suggested.

I don't remember if I agreed or responded in any way. I lost track of time and space. Carolyn got Jennifer's attention as we stood up and passed her her credit card. She gave explicit instructions that that card was to be used to pay the bill at the end of the night. By process of elimination, Carolyn knew Jennifer was the one in the group with the best chance of following directions. We left and strolled along el malecón on the way to our hotel.

Mama Killa, Mother Moon, was full and bright, amplifying her moonlight like a sonata on the rippling oasis. Carolyn softly slid her fingers in between mine, and my whole life started to flash before my eyes. Carolyn wasn't just seducing me. This was something different. I suspected that Carolyn was beginning to fall for me. Not suspected, I hoped. Everything I could have possibly wanted was now literally in the palm of my hand, but I wasn't sure if I could close my fingers and take hold.

"Did you have any idea this place would be this romantic Collin?" Carolyn asked as our hands glanced our hips with the swing of our arms.

"I had no idea. I'm willing to bet there are more unplanned pregnancies per capita here than anywhere else in Perú." I answered and tried to remain relaxed.

"Not romantic, Collin," she said before she swung in front of me, placed her hands on my chest, and asked, "Wouldn't this be a great place for a first kiss?"

"As good as any I guess," I answered less than romantically.

"It could be our first kiss, you know, as a couple. We haven't said that yet. Would you like to kiss me and make me your girlfriend, Collin?" Carolyn asked as the moonlight reflected in her dark eyes.

"Obviously, I'd like to do a lot more than kiss you." I hoped honesty would get me out of this jam.

"I'm serious! Are we doing this or what?" Carolyn demanded to know, as she pushed me away with both hands.

"Wait. What? Doing what?" I asked as I caught my balance.

"You can't be this clueless," Carolyn said in frustration.

"I can if you don't give me any clues as to what you are talking about," I responded with an equally frustrated tone.

"I've been giving you clues since we met!" Carolyn shouted at me.

"You're trying to ruin this trip aren't you?" I asked in an apparent attempt to do anything other than diffuse the situation.

"No, I'm trying to make this the greatest trip of our lives, and you're playing stupid," Carolyn said, clearly disappointed.

"I'm not playing stupid. Back at the restaurant, I thought you were priming me to take advantage of me sexually. Now, I'm not sure if I'm supposed to take a knee and propose, or what?" I snapped back.

"We both know, if someone around here is going to propose, it would be me," Carolyn said.

"Well, I'd have to think about it," I replied.

"I'm not proposing to you, Collin. I'm trying to establish that we like each other, and we actually might have a future together. Why is that so mystifying? Yes, I want to go back to the room to get primal with you, and yes, I'd like for it to be emotionally intimate as well. Are you capable of holding two thoughts in your head at the same time?" The volume of Carolyn's voice rose little by little as she spoke until reaching a volume that reverberated over the water.

"It's not mystifying. It's terrifying," I admitted to both of us.

"I get it. I'm scared too, but aren't all the best things in life just on the other side of breaking through some kind of fear?" she asked.

"And don't you think you should find out who the father is before we commit to anything?" I asked.

"No Maury Povich, I don't. My pregnancy, no matter who the father is, will not determine who I fall in love with," Carolyn said.

"Has it occurred to you that maybe you shouldn't fall in love with me? You're way too good for me. You know that, right?" I asked.

"Actually no, that hasn't occurred to me. I believe we've covered this. You're here because I think you're great. Other than you, I bet everyone is thinking how lucky I'd be to be with you." She couldn't possibly really think that.

"What happens when you get to know me a little better down the road, and you change your mind?" I asked knowing that she really didn't have the full picture yet.

"Collin, you'd be just fine without me. You're rich, you're intelligent, you're funny occasionally. What are you so afraid of? You have everything a reasonable person could dream of having. What more do you want?" Carolyn didn't understand, and she didn't provide any guarantees either.

"I'm not that rich. What more do I want? To be happy for longer than a few months at a time maybe?" I answered.

Carolyn paused for a second and asked, "Haven't we been having a good time together? Don't we click? Don't you think I could make you happy?"

"For sure, but that doesn't necessarily last. Happy is the wrong word. I mean something satiating and lasting. Free of stress, fear, worry, loneliness." I tried to explain but kept coming up short.

"You're lonely. Is that it? I'm right here, you big dummy," Carolyn said before she smacked me upside the shoulder.

"Do you know what's worse than being lonely? Having been in a relationship that should have been perfect—that could have been everything you wanted—so much so that you gave a hundred million percent of your soul to it, and then it's taken away from you. Lonely is a whole lot better than having your heart ripped out." I was breathing hard now.

"How do you know it would end up that way?" Carolyn couldn't understand my pessimism.

"I don't, but the probabilities seem stacked heavily in favor of it going that way. Also, I would be lying if I said I wasn't intimidated by your family. I didn't come from anything like that, and I don't just mean the money," I tried to explain.

"Collin, I barely know these people! Remember when Tío Dan asked about rooms? I was the one who said the same room, and you said separate rooms. If I'm comfortable being with you around my family, then you should be able to be comfortable around my family. Regardless of who's accomplished more, or has a more appealing life, I invited you there. That should be enough. Beyond that, do you think everything is perfect at El Gran Sueño? Do you think that Tío Dan never has problems or self-doubt? Do you think that mis primos have everything figured out and have raised perfect daughters without a tear being shed? Come on, there are more than a few chinks in the armor. I'm sure of it," Carolyn said.

I was unconvinced and didn't say anything, so she continued, "Besides all that, if anyone looked at your life from the outside, they'd think you have it all figured out. You have a multimillion-dollar home overlooking the Pacific. You eat and drink whatever you want. You go wherever you want, whenever you want to go there. What more do you need?"

"I know that, but it's never enough. I wasn't raised in poverty, but times were usually tough. I always assumed lack was the source of my unhappiness, so I've always been hellbent on making money and being successful. Maybe if I accomplished enough, I'd be worthy of being loved," I said.

"Collin, love is not something you can ever earn. It's something someone gives you freely, that you have to accept," Carolyn said.

"Is that what we're talking about? When you ask me if we're

doing this or not, I don't know if you mean sleeping together, starting to date, falling in love, or what. I have no idea. What I want, I don't feel worthy of. What I think I can get makes me think I'd be taking advantage of you in some way, even though I'm pretty sure you can't be taken advantage of. Now that I've said all that, I'm pretty sure you're not going to be horny or interested in me romantically in the slightest." I let it all hang out.

"Honestly, Collin, I feel like both trips I've taken to Lima… no matter which direction I turn in, there's an obstacle. I keep getting tripped up. Something tells me that what I think I'm looking for isn't really what I'm looking for. I can't help but think that while I'm looking for Abuela Rosa's letters, the thing I should be finding is you. I give up. I don't want to keep tripping and stumbling. I want to fall, but you won't let me. Let me fall, and then if you want to, catch me. If not, then at least I can get up, dust myself off, and get on with getting my grandmother's letters and go home."

She was right. I didn't want to let her fall. I had her on a pedestal and wanted to keep her there.

"Fuck," I said as the reality of the moment sank in.

"Yeah, not horny at all now. Nice going," Carolyn said with a somewhat comforting grin.

"Sorry about that," I said.

"Collin, it sounds to me like you are terrified of losing something that you don't have yet. Have you heard the expression, 'It's better to have loved and lost, than never to have loved at all?'" Carolyn asked.

"Whoever said that had a lot left to learn about life," I said.

"Collin, you have a lot to learn about love."

"I'll need a teacher."

"You know what I've learned?" Carolyn asked, and I paused to allow her to answer, "Sometimes the journey is better than the destination. Except when it involves overthinking shit on the Huacachina Malecón on the way back to the bed in our hotel room."

113

THIRTEEN
CLIMBING IN LOVE

Nazca

C arolyn had arranged for a private Cessna to take us all up to fly over the world-famous Nazca Lines. Once we were done touring the Lines we'd go back to the Nazca airport and change planes to a chartered jet that would take us on to Arequipa. Carolyn and I split the rather pricey expenditure that I never would have splurged for, but it was definitely worth it. I'd had enough of driving through the desert. Javi and Jennifer would be taking my Jeep back to Lima since they both had to be back for work.

A little while after we were in the air, Namash began to point out the geoglyphs carved into the dry desert surface below. There were several animals, geometric shapes, and lots of grouped lines. He told us that with the advent of the drone age, they were finding more and more every day. There were more than a thousand dating back over 2000 years that had been discovered.

It was remarkable being able to make our way to find Abuela Isabella through the south of Perú with a native who had a high level of knowledge and deep appreciation for his country's culture and beauty. The wonder, joy, and excitement he had was contagious. Namash was never bored with anything. For him, each moment in time was unique, with a whole new set of possible outcomes. This wasn't sightseeing. This was something different. Everything was magical.

I imagined that people just like Namash had created the world's largest street art display in the expansive desert canvas below. Carolyn stood by her alien thesis. Namash offered the standard explanation that the local Nasca people, who thrived in the area for about 700 years, had probably drawn most of them. The Paracas culture that predated the Nasca people had drawn many of the designs and hundreds of the straight lines and geometric shapes as well.

"I'm fascinated by the stories of why the lines were drawn, as much as the drawings themselves. What do you think, Namash? Astrological calendar? Alien landing pad?" I asked Namash.

"I think people like to draw and play in the dirt." Namash reminded me what it was like to be a child again.

Arequipa

Our stop in The White City, named for the colorless volcanic rock that it was built with, served two purposes. It was second only to Machu Picchu of places Carolyn wanted to see in Perú, and the time here would help us adjust to the altitude in the Andes. At 2300 meters in elevation, Arequipa is a bit more than half as high as we would be on Lake Titicaca to meet Abuela Isabella.

When we went out on the hotel's rooftop terrace, there was just enough light remaining to provide a dramatic dusk vista of the snow-capped Volcánes Chachani and Misti. The terrace overlooked the magnificent Plaza de Armas in the center of Arequipa. The chilled evening air to let us know we were underdressed. The hotel had a beautiful lliklla, which is the Quechua name for an alpaca shawl, they gave Carolyn to warm her up. Her Grace was, as by now expected, attended to flawlessly.

"I know the elevation is a factor for temperature, but it's so weird that it's so much colder here than Lima or Paracas. I wonder why that is?" Carolyn asked.

"Because female praying mantises devour the male after mating," I remarked.

"The sarcastic ones are especially delicious," Carolyn said.

Namash laughed and explained, "Perú has something like 30 different microclimates. The coast is low elevation and always dry, so it follows the traditional winter-summer rotation. The Amazon and the Andes, however, are divided by wet and dry seasons, as opposed to winter and summer. We're here in rainy season. We definitely need to go shopping tomorrow, so you'll be properly dressed for the cold, wet weather,"

En la mañana, we set out down Calle Santa Catalina to acquire appropriate Andean wet season wardrobes. Namash chose all of Carolyn's clothes and accessories. Carolyn chose all of mine. She looked like an Inkan Queen, if they had traveled into the future and were about six feet tall. I looked like an American trying to look like a local tour guide, which for the record, was not the look I was going for. Namash and Carolyn couldn't stop laughing.

We dropped the plunder of our shopping excursion back at the hotel, and like teenagers going downtown without their parents for the first time, we set out into the plaza. Just down la cuadra from our hotel was Iglesia de La Compañía. This Jesuit church had an elaborately carved stone facade reminiscent of the cathedrals in Seville. From there, we walked diagonally across Plaza de Armas to the entrance of Arequipa Catedral, which spanned the entire width of la cuadra. It had two impressive bell towers mimicking Volcánes Chachani and Misti behind it to the left and to the right.

The cathedral housed several breathtaking artifacts made from gold and precious stones. In one of the many secure glass displays, there was an ornate corona for la Virgen Maria that had over a thousand diamonds, many of which were several carats to my untrained eye.

"I see they've taken the utmost care of your crown while you aren't using it," I commented to Carolyn, whose catholic upbringing provided her with the intuition not to laugh at my joke.

Another visitor with a high level of church artifact knowledge didn't care for my joke and informed us, "That crown was worn only by the Blessed Virgin Mary. No one else, not even the Pope or the Cardinal, would wear that crown."

"I don't get it. Was she here? What does she mean the Virgin Mary wore the crown?" I whispered under my breath to Namash as we walked to another display.

"Primo, stop! You're going to get us kicked out of here," Namash whispered back while trying to contain his laughter.

"It would not be the first time I wasn't welcome in one of God's houses," I said.

"Just make sure She is welcome in yours, and it will all work out," Namash said with a grin.

To continue our religious and architectural experiences for the day, we walked dos cuadras to Monestario de Santa Catalina and explored the massive convent that was originally founded in 1579. The living quarters for the monjas, despite their short doorways, were surprisingly large but very dark, as there were only a sporadic amount of small windows in the stone structures. The courtyards and gardens throughout the monestario were beautiful and must have lent themselves to a great deal of time in quiet contemplation in the outdoors.

"This is great. I won't have to go to church for another 10 years," Carolyn commented.

"Or we could leave you here to search for your lost faith," Namash suggested.

"Don't worry. I'll rescue you if I have to," I said.

"I would need no such savior," Carolyn declined.

After lunch, we went to La Ruta Sillar to see several different active and historic quarries where, beginning in colonial times, Arequipa's builders harvested Ashlar, a white volcanic rock. Quarry workers had carved massive shield crests into the towering rock walls, and there were lots of different sculptures to pose and take pictures with like they were celebrities. A few vendors had set up tables with different artistic pieces carved from the white volcanic stone. Namash and Carolyn picked out a small puma sculpture to take to Namash's Abuela Isabella, who was a sculptor herself.

"She'll love this. Lake Titicaca means either gray or stone puma depending on the local language," Namash explained.

"Is there such a thing as a gray puma?" I asked Namash.

"I've never seen one, but that doesn't mean they don't exist," Namash replied.

"Collin, you were wearing gray Pumas the first night we met," Carolyn said cracking herself up.

Namash took us to Sillar Rosado where the composition of minerals in the sand and stone and angle of the sunlight gave the sub-terrain passageway a pink penumbra. Before we descended into the pathway, Namash told us about the thousands of piles of small stones stacked up like miniature stone snowmen. They were called Apachetas and were ofrendas to Pachamama. We slithered our way through the narrow winding canal with the sense we were nearing sacred ground. The canal opened wider, and there were petroglyphs of pumas, condors, and serpents depicting ancient stories on the walls.

The ancient people who had tamed these lands drew upon their faith, the dense desert ground, and their secret stone walls. What was I drawing upon? What story was I leaving behind? If Carolyn decided to keep her pregnancy, what could I tell our child about finding his or her way through the bewildering world? I didn't have a clue how I would do it, but I realized it was time to stop worrying about everything working out the way I wanted it to. It was time to embrace whatever role the universe would assign to me next. I at least suspected that if I did, I would find the meaning and purpose that had been missing my entire life.

We made it back to Plaza de Armas just in time to sneak into Museo Santuarios Andinos before it closed. El museo displayed Inkan artifacts from a 1995 expedition to the summit of Volcán Ampato. The most important discovery was the mummy Juanita, a young girl of approximately 12 years who had been sacrificed to the gods in the mid-1400s by the Inka.

Namash explained that it would have bestowed honor on her family, and Juanita would have willingly made the trek to the sacred sacrificial ground near the top of the volcano. Because the ground had been frozen all these 500-plus years since her sacrifice, Juanita and her ceremonial clothes were almost perfectly preserved and intact. She likely would have been drinking Chicha, a maize alcohol, to give her relief from the elements and to keep her calm as she climbed the mountain. At the top, there was a pre-dug mountain tomb where she would sit down with her knees to her chest and complete her sacrifice to the gods by being struck on top of her head with a blunt object.

While we were staring through the glass at her frozen body, Carolyn whispered, "Can you imagine what it would feel like to sacrifice your child to the gods?"

"I wouldn't let it happen," I said firmly.

THE NEXT MORNING, Carolyn rushed to the bathroom and was sick. I casually followed her in and pulled her hair into a ponytail behind her.

"You don't need to do that," Carolyn said as she wiped the side of her mouth with the back of her hand.

"I don't mind at all," I replied.

"Let me say it another way. Get out of the bathroom, Collin!" Pulling Carolyn's hair back was apparently not the next role the universe had assigned me.

Namash had one of his primos waiting with a van that would take us the rest of the way to Lake Titicaca. The real climb into the Andes was now underway. We stopped a few times along the way to observe the diverse selection of alpacas, llamas, and vicuñas tranquilly grazing the altiplano. At one point, near a stream of snow melt, two local Quechua women had gathered 30 or 40 alpacas and llamas of all different ages, shapes, sizes, and colors on the hillside beside the road. Carolyn had scooped up and was cradling one of the baby alpacas in her arms. Abruptly, she let the baby slide from her grip onto the ground, before scampering down the road a bit and hurling. I took the portable oxygen can out of my backpack and went to offer some support.

"Altitude or morning sickness?" I asked softly and handed Carolyn some tissue.

"Uppercut or straight right hand? Pass me the O, asshole." I wasn't even mad. As we were climbing in elevation, I think I was falling in love.

After the two-mile-high safari, the van took us to the crest of Patapampa Pass to stop at the Mirador de Los Andes, nearly 5000 meters high in the sky. As we strolled amongst the thousands of apachetas, we found Yarita plants sporadically covering the rocky terrain. From a distance, they looked like an iridescent green moss covering the rocks, but when we went in for a closer look, there were hundreds of tiny succulents pressed together into a matte. Yarita plants grow less than 2 centimeters per year and live anywhere from 800 to 1200 years. We were walking amongst living things that had been on the planet before the printing press was invented.

The experience left us breathless as we explored, pulling the thin mountain air into our lungs and the unparalleled views across the volcanic peaks of the Andes into our hearts. Carolyn, Namash, and I placed our own apachetas side by side to honor the experience and leave an offering for Pachamama.

"This might be the highest I've ever been. Literally and figuratively," I announced.

"Probably literally, definitely not figuratively," Carolyn said with a laugh.

"This is indescribable. I can't get over all the colors," I said.

"Now I know the inspiration for the bright traditional clothing here in Perú," Carolyn said.

Namash summed it all up poetically. "This is the thing with Perú. It's yellow, orange, and it's blue. Perú is purple, red, and it's green. It's real, surreal, and it's just a dream. The needle and the thread that Pachamama pulled through, all the colors embroidered together for the dream that you make and the one that made you."

Valle del Colca

Alongside Rio Colca, the Colca Lodge is close to heaven, but it's on earth. After our first dip in las aguas termales at the lodge, we took a relatively short, but arduous, hike from the lodge up the mountainside to Uyo Uyo. This archeological site dated back to the 1200s and was the capital of the Colca Valley for both the Collagua Culture and the Inka who followed. The Spanish had burned the settlement and killed all who lived there, as was their custom to do so in the region. Enough of the stone structures remained to visualize how daily life in Uyo Uyo would have been.

The view from the site revealed countless terraced farms on both sides of el Río Colca, growing Peruvian staples and superfoods: potatoes, corn, quinoa, maca, and kiwicha. There were stone-walled corrals for cattle and sheep, and aside from the luxury lodge we were staying at, not much had changed in 800 years. Unlike the ancient ruins in Lima, here there weren't any tourists or signs of modernity. For the moment, time travel—at least backward— seemed possible and instilled a certain romantic notion of what life could be like.

In that moment, I was transformed from being the kind of traveler who constantly worried about everything working out perfectly to a traveler who enjoyed where they were, simply for the sake of taking in a new experience.

Until Carolyn decided to make friends with a white cow with black spots that had been tied up to a small stake near the trail. All the other cows were grazing freely and paying no attention to us.

My spidey sense had been activated and called out to Carolyn, "Be careful!"

"Lighten up Allweather. It's a cow," Carolyn said as she stroked its nose.

"Just be careful. One sudden move from that thing, and you don't know what could happen," I said.

"Primo, it's a cow. they don't make sudden moves!" Namash said through his laughter.

The cow lowered its head and slowly started to nuzzle into Carolyn.

"See! It loves me!" she proclaimed as the cow started to slowly walk forward with its head pushing into Carolyn. She started to back away, and the cow started walking progressively faster toward her. Carolyn turned and walked away, and the cow picked up speed pursuing its new love interest. She yelled, "Namash!"

"Just slowly walk away. It's tied up, Prima," replied Namash.

"Why did you call for Namash?" I asked.

"Because you don't know shit about cows Collin!" Carolyn said as la vaca continued to gather momentum.

"Oh fuck," Namash said.

"Oh fuck what?" Carolyn asked slowly.

"The stake pulled out of the ground," Namash answered.

"Run!" I shouted, and we all sprinted for the roadside.

THAT EVENING, the mineral-laden thermal waters and the crisp cool evening air awaited us. The stars and Mama Killa shone brightly in the spaces between the passing clouds. The volcanically warmed water stole the shiver from our exposed skin, brought bliss to our muscles, organs, and bones, and sculpted our souls like soft wet clay on the potter's wheel.

That night in each other's arms, our emotional intimacy incubated along with the potential for a family, under the lush linens surrounding us in our sleep. Inkan spirits and mystical Andean wildlife filled my dreams. It was as if I was inside of a painting while it was being made. Drifting between the canvas and the artist's brush as the paint, forming one vision after another. I woke up feeling that real life was the illusion. The universe's dimensions are deeper than I allowed myself to realize, and a vast horizon of quantum possibilities awaited on just the other side of my closed eyelids.

Since Carolyn and I met, we were on a crash course with life-altering experiences. She was born ready. For the first time, like a good wine that had been laid down to mature so that all the flavor could develop, I was ready to be consumed.

We left the lodge early in the morning to go to Mirador Cruz del Condor. Because of the time of year, we had limited expectations of seeing any condors at all, but the clouds had broken open a bright crisp morning, which—against the odds—brought the giant Andean condors out to soar in the sun. The black birds have collars of soft white feathers around their necks beneath their dark featherless faces and have white tips to their three-meter-long wingspans and beaks. They are larger, slightly kinder-looking, versions of their close cousins los Gallinazos en Lima.

The condors were magnificent as they patrolled the 3,400-meter-deep Colca Canyon. They would swoop down towards the canyon floor and then rise effortlessly in a spiral path toward the heavens propelled by invisible air currents.

"Aren't they wonderful!" I shouted.

"They really are awe-inspiring. Especially when they're off in the distance in flight, as opposed to lining up on your terrace, Collin," Carolyn compromised.

"Heavenly, you could say. The condor represents the heavens in Quechua culture. They are an important symbol for carrying our loved ones from this life to the next when they pass away," Namash explained.

"It's nice to think there was someone helping Abuela Rosa when she left us," Carolyn said with tears forming in her eyes.

"They really do look like spirits ascending to the heavens, gliding left and right. For such an endangered species, they don't seem to have a care in the world," I noticed.

Back on the road, we passed through los pueblos Pinchollo, Maca, and Yanque and saw various colonial-era iglesias in each town's Plaza de Armas. It struck me that the condors transporting human spirits from their earthly lives to their heavenly ones didn't have to travel nearly as far in these towns as they do in Lima or Chicago.

We left the serenity of the Colca Valley, and it was onward to Puno to reach the ultimate purpose of our journey: Abuela Rosa's letters. This time there were no views of the volcanic peaks of the Andes. It was dark, and the sky sporadically spat a mixture of snow, sleet, or tiny hail with persistent rain streaking down our van's windows. As my head rested on the cold glass, my breath fogged the window. Carolyn pulled my arm around her and rested her head on my chest. I was warm on the inside as we ascended in elevation along the winding highway. The last two days, we'd been climbing in love.

"We're almost there," I said.

Carolyn searched for my hand and then pulled our clasped hands onto her stomach and said, "I feel like Abuela Rosa is with us, guiding us to her sister. I feel like it's all a dream, and I don't want to wake up. That when I do, no matter how hard I try, I won't be able to remember what happened."

FOURTEEN

THE PUMA AND THE CONDOR

Titiqaqa Qucha

We made our way down through the hillside city of Puno to the shore of Lake Titicaca. We boarded a small outboard motorboat in the darkness to go to the Uros islands. The Uros are small human-made islas crafted from the reeds growing in the lake. The Uru people use the dense root base of the reeds to create the core of the island and cover them with deep layers of cut reeds. We would stay overnight on one of these islas, also called a flotante, where a local Uru family would host us in the largest lake in South America.

As our boat navigated the reed patches, illuminated only by a handheld flashlight, it was as though we were arriving at the beginning of something that never ended as we stared out over the dark waters of the lake. For the Inka, this place was the beginning of time. The short boat ride in the dark gave Namash just enough time to tell us the Inka legend of creation. The same way his father had told him when he was a young boy, and they shared a boat ride on Lake Titicaca.

He began, "Viracocha was the great creator of all. He rose from Lake Titicaca in pure darkness, darker than it is now, to bring forth the light. Viracocha formed the sun, the moon, and the stars to give us light and commanded the sun and moon to travel around the earth to create time. He created giant living beings from stones who occupied the land. His wife was Mama Qucha, the goddess of the lakes, rivers, and seas. They had one son, Inti, the Sun God and two daughters, Mama Killa, who is Mother Moon, and Pachamama, Mother Earth."

Namash paused his explanation to raise his hands toward the sky and declared in Quechua, "A Mama Killa! Kusikuywanmi napaykukiku, k'anchayniykiwan samikuspayku!"

"This means, Mother Moon, with great joy we salute you basking in your great light!" Namash translated, the clouds parted, and a nearly full moon appeared brightly in the sky.

"Unreal!" Carolyn said as we both shivered from the cold and nature's response to Namash's voice.

"Do not be so amazed, Prima. Mama Killa may reveal herself or not. That she chose to do so after my prayer is because we were ready to see her. Mama Killa and Pachamama will provide for us exactly what we need, exactly when we are ready to receive it." Namash's voice was calm, as though he witnessed these kinds of miracles all the time.

"A Pachamama tiyayukuy teqsemuyuq hatun kallpan!" Namash said as he bowed his head downward.

"This means, Mother Earth, we welcome the great power of the universe!" Namash's voice resounded through the dark night sky.

Something came over me, and I spontaneously shouted, "Mama Killa!"

"Collin!" Carolyn smacked my thigh with the back of her hand.

"No, that's good, Prima. His spirit is pure. Often when one reunites with nature, they declare her glory, seemingly out of turn in our social norms." Namash knew I was along for more than just a boat ride.

The clouds had covered Mama Killa once more, and a steady drizzle invigorated the water on the lake's surface.

"Great, Collin, you scared Mama Killa away," Carolyn said.

"Perfect timing to continue our story," Namash said.

"Just saying," Carolyn stated for the record.

"Viracocha was displeased with the beings he had created from the stones. They were living giants, but they were mindless. He brought a great rain that lasted 60 days and 60 nights that drowned all the beings around Lake Titicaca in a great flood we call Unu Pachakuti. Two beings, the children of Inti who were born on Isla del Sol in the middle of Lake Titicaca, survived. Manco Cápac, which means splendid foundation, and Mama Uqllu, which means mother fertility, and together they gave life to the Inka civilization." Namash turned his attention to the small island we were approaching.

"Yes, Isla del Sol! I've wanted to go there. Maybe we can go after we meet Abuela Isabella," I said excitedly, after patiently waiting for Namash to finish the tale.

"Sounds good to me," Carolyn replied.

With that, we'd arrived at our flotante and were taken to our habitación. The family who built the isla installed solar power, so we had lights and hot water for the small stand-up shower in the bathroom. It had an open window frame to ventilate the odor from our ecological toilet. The main room was quite spacious and had a king-size bed with a beautifully hand-carved wooden frame, a second full-sized bed, and there was a little sitting area with a coffee table. The room was beautifully decorated with framed traditional Peruvian tapestries and hand-crafted animal sculptures made from the same reeds we were floating on. The main aesthetic was the floor-to-ceiling windows on two sides of our habitación. We could see the lights of Puno shining off in the distance across the dark waters of the lake.

There was a propane-fueled space heater that was on when we arrived, but the host let us know the heater would have to be turned off before we went to sleep for safety. At that point, we would be relying on the dozen or so heavy blankets available to insulate our body heat. We kept all our clothes and jackets on as we unpacked and settled in for the night. Before going to bed Carolyn told us a dream she remembered from the night before.

"I almost never remember my dreams, but I remember every detail of this one. I was hiking in the Andes with my mother and sister—which is crazy by itself since I can't remember the last time the three of us did anything together. We were looking for a magical waterfall. There was a majestic condor showing us the way by flying overhead. After this morning, I realized that must have been Abuela Rosa. We reached the waterfall, and the condor flew over the top of it out of sight.

We found a path that wound up to the top of the waterfall to try and find the condor again. When we reached the top, the river that had been feeding the waterfall had turned into the mouth of a volcano, and instead of water, it was now lava bubbling up from below. The lava kept rising and was soon to overtake us, when a gray puma appeared and said, 'In this world, we must be strong and brave. One of you will have to give yourself to the volcano to save the others.' The puma bounded over the volcano and sat next to the condor who had led us there." Namash and I listened intently.

"I knew I had to be the one to sacrifice myself, so I walked over the edge and fell into the molten lava. I sank through, but my skin did not burn. And I felt no pain. I fell slowly and landed softly on the ground inside a massive cave beneath the volcano. I sat up to gather myself and realized the cave was behind the original magical waterfall we'd found. Beside me was a river of lava that turned into water, as it met with the waterfall from above." Carolyn stood up and began to pace as she continued to tell us her dream.

Her hands acted out the scenes as she continued, "A serpent slithered through the lava toward me. I was terrified and couldn't move. The serpent wrapped itself around my right wrist and then the left, pulling them together to bind my hands. The serpent said, 'In order for you to return to the world of the living, you must let go.' I screamed at the serpent, 'Let go of what? You're holding me!' The serpent replied, 'Let go, or you will remain here in the cave of the unliving.' Then I woke up."

"Very Disco!" Namash excitedly burst out.

"You keep saying that. Very disco, what do you mean by that?" I asked.

"I can't just tell you. That wouldn't be very disco would it?" Namash asked coyly before he quickly returned to Carolyn's dream. "I can't wait for Abuela Isabella to hear your dream tomorrow. She has wonderful interpretations of dreams."

"What time will we get there tomorrow?" Carolyn asked.

"It's about a four-hour boat ride. We should get to Isla Amantani around lunchtime. This works well since Abuela Isabella is steadfast in her morning rituals. She rises with the sun every morning to paint, sculpt, or search by the shore for a new stone. She says that her creativity peaks in the morning while her dreams are fresh and before she consumes any food," Namash explained.

"I love a good morning routine," Carolyn said.

"I can tell you this much about your dream. There are three very important symbols. The condor, as you know, represents the heavens and the journey from this life to the beyond. The puma represents strength and power manifested in this life on earth, and the serpent represents the beginning of life springing from the underworld, as well as wisdom and knowledge," Namash explained.

"To my knowledge, prevailing wisdom is that there are two kinds of snakes: alive and dead," I commented.

"How very nuanced of you, Collin." Carolyn teased as she went to the bathroom.

"It's literally freezing in there!" Carolyn said as she burst out of the bathroom and closed the door forcefully behind her.

"Yes, Prima! But believe me, this is luxury compared to how the people here, and how Abuela Isabella, live," Namash said while laughing.

"Yes, please tell me what this no-electricity thing is about," Carolyn said.

"There's solar power on the island, like we have on this flotante, but abuela doesn't want to install it. She likes when her flickering candles cast shadows from her sculptures on the walls. If there are lights, she'll end up staying up later and won't wake up with the creative spirits who rise at dawn." Namash explained his grandmother's wisdom for resisting the allure of technological advancement.

"So no TV. Does she have a phone?" Carolyn asked.

"No phone," Namash said.

"If she doesn't have a phone, how does she keep in touch with everyone? Doesn't she get worried?" Carolyn asked.

"No, I don't think that worrying is something she ever does. We have to come visit her. Mi Tío and his family live on the island and make sure she has everything she needs. My father, who grew up on la isla, is now a physician in Puno. He and my mother go every Saturday and spend the day there on the isla. I come to visit every couple of months, to select some paintings and sculptures that I take back to our galleries in Paracas and Lima," Namash explained.

"Increíble. So many more questions, but I don't even know where to begin," Carolyn said.

FIFTEEN

THE SERPENT IN THE GRASS

In the morning, Namash's parents were waiting for us with a boat. Namash's father, Enrique, had a warm charismatic smile and an engaging personality. His mother was named Urpi, which means dove, and her presence was peaceful, free, and graceful. It was clear to see how Namash had developed his personality.

"Does Abuela Isabella know I'm coming today?" Carolyn asked as the boat pulled away.

"Not that I'm aware of, but she does have a way of knowing things. So it's possible," Namash said.

"Such a trip." Carolyn said what I was thinking, out loud.

We arrived at the dock on Isla Amantani in front of Abuela Isabella's home, and Namash's parents led us up to the house, where we had to duck down to enter through the small doorway. She waited in the front room on a small sofa surrounded by dozens of beautiful, hand-carved sculptures placed on shelves and pedestals. Several small paintings of various landscapes hung on the walls. There was not a single mirror anywhere in the house. Abuela Isabella rose off the small sofa, greeted her son and daughter-in-law, and embraced Namash.

"Namash, I see you've brought friends for lunch, wonderful!" Abuela Isabella said as Namash turned to introduce us.

"Abuela, this is our friend, Collin. He lives in Lima. And this is…" Namash began.

"This is Carolyn! You look so much like my sister when she was young, but you're much taller!" Abuela Isabella said with a joyous laugh.

"Mi Tía Isabella!" Carolyn leaned down to give her a hug.

"You must be wondering, 'Why in the world have I traveled all this way to meet this little old lady?'" Abuela Isabella said as they embraced. "I am too," Abuela Isabella said with a laugh.

Namash's parents lead us through the front room to a much larger open area in the back of the small, stone house. The daylight was abundant for the large dining table and chairs. Namash's prima prepared the meal in a dome-shaped stone oven with another open fire next to it heating a charred, stone caldron. Her brother and father served the freshly caught trout, roasted vegetables, and quinoa soup to each of us. Abuela Isabella sat at the head of the table and began to tell us about herself.

"I came to Perú to work at El Gran Sueño when tu Abuela Rosa decided to move to the United States. I would take her place overseeing the cooking in the kitchen. We worked together for a couple of weeks before Rosa's wedding to Samuel. It was a very special time to have spent with my sister. The wedding was a special day, March 2nd. The next day would be the last time we would see each other," Abuela Isabella began.

"So how did you end up all the way out here?" Carolyn asked.

"In my spare time, I would paint as I always had. Cooking was Rosa's art, but mine was painting. Your great-grandparents soon learned of my paintings and removed me from my work in the kitchen, so I could paint full-time. I painted portraits of the family members and landscapes from El Gran Sueño's vast fields, orchards, and gardens. Daniel and Samuel's parents had a space in a centro comercial in Miraflores where I sold my paintings and an apartment nearby where I stayed.

Maybe a year or so after that, I met Namash's Abuelo. We were seeing each other for about six months when we decided to get married. For another year, we lived together in Lima, but Namash's Abuelo missed living here with the lake and the mountains. He felt closer to the gods and could practice his healing and natural medicine here. My husband healed people with his energy. My son Enrique heals people with medicine, and my grandson Namash heals people with their eyes. He helps them see what was there all along. This is my story of how I came to be here. I know you are Rosa's granddaughter, but I want to hear how you got here." Abuela Isabella folded her hands and rest them on the table.

"Namash got me here! Thank God!" Carolyn said with a laugh.

"Before Abuela Rosa passed away, she sent me to find Tío Dan, so I could bring back a jewelry box she'd left in Lima. That's when I met Collin," Carolyn began, as she pointed in my direction.

Carolyn continued, "I was supposed to meet Tío Dan, but Abuela Rosa had the stroke and was in the hospital. So I rushed back to see her. Before she passed, she regained consciousness only for a moment and told me to 'Ask him for the letters.' So I came back to meet Tío Dan and find out more about the letters. He told me you had brought the letters here and sent us to find Namash."

"Yes, I've had them here to remember her over all these years," Abuela Isabella said.

"Our journey has been inspiring. I told Namash and Collin about my dream from two nights ago, and Namash said you can interpret them. I had another one last night. Do you think you could interpret for me?" Carolyn asked.

"I can. After lunch, you can tell me your dreams, and then we can look at Rosa's letters," Abuela Isabella generously offered.

When we finished eating, Abuela Isabella motioned for Carolyn to follow her back to the front room, and they sat down on a brightly colored rug in the middle of the room in front of the sofa. I followed while the rest of the family remained gathered around the table in conversation. Isabella laid her hands above Carolyn's open palms and said lovingly, "Close your eyes, open your heart, and tell me your dream, dear child."

Carolyn described her encounter with the condor and the puma and being frozen by fear as the serpent slithered out of the river of lava and bound her hands.

"Last night, I had another dream. It was much shorter. The dream woke me up, and I couldn't go back to sleep afterward," Carolyn opened her eyes and explained.

"Yes, close your eyes once more. Tell me, dear child," Abuela Isabella instructed Carolyn.

Carolyn began, "Los gallinazos from Collin's condo came flying through the waterfall and began swooping around the cave until they were all inside. You don't know about los gallinazos at Collin's, but they were really scary."

"I'm here to listen to your dream and have no need for an explanation. Close your eyes, dear child, and tell me," Abuela Isabella said calmly.

"They landed on the opposite side of the lava river and lined up side by side in a straight row. One by one they dove into the lava river, and when they emerged, their black feathers were painted brightly with war paint. They formed a circle facing inward around myself and the serpent. One by one they attacked the serpent trying to kill it, so that I could be set free. Each time, the serpent successfully fended off their attack by striking them, and they all died from the venomous bite." Carolyn exhaled.

"Did you look down my child?" Abuela Isabella asked.

"I did, and it was then I realized I had a hold of the serpent's tail. And once more the serpent said, 'You must let go, and I will release you.' I wanted to let go, but my hand wouldn't listen to the command my brain was sending. The serpent hissed, 'Let go, and I will release you.' I made the serpent promise—and it did—but I still could not let go. The serpent grew angry and hissed, 'Don't you want to return to the earth to run with your puma friend? Let go, and I will set you free.' That's when I woke up," Carolyn finished her story.

"The dreams we remember shape our destiny. I believe I can help guide you to discover their meaning." Abuela Isabella assured Carolyn, as I sat quietly in the background in eager anticipation.

"So the condor is mi Abuela Rosa right?" Carolyn asked.

"No, the condor is trying to take Rosa to the life beyond. The puma is Rosa. The river of water is the life force of this world. The lava river is the force of the underworld that prepares energy to take shape in this world. The condor wants to take the puma to the life beyond, but the puma will not leave until she knows you are free of the serpent, to live freely in this world. You said there were 18 gallinazos, correct, my dear?" Abuela Isabella had begun her interpretation.

"Yes, 18," Carolyn said.

"Los gallinazos represent the 18 Inka rulers. They returned from the beyond life to visit you when you arrived in Lima. They were warning you that there was to be a great battle in your life," Abuela Isabella began.

Carolyn clapped her hands and said, "I knew it! I told you they were a bad omen, Collin!"

"Calm your spirit, dear child. You must be still to hear what I'm telling you. They were there to protect you. When they flew into the cave, they were returning to the underworld, and they dove into the lava river to transform back into great warriors to go to battle for you." Abuela Isabella's explanation gave me a sense of relief.

"But why Inka rulers? Why would they be interested in anything about me? That makes no sense," Carolyn said.

"Because you're here. You're in their lands. They want to show you how to be brave like they were," Abuela Isabella said.

"Why couldn't they defeat the serpent?" Carolyn asked.

"Because in some battles, others can fight for us, but they must be won ourselves," Abuela Isabella answered lovingly.

"So who is the serpent? That seems to be the most important thing for you to tell me," Carolyn asked.

"You must see who the serpent is yourself. This is the purpose of your dream," Abuela Isabella instructed.

"So once I get free of the serpent, mi Abuela Rosa can finish her journey to the life beyond?" Carolyn asked.

"You must find out. Remember, it is you who is holding the serpent's tail," Abuela Isabella explained once more.

"I guess it's just a dream. Nothing to get too worked up about," Carolyn said as she shrugged her shoulders and looked over at me completely in awe of Abuela Isabella.

"When you're in a dream state, it is vivid and powerful. Some things can only be seen in the dark with your eyes closed. In order to be awakened to the true nature of yourself and the universe, it is first necessary to sleep and to dream, to rest and to still your mind. When we're busy going about our lives, our minds are like turbulent water, murky and unclear. When we still our thoughts, the waters of our minds, our vision of who we are becomes clear and lucid. You can only find what you're looking for by not searching for it. When you stop looking, everything will settle. The water will be still, and you'll realize that what you've been looking for all along has already found you," Abuela Isabella carefully explained.

"I wish mi Abuela Rosa was here to have this conversation with us. I know she would have loved it. I would love to hear what she would have to say. Do you think she can hear us?" Carolyn asked.

"Yes, Rosa can hear us. We can't hear her with our ears. Ears are only able to hear so much. The best listening is done with the heart. As is the best speaking. All of our ancestors can hear the desires of our hearts. The modern life cuts you off from their wisdom, clouds your mind, and fools you into believing your visions are just dreams," Abuela Isabella answered.

"Tía Isabella, thank you for sharing your wisdom. You know what I am dying to see, though?" Carolyn asked Abuela Isabella.

"Oh yes, Rosa's letters! Let me get them for us to go through some of them now, and you can take them all with you when you leave," Abuela Isabella said before she went to her bedroom to retrieve her hermana's letters.

She returned soon thereafter and began to recall the content of each letter, as she removed them from a wooden box. "This one is the letter Rosa sent me to come to Lima for her wedding, and the offer to replace her en la cocina at El Gran Sueño. This is the letter she wrote when she had first arrived in Lima. Ah, this is my favorite. It's the letter she sent me when your mother Christiana was born, and there should be a photo of the two of them together at the hospital if I remember right."

"Oh my god, I would love to see that photo!" Carolyn screeched with excitement.

"It must be in another envelope. Yes, here, this is the one. This is the letter she sent to Daniel that the photo came with," Abuela

Isabella said as she handed Carolyn the photo and opened the folded letter.

"This photo is amazing! They were both so beautiful! Mi Abuela Rosa was so happy!" Carolyn said as she admired the photo Abuela Isabella had handed her.

Abuela Isabella read the short letter out loud. "Dear Daniel, she's here! The pregnancy was much more difficult than I imagined it would be. However, the delivery was quick and without complications. I am tired but so overjoyed I don't notice. I can't put into words what it feels like to be a mother. One day, I hope you will experience something similar. For now, here is a photo of your newborn daughter, Christiana Victoria. With love always, Rosa."

"You look confused, my dear child," Abuela Isabella said as she stopped reading the letter and began to read the look on Carolyn's face.

"This letter is to Tío Dan, right? Why does she say, 'your daughter, Christiana?' I don't understand." Carolyn reached up with both hands to hold her face as her chin tucked in. It was the first time I had seen Carolyn's body language tell me she was unsure of herself.

"Daniel is Christiana's father. I was wondering why you kept saying Tío Dan. I thought you must have meant his son. My child, who have you been told your mother's father is?" asked Abuela Isabella as Carolyn and I sat there dumbfounded.

"Mi Abuelo Samuel," Carolyn said.

"Then I'm afraid, as a serpent slithers in the grass, the truth has been concealed from you. Samuel married Rosa, but Rosa's child, your mother, is from Daniel," Abuela Isabella revealed.

"I had no idea. My mother has no idea," Carolyn said as she sat there shell-shocked by the secret that had been kept for so long.

Carolyn shook her head back and forth rapidly as if to wake herself from a sudden nap. She grabbed my arm and stormed out of la casa with me in tow.

"What the fuck—just exactly what the fuck—am I supposed to tell my mother?" Carolyn erupted once we were outside.

"I think we need to ask Tío Dan what happened," I said.

"You're damn right I'm going to ask him just what the hell happened!" Carolyn paced like a caged puma.

Namash came out and slowly walked towards us. "You must be so upset right now. Let's see what we can do to talk through this and ease your suffering," Namash graciously offered.

"Upset doesn't begin to describe it. I'm not suffering; I'm furious!" Carolyn screamed.

"Collin, we need to get back to Lima right away and find out why Tío Dan thought it was ok not to say anything about any of this when we were there. I need to know exactly who knows what, and why they haven't said anything about any of this!" Carolyn was screaming.

"Namash, Primo, would you be able to arrange a ride back to Arequipa for us?" I asked in a bit of a panic.

Before Namash had a chance to respond, Carolyn asked, "There's an airport in Puno right?"

"Not Puno, but nearby in Juliaca," Namash responded.

"So that'll be faster than driving to Arequipa Collin. For such a smart guy, there are times your cluelessness is stupefying. How soon can you get us to the airport Namash?" Carolyn took over planning our return.

"If we leave now, it will be about four and a half hours," Namash answered.

"Ok, that's what we are doing. We will be there by 5:30 pm. Collin, get us on the next flight after that. Please and thank you," Carolyn delegated.

"If we leave now, we'll miss Isla del Sol," I protested, as I was unable to hide my disappointment that we would not be continuing on with the spiritual journey through the Andes Namash had been guiding us on.

"I really don't care right now. You'll have to meet Inti another time. Really, your grasp of the moment is utterly breathtaking!" Carolyn snapped back at me and shook her head.

"And Machu Picchu?" I asked.

"Namash, he's brain dead. You've been amazing. Thank you so much. Maybe when I get all this figured out, we'll have some time to go to Machu Picchu. Would you be up for that? Could we meet you in Cusco?" Carolyn asked.

"Cusco? I'm going to go to Lima with you now. I wouldn't miss seeing how this unfolds with Tío Dan. This is my family too, and I promise you there is a lot more than meets the eye. This is so very disco!" Namash was bursting with enthusiasm and curiosity as he spoke. He restrained his demeanor as Carolyn shot him a glare that reminded him this was not the time or place.

"Great, more to the story of people not telling me everything they know, as it pertains to my existence," Carolyn said while rolling her eyes.

When we went back inside, Abuela Isabella had put the letters back in the box and gave it to Namash to make sure it came with us safely. Carolyn gave Abuela Isabella the puma sculpture she had brought as a gift. I was surprised that Abuela Isabella didn't protest for us to stay longer. I suspect she knew that Carolyn needed to go on with her journey and find out who the serpent was. I wanted to protest for us to stay longer. Everything would be alright if we could just keep going. The jewelry box, the letters, the journey through the Andes, all of it was drawing us closer, like the sides of a triangle nearing their apex. What if I was the serpent? What if somehow by going back to El Gran Sueño she figured that out and let me go?

"I want to give you something I saved for many years hoping to give it to Rosa one day. I thought I'd carved a statue of her. Now I think it may have been a statue of you all along," Abuela Isabella said as she held the statue with both hands and allowed the cloth wrapped around the statue to fall open. The polished stone statue was of a woman who had a puma's head, and her hands were bound in front of her by a serpent. One of the woman's hands had a hold of the serpent's tail.

"How is this possible? When did you make this?" Carolyn asked.

"It's been so many years I'm not sure. I carve the date into the bottom of all of my sculptures though. What does it say?" Abuela Isabella responded.

Carolyn looked at the base of the statue below the woman's feet and saw, '27-1-1990.' She froze, staring at the numbers on the base of the sculpture. There was a look of horrified amazement on her face as she stood there silently not breathing.

"What is the date? How old is it?" I asked out of curiosity and to find out if Carolyn still had the use of her voice.

Carolyn didn't respond to me but instead looked deep into Abuela Isabella's eyes and said, "You made this on my birthday."

"Very disco! What year? How old were you?" Namash chimed in.

The rest of us were irrelevant, and still looking deep into Abuela Isabella's eyes, Carolyn said, "You made this on the day I was born. The actual day."

"So it seems you've always been in my heart, my dear child. You must find out who the serpent is, and then you will be able to let go of their tail," Abuela Isabella said as she embraced Carolyn.

The boat shoved off, and after a few moments of silence, I asked Carolyn, "What are you thinking? Do you want to talk about it?"

"What I imagined my family to be like, and what the truth of the matter is, just don't make sense. Why would they keep this a secret for all these years? I wish I had never heard of these goddamned letters." Carolyn slammed her fists into her thighs three times.

She walked to the back of the boat, sat down, and leaned on the glass window with her chin in her hand. Carolyn was staring into the future and the past simultaneously. No, she didn't want to talk.

Namash's father, Enrique, drove his boat at top speed to get us back to the mainland as quickly as possible and then to the airport in his car. We made it in time for the last flight to Lima. Carolyn had called Tío Dan before we took off to alert him we were on our way. Carolyn asked him to wait up for us but made no allusion to the wrath that was coming to El Gran Sueño.

Namash took a taxi to my place in Barranco to get my Jeep and bring it to the estate. Carolyn and I went straight to El Gran Sueño. In Carolyn's mind, there was no time to waste. Despite her family's long-suffering patience to keep this secret, she wasn't going to allow any more time to elapse. This dark revelation would not be allowed to remain mysterious for a solitary minute longer.

On the way to El Gran Sueño, Lima traffic was in full sensory overload mode. Motorcycles growled and zoomed by. A constant barrage of blaring car horns echoed off into the night sky as our taxi would accelerate for half a block and then slam on the brakes. Yet with all that, the silence inside our taxi was even more deafening. I was always quiet in situations like this. I had no idea how to relate to what Carolyn was thinking about the revelation that her grandfather was in fact Tío Dan not her Abuelo Samuel she had known all her life. I'd find out when she told me. Carolyn would never keep a secret like this. After all, that's why I was riding with her now. She didn't have to tell me she was pregnant. She didn't have to come back to Lima.

"I don't really want to see this bastard after he lied by omission about what was in the letters and threw a big celebration like everything was normal. How does someone do that, Collin?" Carolyn broke the silence with a question I couldn't answer.

"Mi Abuela Rosa at least tried. She was more than 50 years too late, but she was going to," Carolyn said.

My stomach felt like I was the one who was pregnant, like the pauses after each time Carolyn spoke.

"And what was mi Abuelo Samuel doing with mi Abuela Rosa if she was pregnant? Did he steal her from his brother? That's exactly the kind of shit that Jacquelyn would pull! It makes me want to throw up," she said.

I should have just stayed quiet but said, "Me too."

Carolyn had a hornet's hive in each of her eyes as she shot me a look that was just a small preview of what Tío Dan would get.

Carolyn jumped out of the cab and stormed into the house with me a step behind.

"I owe you an explanation," Tío Dan said preemptively as he rose from the sofa in the parlor when we barged in.

"I'd say you owe me a lot more than that!" Carolyn lashed out.

"Maybe, I do. Collin, would you give us a moment in private?" Tío Dan graciously requested.

"No! He stays!" Carolyn demanded. I wasn't sure if she needed me there to keep her from murdering her grandfather or to help remove the body.

"Muy bien, Collin stays. It's difficult to know where to begin," Tío said.

"Begin where you stop lying to people!" Carolyn barked at him.

"Bueno. Your grandmother and I were in love. My brother Samuel also loved your grandmother. Rosa loved my brother as well, but her love for Samuel was platonic. Though we never discussed it, I'm sure she thought that we would be married, as did I," Tío Dan began.

"Pick up the pace, Dan!" Carolyn was fuming.

"My brother knew I had a secret. Something deep inside I couldn't explain or really understand myself when I was young. I was the same as all of the other boys, but I also wasn't the same. I was attracted to women, their faces and bodies, but particularly their personalities and conversations. When the men in my family or the other boys growing up couldn't understand the women in their lives, it didn't make any sense to me." Tío Dan was taking his time.

"What's not obvious is why my mother was lied to her whole life. Please make sense of that," Carolyn said.

"When I was a teenager and young adult, I always assumed I would get married and have a family, but I also have a secret desire. I am attracted sexually to men. But usually, I can't connect with them the same way I do women. I don't enjoy listening to them in conversation, and they're bored by the things I like to discuss. My body is masculine. My mannerisms, demeanor, voice—all masculine —but my mind, my heart, my emotions are more feminine. So I always assumed I would have a rewarding relationship and family with a woman and purely physical relationships with men." Tío Dan unveiled the center of his soul as he revealed the truth that he had kept concealed his whole life.

Carolyn's shoulders lowered, and her breathing slowed. Her anger had begun to subside, as she had her first inclination as to why this man in front of her was called Tío instead of Abuelo. She reached for my hand and allowed Tío Dan to recount the story.

"My brother had encountered me with another male when I was

young. He was accepting, but he didn't understand it. Nor could I really explain it to him. I had already been with girls and boys when I was growing up, women and men by that time, and my brother had never had a partner. He was awkward and introverted. He had nothing to hide, yet hid, and I had everything to hide but was very social. I knew he was jealous of that, and I knew my sexuality made him nervous, which I think only made him more shy with girls growing up. Which of course made him more jealous. He knew my secret, and he provided cover for me. Until one day when he did the opposite," Tío Dan explained.

Carolyn placed her hands above her heart and said, "I just want you to know that no matter what the rest of the story is, my acceptance of who you are is unconditional. I'm so sorry we live in a world that forces people to keep who they really are a secret. It's disgusting." Tears of empathy welled up in the corners of her eyes and began to roll down her less angry cheeks.

"Thank you. I knew from our first moment meeting each other this would not be a problem for you. I was, of course, more concerned how my son Daniel would receive this news, and I needed to make sure Tío Patricio was comfortable living openly, as we now will be," Tío Dan explained.

"Oh my god! Your family is just now finding out as well?" a horrified Carolyn asked.

"Yes, I am afraid so. This is the reason I was unable to tell you right away. I had no idea you would ask for the letters. If you hadn't, I wouldn't upset everyone's lives. So I took the time to tell Carla and Daniel when you were on your way to meet Isabella," Tío Dan explained.

"Rosa had begun to suspect that she was pregnant, and before she went to a doctor, she went to my brother to seek advice. Why she chose to confide in him before telling me, I will never know. Perhaps, she feared my reaction since we weren't married, which of course would have been a big problem for my parents. I suspect that God or Fate or The Universe, or whatever the thing is that works in mysterious ways on our behalf, had a plan for us. Rosa, myself, my brother, your mother, and for you and your sister. Part of that plan was for Samuel to take Rosa to see me with one of the ranch hands

I was having regular encounters with." Tío Dan leaned back into the sofa.

"Abuelo, can I call you that?" Carolyn asked Tío Dan.

"Of course, mi amor! I would like nothing more!" Abuelo Dan hopped back up to the edge of the sofa.

"Abuelo, did Abuela Rosa see you with Tío Patricio?" Carolyn asked.

"You're very intuitive Carolyn. It was Patricio. We've been involved since before I met your Abuela Rosa. Neither of us imagined that one day we could live together, openly and freely. Over all these decades we have become the best of friends. He understood when I married Daniel's mother I needed to have a family in order to continue the legacy of our family and the estate, and he has remained a faithful friend no matter what," Abuelo Dan confirmed before he continued.

"The next day Rosa asked me if I was attracted to men. She said it would be ok if I was, but she just needed to know. I immediately knew she must have seen something or known something, but I couldn't bring myself to tell her. I thought if I did, I would devastate her and hurt her deeply. So instead, I lied." A tear fell from his eye into his mustache.

I told her her question was crazy and asked her why she was worried about it. She immediately confronted my dishonesty. Rosa was furious. Angry like I had never seen her. Angrier than you were when you came to the house tonight. She told me she'd seen me with Patricio. She told me she needed to know because she was carrying our child. She needed to know because she'd wanted to have a family with me and share a life with me right up until the moment I had lied to her." Abuelo Dan had tears rolling down his cheeks now, as he confessed the lie he was most sorry for. A lie that he had suffered for more than 50 years.

"I begged her for her forgiveness. I pleaded and wept on my knees for a second chance. Rosa needed time to think. We didn't see each other for a week. All I was doing was thinking. I couldn't eat much or sleep much. I loved your grandmother with all of my heart. Having sex with other men didn't seem at the time like I was betraying her. It was like drinking too much or eating a second piece of cake when no one was watching. That was how I rationalized it. I would be able to stop if Rosa and I had been married. It was something that wouldn't have hurt anyone, as long as no one found out. Rosa had found out though. She had been hurt, and now I was hurting more than I ever had before or since." Abuelo Dan took a moment to collect himself after sharing his deepest emotions with us.

"I resolved to keep asking her to forgive me and promise her I would be true to her. There was no way I could ever hurt her again. I also knew she may not forgive me, and if not, I needed to make sure she and our future child were taken care of. Though I knew it had to have been my brother who revealed my secret to her, I also knew that besides me, there was no one who loved her more or would take better care of her and our child," he said as he wiped more tears from his eyes.

Abuelo Dan stood up. "So I confronted him. I asked him why he'd betrayed me, revealed my secret, and why he was attempting to destroy my life. He told me he was in love with Rosa. He wasn't going to let her marry me and dedicate her life to raising a family with me without knowing the truth. I hated him for that, but I also knew he was right."

He sat back down and continued, "The next thing was to ask him to be a part of the solution. I offered Rosa a choice. She could stay with me, and we could raise a family. Or she could go with my brother who was moving to the United States to attend medical school in Chicago. I asked Samuel if he would accept that responsibility, and he eagerly agreed. Whatever Rosa decided we would abide by, and he would never tell another soul about my sexuality ever again. It was imperative that my parents did not find out. That would have broken their hearts and destroyed the family. The next day, I arranged to see Rosa and presented her the choice. She took three days to think about it and search her heart. You of course already know what she decided."

"I do," Carolyn confirmed.

"The locket I gave you when you arrived is a photo of your grandparents, but it is I, not Samuel in the photo with your Abuela Rosa. She returned the locket to me when she decided to go with him and move to the United States." Abuelo Dan revealed the real treasure inside Abuela Rosa's jewelry box.

"Thank God she left that jewelry box behind," I said as my eyes watered.

"You and Abuelo Samuel looked so much alike when you were younger. I had no idea when you said, 'This was your grandparents when they were young' that it wasn't him," Carolyn said.

"Nearly indistinguishable. We were twins, mi amor!" Abuelo Dan said with a little laugh.

"You were twins! Jaquelyn is really going to get a kick out of that!" Carolyn said in amazement.

"Abuelo, I've been extremely angry with you, and part of me is extremely angry with mi Abuela Rosa. Why couldn't she have stayed here with you? I can only imagine how amazing our lives would have been if we'd grown up here on the estate!" Carolyn described her mixed emotions and idyllic notion of growing up in this beautiful way of life.

"Yes, she could have stayed, but then your mother would have never met your father in Chicago, and you could never have turned out to be who you are," Abuelo Dan pointed out.

Namash arrived with the Jeep from Barranco. Abuelo Dan excused himself to bed, as it was much later than normal for him to retire after our late arrival and conversation, but he implored us to stay so we could talk more the next day. I was glad that Carolyn embraced this idea, and we would be heading up a flight of stairs to go to bed, as opposed to up the Pan-American highway back to Barranco. Carolyn and I were both exhausted from all the travel and the emotional roller coaster that the day had been. We went straight to bed.

SIXTEEN

THE LIE AND THE REASON WHY

Lurín

O n the way to El Gran Sueño, Lima traffic was in full
sensory overload mode. Motorcycles growled and
zoomed by. A constant barrage of blaring car horns
echoed off into the night sky as our taxi would accelerate for half a
block and then slam on the brakes. Yet with all that, the silence
inside our taxi was even more deafening. I was always quiet in
situations like this. I had no idea how to relate to what Carolyn was
thinking about the revelation that her grandfather was in fact Tío
Dan not her Abuelo Samuel she had known all her life. I'd find out
when she told me. Carolyn would never keep a secret like this. After
all, that's why I was riding with her now. She didn't have to tell me
she was pregnant. She didn't have to come back to Lima.

"I don't really want to see this bastard after he lied by omission
about what was in the letters and threw a big celebration like
everything was normal. How does someone do that, Collin?"
Carolyn broke the silence with a question I couldn't answer.

"Mi Abuela Rosa at least tried. She was more than 50 years too
late, but she was going to," Carolyn said.

My stomach felt like I was the one who was pregnant, like the pauses after each time Carolyn spoke.

"And what was mi Abuelo Samuel doing with mi Abuela Rosa if she was pregnant? Did he steal her from his brother? That's exactly the kind of shit that Jacquelyn would pull! It makes me want to throw up," she said.

I should have just stayed quiet but said, "Me too."

Carolyn had a hornet's hive in each of her eyes as she shot me a look that was just a small preview of what Tío Dan would get.

Carolyn jumped out of the cab and stormed into the house with me a step behind.

"I owe you an explanation," Tío Dan said preemptively as he rose from the sofa in the parlor when we barged in.

"I'd say you owe me a lot more than that!" Carolyn lashed out.

"Maybe, I do. Collin, would you give us a moment in private?" Tío Dan graciously requested.

"No! He stays!" Carolyn demanded. I wasn't sure if she needed me there to keep her from murdering her grandfather or to help remove the body.

"Muy bien, Collin stays. It's difficult to know where to begin," Tío said.

"Begin where you stop lying to people!" Carolyn barked at him.

"Bueno. Your grandmother and I were in love. My brother Samuel also loved your grandmother. Rosa loved my brother as well, but her love for Samuel was platonic. Though we never discussed it, I'm sure she thought that we would be married, as did I," Tío Dan began.

"Pick up the pace, Dan!" Carolyn was fuming.

"My brother knew I had a secret. Something deep inside I couldn't explain or really understand myself when I was young. I was the same as all of the other boys, but I also wasn't the same. I was attracted to women, their faces and bodies, but particularly their personalities and conversations. When the men in my family or the other boys growing up couldn't understand the women in their lives, it didn't make any sense to me." Tío Dan was taking his time.

"What's not obvious is why my mother was lied to her whole life. Please make sense of that," Carolyn said.

"When I was a teenager and young adult, I always assumed I would get married and have a family, but I also have a secret desire. I am attracted sexually to men. But usually, I can't connect with them the same way I do women. I don't enjoy listening to them in conversation, and they're bored by the things I like to discuss. My body is masculine. My mannerisms, demeanor, voice—all masculine —but my mind, my heart, my emotions are more feminine. So I always assumed I would have a rewarding relationship and family with a woman and purely physical relationships with men." Tío Dan unveiled the center of his soul as he revealed the truth that he had kept concealed his whole life.

Carolyn's shoulders lowered, and her breathing slowed. Her anger had begun to subside, as she had her first inclination as to why this man in front of her was called Tío instead of Abuelo. She reached for my hand and allowed Tío Dan to recount the story.

"My brother had encountered me with another male when I was young. He was accepting, but he didn't understand it. Nor could I really explain it to him. I had already been with girls and boys when I was growing up, women and men by that time, and my brother had never had a partner. He was awkward and introverted. He had nothing to hide, yet hid, and I had everything to hide but was very social. I knew he was jealous of that, and I knew my sexuality made him nervous, which I think only made him more shy with girls growing up. Which of course made him more jealous. He knew my secret, and he provided cover for me. Until one day when he did the opposite," Tío Dan explained.

Carolyn placed her hands above her heart and said, "I just want you to know that no matter what the rest of the story is, my acceptance of who you are is unconditional. I'm so sorry we live in a world that forces people to keep who they really are a secret. It's disgusting." Tears of empathy welled up in the corners of her eyes and began to roll down her less angry cheeks.

"Thank you. I knew from our first moment meeting each other this would not be a problem for you. I was, of course, more concerned how my son Daniel would receive this news, and I needed to make sure Tío Patricio was comfortable living openly, as we now will be," Tío Dan explained.

"Oh my god! Your family is just now finding out as well?" a horrified Carolyn asked.

"Yes, I am afraid so. This is the reason I was unable to tell you right away. I had no idea you would ask for the letters. If you hadn't, I wouldn't upset everyone's lives. So I took the time to tell Carla and Daniel when you were on your way to meet Isabella," Tío Dan explained.

"Rosa had begun to suspect that she was pregnant, and before she went to a doctor, she went to my brother to seek advice. Why she chose to confide in him before telling me, I will never know. Perhaps, she feared my reaction since we weren't married, which of course would have been a big problem for my parents. I suspect that God or Fate or The Universe, or whatever the thing is that works in mysterious ways on our behalf, had a plan for us. Rosa, myself, my brother, your mother, and for you and your sister. Part of that plan was for Samuel to take Rosa to see me with one of the ranch hands I was having regular encounters with." Tío Dan leaned back into the sofa.

"Abuelo, can I call you that?" Carolyn asked Tío Dan.

"Of course, mi amor! I would like nothing more!" Abuelo Dan hopped back up to the edge of the sofa.

"Abuelo, did Abuela Rosa see you with Tío Patricio?" Carolyn asked.

"You're very intuitive Carolyn. It was Patricio. We've been involved since before I met your Abuela Rosa. Neither of us imagined that one day we could live together, openly and freely. Over all these decades we have become the best of friends. He understood when I married Daniel's mother I needed to have a family in order to continue the legacy of our family and the estate, and he has remained a faithful friend no matter what," Abuelo Dan confirmed before he continued.

"The next day Rosa asked me if I was attracted to men. She said it would be ok if I was, but she just needed to know. I immediately knew she must have seen something or known something, but I couldn't bring myself to tell her. I thought if I did, I would devastate her and hurt her deeply. So instead, I lied." A tear fell from his eye into his mustache.

I told her her question was crazy and asked her why she was worried about it. She immediately confronted my dishonesty. Rosa was furious. Angry like I had never seen her. Angrier than you were when you came to the house tonight. She told me she'd seen me with Patricio. She told me she needed to know because she was carrying our child. She needed to know because she'd wanted to have a family with me and share a life with me right up until the moment I had lied to her." Abuelo Dan had tears rolling down his cheeks now, as he confessed the lie he was most sorry for. A lie that he had suffered for more than 50 years.

"I begged her for her forgiveness. I pleaded and wept on my knees for a second chance. Rosa needed time to think. We didn't see each other for a week. All I was doing was thinking. I couldn't eat much or sleep much. I loved your grandmother with all of my heart. Having sex with other men didn't seem at the time like I was betraying her. It was like drinking too much or eating a second piece of cake when no one was watching. That was how I rationalized it. I would be able to stop if Rosa and I had been married. It was something that wouldn't have hurt anyone, as long as no one found out. Rosa had found out though. She had been hurt, and now I was hurting more than I ever had before or since." Abuelo Dan took a moment to collect himself after sharing his deepest emotions with us.

"I resolved to keep asking her to forgive me and promise her I would be true to her. There was no way I could ever hurt her again. I also knew she may not forgive me, and if not, I needed to make sure she and our future child were taken care of. Though I knew it had to have been my brother who revealed my secret to her, I also knew that besides me, there was no one who loved her more or would take better care of her and our child," he said as he wiped more tears from his eyes.

Abuelo Dan stood up. "So I confronted him. I asked him why he'd betrayed me, revealed my secret, and why he was attempting to destroy my life. He told me he was in love with Rosa. He wasn't going to let her marry me and dedicate her life to raising a family with me without knowing the truth. I hated him for that, but I also knew he was right."

He sat back down and continued, "The next thing was to ask him to be a part of the solution. I offered Rosa a choice. She could stay with me, and we could raise a family. Or she could go with my brother who was moving to the United States to attend medical school in Chicago. I asked Samuel if he would accept that responsibility, and he eagerly agreed. Whatever Rosa decided we would abide by, and he would never tell another soul about my sexuality ever again. It was imperative that my parents did not find out. That would have broken their hearts and destroyed the family. The next day, I arranged to see Rosa and presented her the choice. She took three days to think about it and search her heart. You of course already know what she decided."

"I do," Carolyn confirmed.

"The locket I gave you when you arrived is a photo of your grandparents, but it is I, not Samuel in the photo with your Abuela Rosa. She returned the locket to me when she decided to go with him and move to the United States." Abuelo Dan revealed the real treasure inside Abuela Rosa's jewelry box.

"Thank God she left that jewelry box behind," I said as my eyes watered.

"You and Abuelo Samuel looked so much alike when you were younger. I had no idea when you said, 'This was your grandparents when they were young' that it wasn't him," Carolyn said.

"Nearly indistinguishable. We were twins, mi amor!" Abuelo Dan said with a little laugh.

"You were twins! Jaquelyn is really going to get a kick out of that!" Carolyn said in amazement.

"Abuelo, I've been extremely angry with you, and part of me is extremely angry with mi Abuela Rosa. Why couldn't she have stayed here with you? I can only imagine how amazing our lives would have been if we'd grown up here on the estate!" Carolyn described her mixed emotions and idyllic notion of growing up in this beautiful way of life.

"Yes, she could have stayed, but then your mother would have never met your father in Chicago, and you could never have turned out to be who you are," Abuelo Dan pointed out.

Namash arrived with the Jeep from Barranco. Abuelo Dan

excused himself to bed, as it was much later than normal for him to retire after our late arrival and conversation, but he implored us to stay so we could talk more the next day. I was glad that Carolyn embraced this idea, and we would be heading up a flight of stairs to go to bed, as opposed to up the Pan-American highway back to Barranco. Carolyn and I were both exhausted from all the travel and the emotional roller coaster that the day had been. We went straight to bed.

SEVENTEEN
BEFORE IT'S TOO LATE

W e woke up late the next day. Namash had waited for us to eat, so we all went down to Cocina Rosa for a late desayuno. Carolyn brought Namash up to speed on Abuelo Dan's account of how and why his identity as Carolyn's grandfather had happened. Abuelo Dan joined us at Cocina Rosa.

"Do you know what your Abuela Rosa would do right now?" Abuelo Dan asked.

"She would probably slap you across the face," Carolyn answered truthfully.

"Yes, and after that, she would take a nice long ride on horseback. You two didn't get the chance to ride los Caballos del Gran Sueño when you were here before. I've asked your Tía Carla and Tío Daniel to take you on a ride and show you the land," Abuelo Dan said.

"That's right! I knew he was my other Tío Dan! As per usual, Collin, you were wrong!" Carolyn slowly and emphatically declared upon the confirmation that Daniel was Carolyn's mom's half-brother and not her cousin. That put a smile on her face and gave me a little chuckle.

"I meant to ask last night. How did Daniel and Carla take it?" Carolyn asked.

"They're just fine. They have always loved Tío Patricio, and I think the last several years after Daniel's mother passed away, they began to wonder if there was something more to our relationship. Obviously there is more for Daniel to think about, but mi preciosa Carlita is as wise and caring as they come and will help him work through any emotions that need to be," Abuelo Dan explained.

"You know what? I could use some time to think and process. That horseback ride does sound like the perfect thing. Let's do it. Are you up for it, Bubba?" Carolyn looked up at me.

"You bet," I said.

"Namash, you should join us!" Carolyn said.

"I would love to, but this is a good time to catch up on some alone time and find a good place to meditate in one of the gardens," Namash politely declined.

Abuelo Dan motioned for one of the restaurant staff to come over and instructed, "Please send word to Carla and Daniel that Carolyn and Collin will be going for a ride with them, and tell the stable to ready our best horses."

Then he tossed me his cowboy hat and said, "Collin, bring her back to me in one piece."

Carolyn and I caught a ride in a golf cart with one of the maintenance workers to Carla and Daniel's house nearby. It was even larger than the main house. Tío Daniel greeted us out front and explained that his father had built this house after he'd been married, so he could raise his family in it. After Daniel had married Carla, Abuelo Dan moved back to the main house, so Daniel and Carla could raise their children here. The main house where Abuelo Dan had grown up was full of family heirlooms from the Italian Rosso side of the family from his father, as well as the Peruvian Flores family from his mother. The priceless Inkan and Spanish Colonial artwork and artifacts made the house feel like a cross between a museum and a royal palace. It definitely wasn't child proofed.

Carolyn and I followed Carla and Dan up to their bedroom, so we could borrow some clothes and boots more suitable for riding. We changed into our riding garb, and upon meeting each other in the hallway, admired one another in a large mirror on the wall.

"Collin, you totally look like a cowboy!" Carolyn said enthusiastically.

"Well, I am a gotdamm cowboy," I said in my best Texas drawl.

"I have never so badly wanted to—" Carolyn started to say when Carla took Carolyn's arm to lead us down the hallway.

"Vamos!" she shouted.

Carla took Carolyn with her to ride in one golf cart, and Daniel drove us behind them to the stable. The air was fresh, the temperature perfect, and the skies were mostly clear blue and sunny. We could not have asked for a better day to go out riding. Daniel sensed how much I was enjoying the moment, put his hand on my shoulder, and said, "Collin, when Carolyn goes home, you are welcome to come back anytime. We would love to have you, and I know it would do you some good to get out of the city every once in a while. Of course, we would expect you to have us over to your beautiful ocean-view condominium we have heard about."

"I'm getting the better end of that bargain for sure, but you have yourself a deal. Thank you," I graciously accepted. Daniel wasn't wrong. Getting out of the city would do me more than a little bit of good. I was really looking forward to this horseback ride in the countryside.

We arrived, and three of the most beautiful horses I'd ever seen were waiting. Daniel mounted a dark brown stallion with a black mane and tail and a distinct white streak down its long handsome face. Carla gracefully elevated herself onto her saddle and introduced us to Gracie. The beautiful gray mare with white speckles on her legs and face began to rear back and shook her white mane and long, flowing, snow-white tail. Carla directed Carolyn to a pure white stallion whose only coloring was its fierce blue eyes and black hoofs. When I looked at this horse I assumed it could fly and possessed mystical powers. It was perfect. Apparently for me, a dirty, brownish-gray donkey awaited.

"Sorry Collin, all the other horses haven't had enough rest, but this is our finest burro named Jefe. He'll give you a steady and sure ride," Carla said convincingly before looking down at Carolyn and not at all whispering, "I would too." They both chuckled.

I ignored the innuendo as I looked Jefe up and down and asked, "Are you sure I'm not too heavy for him?"

Carla, Daniel, and the stable hands suddenly burst out laughing. Daniel raised his fingers to his mouth and whistled, bringing another hand out from the stable who introduced the imposing horse, Generalissimo, to me. Carolyn and I started laughing as well, and I could only hope that little Jefe had no idea what was going on as he was taken away.

Carolyn went to put her foot in the stirrup, but it slipped. She turned her ankle and stumbled backward. She hopped three times trying to gain her balance but eventually fell and slid backward on her butt, with a surprising amount of grace. I rushed to her side to help her up and see if she was ok. She informed us all she was fine as she began to limp back toward the horse.

Carla took her hat off and swatted the air in the direction she wanted her husband to move. "Daniel get off your horse and help her! You need to take her back to have that looked at. I'll take Collin out for a little ride, and we will meet you back at the house."

They left, and I mounted the solid-black, muscular, and imposing stallion. There was no doubt that if necessary, he could raise an army. The feeling of power that rushed from my boots up my legs, through my body filling my chest, down my arms and into my hands as I took the reins was incredible. Carla turned her horse to head out, raised her hat off her head, and then rapidly swatted the horse's rump with the hat as she said, "Listo? Ya! Vámanos!"

We trotted through an avocado grove into the open countryside. Carla slowed and came beside me to explain that Generalissimo had a crush on Gracie, so she liked to ride them together. Then she explained, "It hadn't occurred to Carolyn, but she can't ride a horse in her condition. And she can't tell anyone that she can't ride a horse because of her condition right now. I waited until we were in the cart on the way over to help her devise the plan."

"You're a genius," I said.

"I'm a woman. 90% of your life has been orchestrated the same way, you just don't know when it's happening." Carla was blunt.

"Collin, what are your intentions with Carolyn? More than a

sure and steady ride I hope," Carla asked me slightly playfully, but mostly directly, with a wink at the end of her question.

"I can't say I have any intentions. I like her very much, if that is what you're asking." I sensed a vice was about to tighten around my masculine reproductive apparatus.

"That's obvious. That's not what I was asking. You don't have any intentions? Now that is a problem," Carla said in a disappointed tone.

"Abuela Rosa worked here on the estate for the family when she met my father-in-law and his brother. She came from a simple family and had no aspirations of living a privileged upper-class life. The likelihood was that she would end up marrying one of the stable hands, and they would raise a family and live on the estate. There are three generations and over two hundred people who live here, the staff with their families. That's how Tío Patricio has blended in so well. He has worked this ranch his whole life. They all have a good life, but they don't have my life or your life or Carolyn's." Carla reached down to stroke Gracie's neck.

She raised her body into an erect posture firmly straddling her saddle and turned in my direction. "I know because, like Rosa, I moved here from a simple family in Venezuela to pursue my dream of running a kitchen and creating beautiful food as well."

"Now look at you," I interjected as we continued to ride.

"Now look at me. I couldn't have possibly ever imagined all this would be the life I would enjoy and give to my daughters. Carolyn can imagine this life. In fact, I suspect she is quite distressed right now that this hasn't been her life. Almost cheated," Carla surmised.

"You know her family back in Chicago has done pretty well, and she is quite successful herself," I interjected once more.

"Collin, you clearly don't understand what I'm talking about. This isn't about wealth or achievement. This is about building something. Having a place of your own that you share with your closest loved ones. A place where you're all connected, and no matter what happens, you all belong," Carla said.

"That would be something." I couldn't relate.

"Since my husband Daniel started courting me, his father has treated me as his own daughter. I was the princess of this fairy tale, and now I am the queen," Carla said.

"So is Carolyn, and I am just a commoner. That is why I don't have the intentions you think I should," I said.

"Just because you can't see yourself for who you really are, doesn't make you common, Collin," Carla said. "Let me ask you. When Carolyn's mom finds out, does she want to come meet her father? Does Christiana come and assume her rightful place as the matriarch of this family?" Carla solicited.

"From what Carolyn has told me, her mother wouldn't have much interest in anything more than visiting here, if even that. She's a city dweller. To be honest, I don't think Carolyn would want to live here either. I agree that she is picturing what her childhood and growing up here would have been like—every little girl wants a pony—but now she loves her career, the city, the jet setting," I offered my opinion.

"Collin, I think you are right, which is why I have asked what your intentions are. My daughters, Rosa and Isabella, are blessings from heaven, beautiful inside and outside, but they are not suited to run the estate. They inherited their father's temperament and personality. He has me to steer the ship and run the estate. So what happens to the estate when Daniel and I are gone? Who keeps it running? Who keeps the legacy living?" Carla paused for several moments while we continued to ride.

She began again, "Collin, whether you know it, or not, God has brought you here to Perú and placed Carolyn in your path for a reason. Do you know what I mean by that?" Carla asked me.

"Yes, I too have come to believe we all have a purpose," I answered, as I tried to ignore the audacity of someone telling another human what God has planned.

"I don't think you do know what I mean. Collin, God has given you a great mission. It is your destiny to marry Carolyn and raise a family together here at El Gran Sueño," Carla said.

"And how exactly do you know that?" I asked.

"This was shown to me in my dreams the night that Carolyn's abuela passed away," Carla announced.

"You had a dream, so I should ask Carolyn to marry me?" I was flabbergasted.

"You have a choice. You can take charge of this assignment from God trusting that you will be blessed more than you can imagine. Or, you can passively wait for Carolyn to decide if she wants you to be her boyfriend at some point down the line, and by doing so, allow your destiny to slip by you altogether. Carolyn needs to see that you know she is what you want, that you have unwavering doubt. If she does not see that, she will not waste her time with you." Carla's audacity was on full display.

"I have absolutely no idea how to respond to any of what you've said." I was being honest with Carla and myself.

"You think I am crazy, no?" Carla asked.

"I think you are mistaken," I replied.

"I am not. I have never been so certain of anything in my life. The question is if you want to seize the moment now, or if you want to spend many years of your life wondering what if. While also leaving Carolyn to pursue the life she thinks she is supposed to live, as opposed to her rightful place here, as the head of El Gran Sueño." Carla had the most powerful thing in the world: passion combined with certainty.

"How can you be so certain that this is Carolyn's destiny? That this is my destiny to bring her back here?" I asked.

"We are never really sure, are we? We always have a choice. I was chosen to reveal your purpose in life to you. No matter what you choose, you and Carolyn will be just fine. It is El Gran Sueño that I am not so sure will survive," Carla answered.

When we arrived back at the house, Carolyn and Daniel were talking in the parlor, and her ankle was just fine. I noticed a grand piano en la sala and, without thinking about it, went over to play something. I tinkered for a minute, deciding what to play, and elected to stay with the western theme from our horseback ride. As I played the first few iconic bars of Desperado by The Eagles, Carla and Daniel came in followed by Carolyn, with just a slight limp.

By the time I sang, 'Don't ya draw the queen of diamonds' Carla and Daniel were dancing something like a Bolero. When I came to, 'You ain't getting no younger' Carolyn sat down next to me on the piano bench, and by the time I reached, 'Don't your feet get cold in the wintertime' some of the staff had gathered as well to listen. As I neared the finale and sang, 'It may be raining, but there's a rainbow above you, you'd better let somebody love you' in unison, everyone including Carolyn sang back in perfect harmony, 'Let somebody love you', and I concluded, 'Before it's tooooooooooo late'.

"I had no idea," Carolyn whispered in my ear before she kissed her cowboy on the cheek.

"Bravissimo!" Shouted one of the staff members as Carla and Daniel lead everyone in applause.

"I think I know what we'll be doing after dinner. Make sure there's plenty of Pisco!" Daniel prophesied.

We had a wonderful family dinner all together, Abuleo Dan and Patricio, Carla and Daniel, Rosa and Isabella, Carolyn and I, and Namash. For the moment, I thought to myself, 'The Eagles don't know what they're talking about. It's never too late.' I also couldn't stop thinking about Carla's dream and raising a family with Carolyn here at El Gran Sueño.

The next morning, Abuelo Dan was having coffee in the parlor when we came down. There was an old shoe box sitting on the sofa next to him with a card on top.

"Buenos días!" Abuelo Dan greeted us, and then he requested the staff bring café pasado for the two of us.

"I meant to ask you yesterday. Did Isabella allow you to take the letters she had been keeping?" Abuelo Dan asked.

"She did," Carolyn answered.

"Good. I want to reunite them with these," Abuelo Dan said as he pointed to the box beside him with a card on top.

"These are all the letters I had written to your Abuela Rosa both before and after she moved to the United States. She sent them back to me in this shoe box from your mother's first pair of baby shoes. The card, I'd intended to give you to return to your Abuela Rosa on your first trip here. It's still sealed, but you can open it." Abuelo Dan concluded his explanation, stood up, and brought the box over to Carolyn.

"Muchas gracias, Abuelo. I definitely will. I don't think right this instant is the best time. I'd rather not have an audience when I read the card and the letters," Carolyn said as she took the box from Abuelo Dan.

"Of course, they are there when you are ready," Abuelo Dan said.

"Abuelo Dan, may I ask you something?" Carolyn seeking permission to ask a question had a certain implication to it. My stomach sank like the Titanic.

"Of course, mi amor." Abuelo Dan lovingly responded with no idea he was heading straight into an iceberg.

"What do you expect my mother, your daughter, to say when she finds all this out? I mean how do you think she'll respond, and what do you imagine your relationship to be with her? You've never met, and you've never spoken, correct?" Carolyn, like her aunt Carla, was always a step ahead of the rest of us.

"I don't have expectations. I guess I would like for her to come visit." Abuelo Dan had the same amount of expectations as I had intentions when Carla cornered me.

"What if she doesn't want to come visit? What if she doesn't want to have a relationship with you at all?" Carolyn asked poignantly.

"I would hope that with a little time, she would change her mind," Abuelo Dan said with a consternated expression.

"You haven't thought about this have you?" Carolyn asked.

"Until recently, I never thought that the truth would be revealed," Abuelo Dan replied.

"That certainly says something, doesn't it?" Carolyn asked her Abuelo and turned to me as well.

"What does it say? I'm not sure I understand." Abuelo Dan seemed bewildered.

"It says you were willing to live with a lie all the way to your death. It says you were willing to go on without a relationship with your daughter. But now, 'the truth has been revealed' as you say. Will you just wait and see what happens after your granddaughter tells your daughter who her real dad is?" Carolyn said indignantly, and I wondered if I was the real dad for Carolyn's pregnancy.

"You don't understand! Your Abuela Rosa wanted to tell

162

Christiana! And she chose you for this moment, for this responsibility! I'm just trying not to overstep my bounds," Abuelo Dan pleaded.

"I understand perfectly. You have a wonderful life here, and whether my mom or the rest of her family were ever a part of it isn't important to you. After you told us the reason for the secrecy, the next thing you should have done was ask if I would take you to Chicago to meet your daughter." Carolyn's voice was powerful, and Pachamama quivered with the words, 'Your daughter.'

"You don't understand," Tío Dan said, shaking his head.

"I understand more than you think I do. If I had a daughter, there isn't a thing in the world that could take her away from me," Carolyn said with absolute certainty.

"Collin, text Namash. Tell him the carriage turned into a pumpkin, and I have to go try on some glass slippers," Carolyn instructed.

"Abuelo Dan, I love you. I'm so glad to have met you. Thank you for the locket and the box of letters. They really are lost treasures. I'm so glad all of this has happened. It's still happening, isn't it? But for now, we need to go. Don't worry, after we pack to head on our way, we'll say our goodbyes. One day soon, I hope, my mother and I will be back in touch with you," Carolyn said as she carried the box of letters in one arm and grabbed my arm with the other to take all of us upstairs.

"Carolyn, it's not too late. We can call Christiana right now if you want?" Abuelo Dan pleaded as we walked out of the parlor.

Carolyn let go of my arm and slowly turned around to say, "Abuelo Dan, with all due respect, 'If *I* want? It's not too late.' It's never too late. Wait, until it is."

Carolyn was done with El Gran Sueño for the time being. Yet for some reason, after all that had happened, after my conversation with Carla, part of me felt like we were checking out, but we could never leave.

EIGHTEEN
MAMA KILLA

Barranco District

Namash came back to my place with us and planned to guide us to Machu Picchu as requested by Carolyn. She wanted to get away and reflect upon the newly discovered revelation of her family's past, as well as the recently discovered future patiently awaiting the two of us in her belly. Carolyn invited Javi and Jennifer to come with us as well. They were constantly working their asses off, and they deserved at least a small vacation. She insisted they come, and they were powerless to resist. They came to stay over as well, so we could go to el aeropuerto all together en la mañana.

Javi broke out one of my bottles of Johnny Walker Blue; the three of us had some catching up to do. Namash sipped on Pisco. Carolyn and Jennifer were enjoying juice on the terrace. Carolyn needed to exhale, and it was good for her to talk with someone who didn't have any interest in her family or the dark secret revealed in her grandmother's letters.

Carolyn had noticed the unusually frequent amount of trips to el baño that Javi and I were taking. She texted me, "Really?"

Namash, who had been refraining from paying any attention to the extra-curricular activities, decided to chime in, "If I may, as we make this next journey together, you should refrain from using that. I don't say this out of judgment, but I would like to show you a more natural and sacred way to ease the pressure from our minds. If you will allow me, I can open a gateway that allows you to feel any way you desire at any time without having to take something to help you feel better." Namash spoke to Javi and me in a gentle voice.

Javi and I sat quietly and didn't respond.

"Don't get me wrong, I'm all for fun. I take a little Pisco when I am socializing. Here is the main thing. I would like for your bodies to be clear when we have our Ayahuasca ceremony in the Sacred Valley. When I introduce the medicine, it will be most useful if it is flowing through your system by itself. One night of Ayahuasca, and you won't need to use la cocaina for 10 years." Namash smiled from ear to ear.

"I need this tonight. This last week has been a lot more than I signed up for," I bargained, realizing that neither Namash nor Javi had any idea what I was really talking about.

"Ok, but just tonight. Then when we are in the Sacred Valley, let's treat our bodies as sacred. For this trip, we want to be very disco," Namash concluded the negotiation.

"Oh, we'll be disco. Don't you worry about that!" Javi said.

"It's fine with me if I never use this stuff ever again. It's like trying to fill a hole with steam," I said.

"I don't really care for it myself. It just smells so good," Javi joked.

"I've quit before, but I keep coming out of retirement. I'm not sure since when, but it hasn't been that much fun for a long time," I admitted.

"Maybe after tonight, you can retire for good," Namash suggested.

"Yes, maybe *after* tonight, Señor Collin," Javi said. He was most concerned with how good a time he was having right then.

An hour or so later, Namash was the first to go to bed. Jennifer wasn't too far behind him and brought Carolyn in from the terrace when she went to tell Javi good night. Carolyn was clearly not thrilled with me and went to bed. That left Javi and me to our own devices. We rotated through the washroom a couple more times each and called it a night.

Cusco

The five of us walked out of the small Cusco airport, took a right turn past the row of waiting taxis, and continued to the small parking lot in front of the terminal. Families and private drivers waited for incoming travelers. Amongst all the professionally dressed tour guides was an eager young man with a big smile, bright traditional Peruvian clothing, and a handwritten sign that had 'Namash' on it.

"Namashi! Namashi!" The energetic young man said while hopping up and down exuberantly.

"Primo! Good to see you! Thank you for coming!" Namash shouted out as we exited the airport parking lot and made our way through the other gathered drivers and tour guides.

"Hey everyone, this is Puma. He knows the Andes from here to Machu Picchu like the back of his paw. Puma, this is Javier and his girlfriend Yanaquyllur, but she likes to be called Jennifer. This is Collin and mi prima, Carolyn. She's one of us Puma." Namash put his arm around Carolyn and pulled her in for a side hug.

"Mucho gusto!" I said enthusiastically as I shook Puma's hand.

"Puma prefers either Quechua or English," Namash directed me, as well as the rest of the group.

"I speak Spanish, but I like to honor my family and ancestors by speaking Quechua—or practice my English to improve my communication with tourists. Pero, mucho gusto, nice to meet you as well!" Puma said while still shaking my hand and bouncing ever so slightly from his left foot to his right foot.

"What about Spanish-speaking tourists?" Javi asked.

"I try to teach them Quechua," Puma said while laughing.

"Jennifer has been trying to teach me for years," Javi said while lowering his head in shame.

"Can you really teach us Quechua? That would be amazing!" Carolyn inquired.

"I told you Primo, she's one of us," Namash said to Puma, and it occurred to me what he meant. Not that she had family from Perú, not that she fit in with their culture, but Carolyn had a voracious curiosity and enthusiasm to discover the magic around every corner of everyday life. Discovery, that's what Namash kept saying. And to that point in my life, I had not been very disco.

Namash faced the group again and announced, "Ok, everyone follow Puma to the van. We are going to take a quick ride, and if Carolyn's credit card is still good, take the train to Ollaytantambo. We'll get off there, the beginning of the Inka Trail."

Namash told everyone to listen up and gave instructions. "Chicos, escúchame! We will assemble as a group to start the hike, and we will stay as a group the whole time. This is very important. If you do not see myself or Puma, stop walking. You are lost, but we will find you. Just call out 'Puma' every minute or so until you hear one of us reply 'Picchu.'

"Puma!" Namash called out.

"Picchu!" Puma rang back as they demonstrated how we would find each other like playing the game Marco Polo.

"This is all very important. You don't want to get lost," Namash said.

Carolyn looked at me and said, "Getting lost is exactly what I want to do."

Javi walked up next to me and quietly asked, "Are we really hiking in from Ollaytantambo?"

"That seems to be the plan amigo. Were you not aware of this?" I asked.

"Señor Collin, you know that is like four days, right?"

"I had some indication of that when Namash gave Carolyn the packing list."

"Madre Maria, does Carolyn know we are walking for four days?" Javi asked.

"I believe so. She said it would be great to blow off some steam," I replied.

"That is what cóctels and la blanca are for. This is not blowing

167

off steam. This is me suffering with back pain for the next month at the bar." Javi was not a fan of the plan.

"Javi, really, I think we will be ok. Namash said he has lots of coca leaves for us to chew on," I said.

"You know they don't get you high, right?" Javi asked.

"No, I did not. Not even a little buzz?" I asked.

"Not even a little," Javi said

"Grancha!" I shouted.

"Got that right." Javi nodded his head up and down.

"I thought you and Jennifer had been to Machu Picchu before?" I asked.

"Yes, Jennifer and I have been to Machu Picchu before. It was an hour-and-fifteen-minute flight to Cusco from Lima. From Cusco, we took a van to Ollaytantambo, and from there, the train to Machu Picchu Pueblo. Then from town, you can either hike for several hours or take a 20-minute bus ride up to the entrance. Señor Collin, I'll let you guess which option we selected." Javi raised his index finger to his temple and tapped three times.

"Carolyn is seeking the authentic Inkan experience. She also paid for the flights, the train, and our entrance tickets, so this trip will be as authentic as she would like it to be," I told Javi.

"Does she also authentically hate her backs and legs?" Javi asked.

"You two know I can hear you, right?" Carolyn turned over her shoulder and asked as we arrived at the van.

Once we were all aboard the train, Puma still hopped and bounced and shouted, "All aboard! Choo! Choo!"

Jennifer and Carolyn faced Javi and me, cheerfully chatting and forming a bond. As the train descended from Cusco into the Sacred Valley, Javi leaned in and quietly said, "I'm serious Collin. I'm not sure I'm up for this. I'm going to do my best, but if anything happens to me—like a heart attack or something crazy—you have to promise me you'll take care of Jennifer and my sister and her kids."

"Javi, really, get a grip on yourself. This is going to be good for us." I was losing my patience with El Mago's drama.

"No, I'm serious. Promise me. Nunca se sabe hermano." Javi reminded me that we never knew what could happen.

"Ok, Javi, I promise. You know I love you hermano." I was being sincere, and I'd started to worry a little bit for Javi. I wasn't in the best shape of my life, but I surfed a lot. And for the most part, ate properly. The only cardio Javi got was from smoking at least a pack of cigarettes a day and doing the bump and blow cha-cha four nights a week.

Camino Inka

We got off the train, and another van loaded with all our camping gear and supplies for our trek waited for us. Thankfully, for the likes of Javi and myself, Puma had a crew Andean superheroes who would carry large backpacks loaded with everything needed to prepare our meals and campsites. Puma introduced us to the crew, who were ready to go, and repeated the instructions Namash had given earlier.

"On our journey to Machu Picchu, we'll be hiking on just one section of the Inka Trail. The Qhapaq Ñan, which means beautiful road, is over six thousand kilometers long. It connected the entire Inkan empire, which spanned across five countries. So when you get tired, just be grateful we aren't going all the way to Quito in Ecuador," Puma said cracking himself up.

"Vamos! Let's go! Hakuchis!" Puma shouted in Español, English, and Quechua.

Carolyn matched Puma's pace as he led the group. Her determination suited his energy, and she bounced through the relatively easy first portion of our trek. I chose to stick with Javi and Jennifer, and Namash joined us to form a group at the rear of the pack. Any of us could have easily been eliminated on the first episode if this were a reality TV show. Team Puma Picchu was well on our way, and there was no looking back.

Puma directed our attention to the first Inkan archeological site on our journey and gave us a brief description of its purpose. "Patallacta was an Inkan checkpoint for the approach to Machu Picchu. Many different tribes would have to pass by this small

169

settlement on their way to reach Machu Picchu or the capital Cusco."

Jennifer said, "I wonder if any of my Huancan ancestors ever made the journey here from where I grew up in the Junín Valley."

"What made you decide to move to Lima?" I asked Jennifer.

"You'll think this is ridiculous, but I saw the movie Pearl Harbor when I was a little girl. I knew then I wanted to be a nurse and help during traumatic situations. You know, Jennifer Garner played one of the nurses in the movie, right?" Jennifer was blushing at first but then proudly beamed as she gave her explanation, and then she blushed again.

"I did not know that," I answered.

"So, I came to Lima to get my nursing education and loved living in the big city. I stayed to work as a nurse, and then I ended up going to medical school. And as of tomorrow, I have been a pediatrician for one year now," Jennifer explained.

"What made you decide to be a pediatrician?" I asked.

"When someone is sick or scared, being able to help bring them comfort is the most rewarding thing I can do. I love working with children because they usually aren't scared. But their parents are terrified, and I can help them feel that everything is going to be ok. The most terrifying thing in life is when something happens to your child," Jennifer said.

"One day I would like to move back to Junín, or somewhere else in Perú, to help children in a rural area. Basic medical services we take for granted in Lima often aren't available in small, Quechua communities." Jennifer made a closed mouth smile and then turned towards Javi.

WE MADE it through the first day and reached the campsite prepared in advance by the crew. Like so much in our modern life, without the hard work of others, we wouldn't have been able to make this journey. After dinner, Namash got us together for a light yoga session.

"This will just be some light stretching and deep breathing in order to let any tightness or discomfort leave our bodies, get a good night of sleep, and help our bodies recuperate for the journey ahead." Namash led us through 20 minutes or so of relaxing movements and breath-work before concluding the session with a gratitude meditation.

"Now, if you would like to, say one word that expresses what you want to receive from our journey. And as you say the word, feel the gratitude in your heart that you will feel when we arrive in Machu Picchu. The universe grants you the desire of your heart you went there to find. Let's close our eyes. Think of your word. Feel the gratitude for having already received it. Place yourself in that moment. I want you to really feel it. It's happening right now." Namash set the stage.

"Let's start with you, Jennifer. If you would like to. Say your word out loud, and we can work our way around the circle," Namash encouraged.

"The Sacred," Jennifer said.

"Friendship," Javier said.

"Energy!" Puma shouted.

"Discovery," I said thinking about how it would feel to one day enjoy finding out what happens next.

"Very disco! You got it, Primo!" Namash whispered as he broke momentarily from the exercise.

"Family." Carolyn reached over and clasped the back of my hand that was suddenly gripped onto my knee for dear life.

"Our bodies, our minds, and our hearts are all connected. If one is not in harmony with the other two, we'll experience discomfort. The longer we go without bringing them back into harmony, the longer our suffering will continue. Gratitude is the one emotion that can quickly alleviate stress, anxiety, or suffering, and it can bring peace and harmony to our body, mind, and heart. Thank you. I am so grateful to have been able to share this moment with you and look forward to all the moments along the way. Namaste." Namash completed our yoga and meditation session with a bow of his head.

"Namaste," we all concurred as Mama Killa shone brightly above, keeping a watchful eye on our journey.

Just as Namash said, we woke up refreshed and ready to take on what would be the most arduous day of our trek to Machu Picchu. We were set to climb nearly a thousand meters in elevation to reach the foreboding Warmiwañusqa, Dead Woman's Pass. The first four hours of the day during the ascent to the top of the pass were free of conversation for the most part. At just over 4,200 meters high, the view was spectacular. Between the mountain ridges we would descend into, the Inka trail meandered on far below. I had a sense of relief for having reached our highest climb on the trek. There was also a sense of wonder as we gazed onto the trail below and thought of the Inka making this journey 500 years earlier.

From there we descended into Pacaymayu, or Hidden River Valley. If there was going to be ranch dressing in Perú, obviously, this is where it would be made. After lunch, we climbed elevation again. The harsh realities of the kilometers we'd hiked and the kilometers we'd yet to hike made their presence known in my legs. Javi seemed to be holding up really well and hadn't complained a bit since we began. I wasn't about to make a peep and admit fatigue before he did. Carolyn mentioned her back was bothering her.

As we neared the top of the pass, we came upon Runkarakay. The tiny circular structure looked like it was constructed as a lookout point, as well as a safe round protective chamber on high ground. I pondered the need to feel safe when there is no way to know what might come your way. We'd had one helluva day of hiking, and the sun began to set over the Vilcabamba mountain range. I hoped Puma and the crew would interpret that as a sign from Inti it was time to set up camp for the night. Thank Mama Killa, they did. We rested as Puma and his crew prepared dinner. Namash went around to each of us individually to share some words of encouragement and let us know that tonight would be the Ayahuasca ceremony. He promised that both our bodies and our spirits would be more than ready to complete the journey we'd begun.

"We need to pass on the ceremony, Collin. You know that right?" Carolyn asked.

"I'm sorry. I hadn't thought of that being an issue."

"I hadn't either, and I don't really know. But obviously, I can't take that chance."

"No, of course not."

"My back won't stop aching, and my legs are unusually fatigued. So I'm going to just say I'm not up for it," Carolyn said.

"Sounds reasonable to me, and I'll say I want to stay with you in case you start having leg cramps." I took her hand.

"Thanks, Collin."

The evening air was chilly, and there was a steady drizzle. As the rain fell, Namash set up a large circle with lanterns and mats. He placed a wooden cup on each mat. In the center, Namash brewed thick brown Ayahuasca tea in a large brown bowl and placed items for the ceremony around it.

He was disappointed that Carolyn and I would be sitting out but presented no pressure to participate. He invited some other sojourners from a neighboring camp and set up for the ceremony in a small clearing beside their campsite. When Namash had prepared everything and was ready to begin, he called for Javi and Jennifer. "Please follow me to the ceremony circle where we will travel together to a different world, a world that has been inside of you all along. We will walk, then dance, then fly through a gateway opened by the Ayahuasca tea."

The clouds parted, and Mama Killa's light shone brightly in the dark night sky. Carolyn and I took a blanket outside our tent to relax in Mother Moon's magical glow. We could hear the ceremony begin in the background as Namash began singing and chanting Quechua Ikaros to stir the magical spirits.

"Ayahuasca, wasn't that the name of that cool restobar in that huge colonial mansion around the corner from your place in Barranco?" Carolyn asked me.

"Yes, indeed. I'm surprised you remember that night."

"How could I forget?"

"I'm remembering every detail as we speak."

"Collin, I think it was that night."

"What was that night?"

"I'll give you three guesses, and if you don't have it by the first one, it's going to be a painfully quiet walk the rest of the way to Machu Picchu," Carolyn said.

"Ah, that night is when it happened."

"Collin, I want this baby."

"Are you sure?" I asked as a drum beat started in the background.

"With all my heart," Carolyn said as Mama Killa left behind the clouds and a light rain began to fall.

"Let's go in the tent," I suggested.

"Oh, now you want to use a tent!" Carolyn laughed. "I'm actually kinda hot. Let's stay out here. It's refreshing," Carolyn said as a loud singular drum beat silenced the ceremony in the background for the moment.

"Sounds good. It's so beautiful out here."

"My back really is starting to kill me. It's been getting worse and worse all day," Carolyn said as chanting began in the background.

I began rubbing her shoulders and felt her forehead. "You are warm," I said.

"Really warm," she said as the chants grew louder and the drum beats grew faster.

There was an engorged vein on her forehead, and I could see her pulse in her neck veins. I felt for her pulse in her wrist. It was getting faster, and her blood pressure was rising. She let out a gasp and doubled over her stomach like she'd been punched and shouted at me, "Let go of my wrist you're hurting me!"

"I'm not holding your wrist!" I shouted back. Carolyn looked down and realized her right hand was smashing the radius and ulna bones together in her left forearm, as she struggled through the pain in her stomach and back.

The pain eased for a moment, and Carolyn had an epiphany. "Oh my god, it's so obvious! I'm the serpent from my dreams. I have a hold on myself, and I have to let go."

"You can hold onto me instead," I said and feigned a brief smile to mask my concern for her discomfort, until another horrific stomach cramp gripped Carolyn. She winced in duress.

"Collin, something, is, something is, not right." She could barely get the words out through her grit teeth and forced breathing.

I shouted for Puma, and he came quickly.

"Puma, I need you to go to get Jennifer from the ceremony as fast as humanly possible," I directed.

He heard the urgency in my voice and took off sprinting.

Puma came back with Jennifer and Javi, and I got up to stop them before they came near Carolyn.

Javi was under the hallucinogenic spell of the Ayahuasca tea, smiling like a circus clown and began to tell me about his visuals, "Oh man, it's like traveling light speed through a hall of mirrors…"

"Not now, Javi. You need to go back to the ceremony. I just need Jennifer. Please don't question me, and just go," I said. He didn't understand, but Puma grabbed his arm and pulled him away.

"Are you ok right now? I need you," I asked Jennifer.

"Yes, I'm fine. This was Javi's first experience, so I didn't drink any tea to make sure he'd be ok," she said.

"Jennifer, Carolyn is pregnant. Her back has been hurting her, and now she's having unbearable stomach cramps." Jennifer started marching toward Carolyn before I finished.

As we went to Carolyn, blood was starting to slowly seep through her jeans. Carolyn saw the small crimson blot slowly expand away from the seam and began to cry. Jennifer was on one side, and I was on the other. Jennifer was soothing her nerves and guiding her to be more calm.

"What do I do? I don't know what to do." Carolyn was pleading with Jennifer.

"All we can do is pray. I'm going to have you lie down. We need to try and calm your body," Jennifer directed.

"Collin, I need you to rest her back in your lap and support her weight," Jennifer instructed me as more cramps seized Carolyn, and she writhed and howled from the emotional anguish of what was happening to her body.

Jennifer began to remove Carolyn's blood-stained jeans, and Carolyn lunged forward to stop her and shouted, "What are you doing? No!"

"I need to be able to see how much you're bleeding to know what we need to do," she explained and continued removing the jeans from Carolyn's legs.

Carolyn raised her hand to her mouth and bit down so hard she broke the skin as she seethed with rage and heartbreak. Her back cramped and sent her torso into a 90-degree angle with her legs. She looked down and could see that a small puddle of blood forming beneath her and shrieked like a prehistoric raptor.

"I have to tell you what is happening, and after I do, the three of us will work together. Ok, Carolyn?" Jennifer said calmly.

"No!" Carolyn shouted not wanting to be told. She dug her heels into the ground, raised her knees, and pulled her body up into her thighs. Her feet anchored her to the soil as she rocked in mental anguish, trying to hold on to dear life.

"Carolyn, you've already lost the pregnancy. Your cervix has dilated to let it out. Everything that is happening to you right now is a natural process that cannot be stopped. You just have to let go and let it happen." Jennifer was the only person who could say out loud what we all already knew.

"No!" The terror and distress from 30 years of being the best she could be, and now being completely helpless when it was needed most, erupted in a titanic howl of inconsolable torment. That one word echoed off every mountain in the Sacred Valley. The reverberation of the terror in her voice rang through all of our ears, bones, and hearts.

The life left her body and Carolyn's head slumped forward. She stared at the soil drenched in blood where she had lost her child beneath her crouched legs and body and began sobbing.

It didn't matter who the father was anymore. There was no burden that could be shared. Misery and anger were all I felt, and I couldn't be feeling a fraction of the pain Carolyn was. This was helplessness. I could only hold her for as long as she needed to sob. Why was it that anyone who ever entered my life always exited with tragedy?

Jennifer gently rocked her backward out of her crouched stance as I cradled her shoulders. Her feet let go of the ground and slowly slid forward. Jennifer gracefully began to gather and pull the blood-soaked soil and tiny clots of tissue away from Carolyn.

She whimpered, "No, don't."

Jennifer left but soon returned with toilet paper and various other linens to clean Carolyn's thighs. She slid underwear and loose sweatpants onto Carolyn and gave us a blanket. She would lie in my lap continuing to lightly bleed for the next several hours. Carolyn's closed eyes gushed tears over her cheekbones, and as her chest cavity throbbed.

She wept.

NINETEEN

THE TEMPLE OF THE CONDOR

A t some point in the middle of the night, Carolyn asked me to help her into our tent, and her exhausted body and soul managed to sleep for a few hours. She woke up and asked me to get Jennifer. When I opened the tent to leave, Jennifer was seated nearby watching and waiting. I motioned for her to come in, and I stepped outside.

Puma was nearby as well and brought me coffee.

"I'm not going to ask. I know enough to know I shouldn't ask until I'm told. Whatever she needs, just tell me. We can send the rest of the group ahead, and she can stay here another day to rest. If she wants to get the hell out of here, I'll take Javi and Namash and have a couple of the guys go slow with the two of you and Jennifer." Puma spoke without a single bounce from one side to the other.

"Jennifer, thank God she's here. I'll let you know what Carolyn wants to do. Thank you," I said to Puma.

I saw Jennifer take Carolyn out of the tent to go get cleaned up more thoroughly. I tried to drink my coffee, but I didn't want it and tossed it on the ground. Full of disdain and contempt I uttered, "Pachamama."

Jennifer brought Carolyn back to the tent and motioned for me to follow them in. The three of us discussed whether it was best to stay and rest for a day or to keep moving. Carolyn wanted to leave.

I spoke with Puma, who had two crew members pack up everything we might need, and he had them guide Carolyn, Jennifer, and me to the next campsite. Jennifer told us this stretch was the easiest terrain and shortest distance. The next morning, Carolyn could choose to either take the walk through Machu Picchu or go to the main entrance to get transportation into town.

Wiñay Wayna

Carolyn handled the hike to the final campsite better than I could have imagined. We would have all afternoon and evening to rest near an ancient Inkan city named Wiñay Wayna, or as Rod Stewart sang in the Queen's English, 'Forever Young.' I couldn't help but think of some of the lines, 'Be courageous and be brave,' 'May you never love in vain', and think of the cruel irony as the crew built our tent there. Jennifer took Carolyn inside and made sure she was comfortable. She slept.

"You need to try and get some sleep as well," Jennifer told me.

"I know. I'm going on adrenaline right now. I'm afraid if I turn that off, I'm going to sleep for 2 days straight," I said.

"She told me she's proud of how well you've supported her," Jennifer told me.

"You've been the one. I don't know what we would have done without you. What can we do for her now?" I asked Jennifer.

"The bad news is not a lot. I've given her a mild pain reliever she can take for the next few days. The good news is we can't do a lot for her because there is nothing wrong with her. This happens more than any of us want to know, and her body is going through a completely natural cycle. Her bleeding has almost stopped, though it will likely reappear with spotting for the next several days or weeks," Jennifer said.

"Is it best to try and talk to her about what happened or not bring it up?" I asked Jennifer.

"I don't know. She'll need to talk about it, and she'll need to be distracted from it, at different times. We'll have to pay close attention to know which. Right now, I want to get her distracted from it. When she wakes up from the nap, I'm going to walk with her into Wiñay Wayna. She needs to rest and go slow, but I'm going to try and keep her going all the way through as planned," Jennifer explained.

Carolyn woke up before the rest of the group arrived at the campsite. She ate.

Jennifer didn't have to persuade her to go for a walk in the nearby site she called mini Machu Picchu. Puma sought me out after the group arrived to let me know he'd told the group Carolyn was under the weather and needed lots of rest. I was in the tent when Carolyn and Jennifer returned. Jennifer gave us some time to ourselves.

"How are you feeling?" I asked.

"Worst question ever, Collin."

"I mean after the walk."

"Worst recovery attempt ever. You're two for two," Carolyn said with just a tiny smile.

"I'm sorry."

"I know, Collin. There's nothing you can say or ask that will be right. It's not going to be possible. So don't try," Carolyn said.

"Ok, just promise me when you want or need something, you'll tell me," I said.

"Collin, I'm, I—I lost our baby. I'm sorry," She said breaking down crying.

She steadied and said, "Collin, I talked with Jennifer while we were walking. I want to tell everyone what happened. I can't stand the thought of everyone trying to figure out what's going on. Do you think anyone has any idea what happened?" Carolyn asked.

"I think Puma has a pretty good idea of what happened, but he's gone out of his way to make sure no one else does," I answered.

"I can't stand the thought of Jennifer having to lie to Javi about what's going on either. She's been incredible. I don't know where I would be without her right now," Carolyn said.

"I don't have the words for what she's done. It's not possible," I said.

"So, I'm going to tell everyone before dinner. Will you stay by me while I tell them?" Carolyn asked.

"Yes, and anything else you want me to do," I said.

"Bubba, just be yourself," Carolyn said.

For the first time since it happened, we cried together. About an hour later, she decided it was time. We changed our clothes, and I went out to find Puma and have him get everyone together.

She prepared.

The group had gathered and sat, waiting in the center of the campsite. Carolyn and I walked up, and Jennifer and Namash grabbed chairs to bring over for us. We sat down, and Carolyn took a deep breath in and let it out. She took hold of my hand and squeezed before placing her hands atop her thighs.

She spoke.

When she finished, everyone cautiously approached one by one and hugged her, sharing the grief of her loss. As each individual peeled away, quiet-side conversations began to form. No one was leaving the area. When everyone had had a chance to connect with her, she stood solitary, surrounded by her friends. She wiped the tears from her cheeks and her nose as she sniffed.

"So how was everyone else's day?" she asked with a laugh through her subsiding tears.

We all laughed.

After dinner, Namash, Javi, and Jennifer came over to sit with Carolyn and me. Namash had a bottle of Pisco, and Javi had a bottle of wine.

Javi took the bottle of Pisco from Namash and said, "Here, you guys could stand to take the edge off."

"I'm going to pass. You?" I asked as I looked at Carolyn who shook her head side to side.

"Wine then?" Javi asked.

"No, I'm good," I responded.

"Do you need a glass? Is that it?" Javi asked.

"No, it comes in one," I delivered the punch line.

"I have to face this without trying to alter my mood and see how it goes," I said.

He didn't press the issue. Puma came over and joined us as well.

181

"Pisco?" Javi offered Puma.

"No, thank you, though," Puma said.

"Wine?" Javi offered as he raised the other bottle in Puma's direction.

"Thank you, but no. I don't take alcohol." Puma's response instigated a horrified expression on Javi's face.

"Ever?" Carolyn asked.

"No, not even for special occasions," Puma answered.

"That's got to be so hard," Javi said.

"Not really, now. I create a state of physical and emotional wellness that allows me to enjoy life on a consistently higher level. I used to think I was consuming alcohol, but I came to terms with the fact that it was consuming me. At first, when I decided to no longer take alcohol, it was difficult. You know, like forbidden fruit. These days when I am offered to drink, I picture forbidden vegetables, and there is no temptation," Puma explained.

"Forbidden vegetables? There's no such thing." Carolyn was flabbergasted.

"Exactly, no one has ever forbidden vegetables. We can eat all the vegetables we want. Not very tempting is it?" Puma said with a laugh.

"That works for you? I might have to give it a try," I said.

"Yes, it works perfectly. Our minds convince us we want what we think we can't have. When we have access to an unlimited supply of something, it becomes uninteresting to us." Puma explained his mental conditioning.

Namash jumped in to take the conversation up another notch. "It's like joy. If we think we can't have it, then we crave it. The more we crave it, the less of it we experience. The truth is, we can receive any emotional experience any time we want. If we tell our subconscious we're happy, our minds will immediately begin to find reasons why that is true. If we tell our subconscious we're missing out on something, our minds will immediately begin to find reasons why. Puma is right about forbidden vegetables, if I tell you that an unlimited supply of joy is available, you'll be less interested. It's the sense that we deserve to be happy, that we deserve to be loved. That is what we all really want."

That was what I wanted. To feel like I deserved to be loved by Carolyn. She raised her hand and said, "I have a question?"

"Go for it, Prima," Namash said.

"What experience should I be telling myself to have right now? Namash, you know, sometimes you are so full of shit."

She left.

Machu Picchu

We rose before dawn to hike up to Inti Punku, the Sun Gate. From there, we'd take in our first views of the hidden gem we'd been questing for. Three days ago it seemed to mean everything. When we reached the summit, the Sun God Inti rose to greet us at his gate.

"Behold! The unhidden gem of Machu Picchu!" Puma declared with gusto.

"I think you mean the hidden gem," Carolyn corrected.

"We can see it now. It's unhidden, no?" Puma knew he had said what he meant to the first time.

"Have it your way. Looks like we still have a ways to go to get to the main site," Carolyn said.

"Yes, we have a little ways to go. Once we reach the agricultural zone above the city, we'll have the iconic view of the site with the towering peak Huayna Picchu in the background. The one you've seen in all the fotos," Puma told us.

"The agricultural zone, is that where the Inka grew all their forbidden vegetables?" Carolyn asked sarcastically.

Jennifer came alongside Carolyn and let her know when we reached the agricultural terraces she could continue through the site or she could leave through the main entrance and get transportation into town. As we continued down the slope, Carolyn asked me for a favor.

"When we get down there. I want you to take a video of me. I've been planning this stupid video for a month. We might as well go ahead and do it," Carolyn said to me.

"Sure, of course," I said.

"Ok, I've got this little dance planned and the music all picked out. You just need to hold the camera high up over my head and walk around me in a circle so you get a 360-degree view of the whole surrounding site. Got it?" Carolyn explained.

"Got it," I said.

The view from the agricultural terraces was spectacular, and Carolyn's body language lifted with just a little spark of excitement. Which made me excited. We set up and started the video. Carolyn did her little dance as I began to circle. From behind me, someone yelled, "Señorita! Señorita! Stop! Stop! Stop!"

I maintained my focus, but when I came around, a security guard for the site charged toward us. Puma and Jennifer went to head him off. He demanded we give him the phone to delete the video, or we would be kicked out.

"You know what? Fuck you! That's what!" Carolyn screamed over the top of Puma and Jennifer, thankfully in English.

Jennifer turned to calm Carolyn down and walk her away from the situation, while Puma pacified the security guard.

"I told him it was my fault. It is my fault. I should have made sure to let this group, in particular, know that dancing is strictly forbidden in Machu Picchu," Puma said.

"You're kidding, right? Why is dancing forbidden? All dancing or just the Lambada? Did you know that Carolyn loves to Lambada on TikTok?" I asked for clarification.

"All dancing. They don't want 50 people up here spinning around or replicating flash mob dance moves at the same time. They'll tell you it's because this is a sacred place, but besides making crowd control impossible, someone will fall off the mountain," Puma explained while laughing.

"That makes a certain amount of sense," I replied.

Carolyn smashed her fist into her palm. "Fuck. That. Guy. He's not going to ruin my day in Machu." With that, Carolyn informed us of her decision to walk through the ancient city.

Puma got the whole group together for a photo, and then we all took turns taking pictures of each other. I hoped one day Carolyn and I would be able to look back at the photos and remember just this moment without anything that had happened two nights prior.

The deep greens and blues of the cloud forest that surround the city were profoundly healing, with each deep breath inhaled, gazing in any direction. The idea that this was a vacation or seasonal home of the Inkan ruler made perfect sense. We stood in one of the most beautiful places on the planet. After three days of trekking through the Andes in the Sacred Valley and seeing all kinds of spectacular views and natural scenery, this was the spot.

Puma pointed out the most notable structures as we went. The Sacred Plaza for important elder meetings, the massive central plaza for gathering the whole community, and the Guard House were some of the standout locations among the various storage houses and residential buildings. Like Larcomar where Carolyn and I first met, Machu Picchu was comprised of functionality and aesthetic beauty. It was a masterpiece of science and art that humans had set inside Pachamama's providential palm.

Puma took us up to view the imposing Intihuatana stone and explained, "This ritual stone was placed to point directly at the sun during the winter solstice. The name translates to 'hitching post of the sun,' and the Inka believed this stone would tether the sun as it made its journey around the earth. The shadows cast would have told them not only the time but also the days of the year. So they would know when the seasons changed."

"Tethering the Sun, I guess the Inka had their attachments too," Javier joked with Namash.

"Seasons change," Carolyn said.

The Temple of Three Windows and Pachamama's Temple were reminders of how prevalent the spiritual and mystical side of life were in Inkan civilization. There was no reason to believe that human sacrifice didn't occur here, as it did at all Inkan settlements, and the Temple of the Sun looked exactly like the kind of place those sacrifices would've been made. The doorway to the temple, gave passage to the heart of the temple, enclosed by a parabolic stone wall. A large rectangular stone platform occupied the center. In one corner of the altar, a step up led to an opening in the wall that Puma called a 'serpent's door.' Through that door, Huayna Picchu was visible behind several stone pools. Two other windows in the temple aligned with the Qullqa constellation and the winter solstice respectively. The divine nature of the highest human aspirations, as well as the darkest base response to fearing the unknown, resided in that building and had been laid bare on that altar.

Puma told us we were approaching The Temple of The Condor, and it would be the last significant building we would see on our way out. Jennifer asked if Puma would wait with the group and took Carolyn and me to stand in front of the large stone that formed the body of a condor in the center of the temple. The Inka built the temple structure around two massive naturally existing rock formations to the left and to the right of the center stone that created the image of a great flying condor. They had carved the head of a condor into the center stone, lodged in the floor of the temple. Jennifer knelt down before it.

She lowered her backpack from her shoulders to the ground beside her and took out a bunch of wildflowers. She began to sing in Quechua, as she peacefully arranged the white flowers into a circle. Jennifer continued to sing as she withdrew a folded white cloth. She set the folded cloth on the ground and continued her song. When she finished the song, she paused before unwrapping the white undershirt she'd used to gather and carry the soil from Carolyn's lost pregnancy. Carolyn already sobbed profoundly, yet quietly, when Jennifer began to sing again.

Jennifer picked up the shirt by its corners and then released the soil into the circle of flowers she'd made. Inti was high above in the sky. Carolyn inhaled her tears and running nose, exhaled, and lifted her face to the sun shining brilliantly within the deep blue sky and billowing, white clouds. Mama Killa wasn't there to witness the beautiful moment Jennifer had created in the daylight. She would come back later, though. Mama Killa would know the best time to shine her light to lead us through the darkness.

TWENTY
SELF-INFLECTION

Laguna Azul

As we walked out of the airport terminal in Tarapoto, Carolyn said she needed a laugh, so we grabbed a mototaxi from the airport to the heart of town. The mototaxi bounced us around like we were on the Millennium Falcon racing through an asteroid field. Once more, I realized my life was in the hands of the cosmos, but it was up to me whether or not I enjoyed the ride. Carolyn's unrestrained laughter each time my head hit the roof of the mototaxi helped as well.

We caught a van to go to a resort on Laguna Azul in the remote Peruvian rainforest to recover, rejuvenate, and reflect. The road brought us to the shore of Rio Huallaga where the van would drive onto a ferry to cross the river. Crossing the orangish-brown, muddy waters of the huge waterway, it became obvious we were in a different part of Perú. This was the rainforest. Muddy river banks tried their best to contain the voluminous amounts of water moving through the rainforest from the south to the north. The flowing river tides would eventually turn east to join the Amazon and be deposited into the Atlantic Ocean, on the other side of the continent.

As we arrived in the little town of Sauce where the resort was located, we noted that it too had a Plaza de Armas. There were no large fancy buildings though, just a cute little square with a non-working fountain in the middle. We checked in and were escorted to our bungalow that faced the lake with floor-to-ceiling glass windows. The view of Laguna Azul, and the hills surrounding it, from our own private terrace and pool was spectacular. This was the perfect place to gather one's own heart and mind. I had arranged for a romantic dinner to be set up on a gazebo floating on the lake.

Carolyn and I walked hand in hand over a floating bridge that tethered the gazebo to the lakeshore and admired the sunset. The angle that the sun fell over the two separate ridges of mountains created an amazing inflection point on the lake. On one side of the lake, nearest to us and to the right, the sky was blue with bright orange while the reflection of the sun on the Laguna Azul water was bright and radiant, much like a sunrise. To our left on the far side, the contrast was stark. The lake was dark and mysterious, and the sky was dark pink and purple. It was breathtaking and mind-boggling. One body of water, one sun, and yet two completely different manifestations of color. There was brightness, and there was darkness.

"Collin, I think this is just what I needed," Carolyn said leaning on the gazebo rail overlooking the lake.

"This sunset over the mountains and lake is mystical. It feels like we're witnessing the moment time was created," I said.

After dinner, we continued floating on the lake in our candle-lit gazebo. I topped off Carolyn's glass, and as my wrist turned to finish the pour, a few more decadent burgundy drops dribbled into her glass. Carolyn remarked, "There is still too much wine in that bottle."

"We can take it back to the bungalow for you," I said.

"Let's," Carolyn said while smiling off into a darkness penetrated by the trillions of shining stars.

"This place is perfect," Carolyn said as she fell into the plush outdoor sofa on our terrace.

"You're right. It's perfect. Out there, in that rainforest

surrounding the lake, there's like 19 different snakes that can kill you in less than 30 seconds," I said in a dead-serious tone.

"Are you afraid of dying, Collin?" Carolyn asked.

"Of course. Aren't you?"

"Less, now."

"For me, the fear of dying isn't what happens after death. What bothers me is the realization the party is going to keep going, and I won't be able to get back in. It's like getting tossed out of a bar when you're over-served. You know it's time to go home, but all you want is one more drink," I explained.

"You're hilarious! You've been thrown out of a bar for being over-served? That is nearly impossible in Chicago." Carolyn was telling the truth.

"I'm an overachiever. It's happened a few times," I replied.

"I can't picture that, Collin. Weren't you an executive when you lived in Chicago? How did you get away with that?" Carolyn asked.

"I was, and I didn't. For a while, yes, but it all caught up to me and came crashing down," I answered.

"How? What happened?" Carolyn asked.

"Do you really want to know?" I asked.

"I do, and I think I should, don't you?" Carolyn asked.

"That's fair. As a general rule, I don't like to talk about that time in my life. Honesty is attractive, but less so when telling someone that for years you spent almost every moment of every day contemplating whether or not life was worth living," I explained.

"Yes, but if they accept you, maybe they can help you," Carolyn said.

"Or they think they can change you, but they can't. So really quickly, it gets tenuous. Then it becomes quiet. The conversations are superfluous so they don't end up treading into dangerous territory of real emotions. That person goes from accepting you and thinking they can help you, to worrying about how much of a toll it will take on their life. It's a normal response. Sometimes it takes days, sometimes a few months, and sometimes years," I responded.

"Then they weren't the right one for you," Carolyn said.

"Just like the boyfriend that cheated on you with your sister?" I compared.

"That's a low blow. Not the same at all. I'm going to give you a pass this time, but don't you dare ever throw that in my face again." Carolyn clearly defined the boundaries of our banter, and bringing up her sister's trysts with ex-boyfriends was not inside of them.

"You know the night we first met? When you asked me if I was suicidal after I'd made a comment about Hemingway killing himself? I was pretty sure it was just a throw-away question on your part, but I dodged the hell out of it anyways," I confessed.

"I remember. The question just slipped out, and it was obvious from your body language you weren't comfortable talking about it. Wasn't sure if you had contemplated it, or someone close to you had gone through with it," Carolyn said.

"Both. I've never told anyone this. I got to a place where I didn't care if I lived or died. The stress from my career, the lingering pain of a heartbreaking divorce, bank-breaking bad investments, and the unfairness of the universe all haunted me. I couldn't carry the weight any longer," I began.

"You were married?" Carolyn asked.

"Yeah, I must have mentioned it before," I answered.

"If you did, I missed it," Carolyn replied.

"Anyways, binge drinking and using drugs were my escape. Nothing made sense. I didn't care about anything anymore, yet I was on the verge of tears at all times because I felt like anything I'd cared about was lost. I thought everything I'd done had been wrong and desperately wanted just one thing to give me hope, or turn out right," I said.

"That's life, Collin. You were in a rut. It's not all rainbows and unicorns. You know that," Carolyn said.

"For sure. But at the time, I didn't think there were ever going to be any more rainbows or unicorns. I will tell you the moment the dam broke, and things might make more sense to you," I said.

"Ok, I'm all ears," Carolyn replied.

"You know the movie 'A Star Is Born,' the newer one with Lady Gaga and Bradley Cooper?" I asked.

"Of course," Carolyn confirmed.

"The Bradley Cooper character, all my life I wanted to be the rock star. I wanted to have the success and fame with the partying, drinking, drugs, and indulgences. Then the comeback story. I wanted all of those highs and lows. Then it ended for him. The same way it almost ended for me. I'd felt like a failure because I hadn't lived my dream, but I realized that everything I'd wanted in life would have led to my undoing. The universe gave me exactly what I needed by not giving me what I wanted. I was balling. I had another chance to make the most of my life." I teared up as I spoke.

"At the time, I was still self-medicating by binge drinking and inhaling as much Vitamin C as I could on a given night. I knew that had a shelf life, so I sobered up for about four months, started eating right, and worked out regularly. I was on the right track, but I knew I needed new soil to grow in. I'd loved Chicago, but it was time for a change." I smiled realizing that I had been right.

"So I packed a couple of suitcases and moved to Lima. When you move halfway around the world where you don't speak the language, and you have to start from scratch, you find out who you really are—really quickly. You figure out you're better served focusing on the person you want to be, as opposed to trying to impress anyone in your social sphere. Their opinion doesn't affect your life one way or another. That was true when I lived in Chicago as well, but it became so obvious after I moved to Lima." It was even more obvious to me as I turned and looked into Carolyn's eyes.

"So when you asked me the first time we met if I was suicidal, I avoided the question because yes, I had been suicidal. I still get those feelings from time to time but manage them much better now. When you left after your first visit, I fell back into the same old emotional patterns of fear of missing out and not measuring up. I missed you, and I felt like we had missed our chance. The light had been shone on the fact that something bigger was missing inside, and I tried to fill it up with all the drinks and lines I could handle. I felt guilty and debauched, depressed and disillusioned." I had rambled on way too long and looked away over the water.

"Thank you for sharing all that with me. It definitely connects the dots on a few things I was wondering about," Carolyn said as she pulled the blanket off the back of the sofa and wrapped it around us. It wasn't cold.

"Namash told me something, the first day we were hiking on the

Inka Trail, that I've been trying to wrap my head around. He said, 'We experience inner peace by taking things out of our lives, not by putting them in,'" I said while staring out over the lake.

"It's so peaceful here. How did you find out about this place?" Carolyn asked.

"I first came here about a year ago. I was looking for land to invest in. Developing a property up here turned out to be a little more complicated than what I was interested in doing, but I told the manager here to let the owners know if they ever wanted to sell, I'd be interested," I explained.

"How much would a resort like this go for here in the Peruvian Amazon?" Carolyn asked.

"A lot of millions."

"Exactly how many millions, Collin?"

"Well, we'll find out tomorrow at lunch. I'm meeting with the owners to see what they have in mind and possibly finalize a deal while we are here."

"You want to run a lakefront resort now, Bubba?"

"No, but I know the perfect couple to do it."

"No! Would they do it?" Carolyn knew I was referring to Javi and Jennifer.

"Before our trip to Machu Picchu, there was no way Javi would move up here. Now it's a different story. He and I have had a lot of conversations over the last several months questioning if we were living life to our potential. Javi could easily run this place, and there's a huge vacant area on the town side of the resort that could be cleared to build out a medical clinic for Jennifer," I said.

"It's genius. I'll finance the clinic. After what Jennifer did, I'll make sure she's going to open her clinic no matter what. They must be so excited. What did Javi say when you told him?" Carolyn asked.

"I haven't said anything yet. I want to get the deal in place before I talk to them about it. I've got a ceiling of what I can afford to put into the deal, and it may go through that. The owners don't really want to sell. They're just seeing what they can get, so I'm expecting their price to be high," I said.

"What's the ceiling?" Carolyn asked.

"If I get a good price for my Barranco condo, $15 million," I answered.

"What do you mean, 'If you get a good price for my condo?' You're not selling that place, Collin!" Carolyn was beside herself.

"I may have to. For this, I would," I affirmed.

"I don't know what to say. Where would you live?" Carolyn asked.

"I don't know, not here. I do want to get away from the city life though. Your Tía Carla said I could come to El Gran Sueño, and I wouldn't have to do much to earn my keep," I answered and gave Carolyn a wink, like the ones she was so good at giving me.

"That woman wants to be stranded with you on a desert island, with the continuation of the human race hanging in the balance. And she has no problem letting everyone in the world, including her husband, know," Carolyn said.

"If she wasn't married to your Tío, I totally would," I said.

"Her daughters couldn't stop whispering, snickering, and making eyes at you either. They aren't married. You like younger women. You should take your shot with one or both of them," Carolyn said while laughing.

"I couldn't possibly do that to their mother," I said without laughing.

"Whatever. So now let's talk about us," she started.

"What about us would you like to talk about?" I asked with a nervous laugh.

"Oh, I don't know, Collin. The same thing I've been trying to talk about since we walked back to the hotel from Huaca Fucking China!" Carolyn said in an agitated voice.

"If you're not that into me, or if you just aren't ready to commit to a relationship, that's fine too. Is that it? That you don't want to commit? It seemed like we were going to commit, and then the miscarriage happened. You're here; you've been right beside me. You've been amazing, but I don't know where we stand." Carolyn crossed her arms and legs.

"I'm definitely into you. You're the most remarkable person I've ever met, but let me ask you a question." I began. "Take me out of it for now. Would you be willing to quit your job and leave your home in Chicago for a relationship?" I asked sincerely.

"I'd take time to think about it, and consider it, but honestly? No, I don't think I would. I definitely wouldn't want a relationship with someone who would ask me to do that," Carolyn answered honestly.

"I agree. You shouldn't, and I wouldn't ask. You won't ever have to worry about that from me. I would always support your career and your aspirations, however they might change or evolve. We have to do what makes us happy. For that exact reason, I'm not moving back to Chicago either. Since I left, my life has been challenged in a hundred different ways, and I've grown exponentially as a person because of that. I'm not done growing. In fact, I feel like I am just beginning," I shared my thoughts, as Carolyn sat quietly listening.

"So if you're not leaving Chicago, and I'm not going back, where does that leave us?" I asked before continuing.

"I haven't brought it up because the last thing I want to do is close this door, but for us to be happy together, we have to be happy as individuals. I'm really just getting started on that journey, but these last few weeks have shown me I'm on the right path. And I'm in the right place. Following you back to Chicago, as tempting as it is, wouldn't work. You leaving Chicago, right now anyway, probably wouldn't work either. You're probably out of tears, but if at any point during this conversation you would like to cry, please do. That way I can go ahead and cry as well and not feel like a loser," I said as the tears welled up in our eyes.

So we cried. We laughed too. Simultaneously, we were all the way in all of our feelings, together and separately.

Whatever our relationship was, hadn't turned out the way we intended. Instead, it had turned out to be what it was meant to be all along.

"Bubba, let's go to bed, and I'm going to pretend I'm Tía Carla." Carolyn knew just what to say.

"Please don't hurt me," I said as she took my hand and led me inside.

As planned, the next day we went to el restaurante to meet the owners, a father and his two sons. They greeted us warmly, and we sat down. The father introduced himself as José, and his sons were Gabriel and Fabio. He ordered a café pasado, as did I and his eldest Gabriel. Carolyn asked for jugo de piña, and the youngest son Fabio ordered a scotch. His older brother cringed a little bit while the father momentarily closed his eyes with a disgusted look.

"Forgive my youngest son. He watches too many movies," José began.

"Collin, it's nice to meet you in person after our phone conversations. We very much appreciate your interest in the property. If I may, Carolyn, what is your relationship with Señor Allweather and purpose for joining us today?" José asked politely.

"I'm visiting from Chicago, and while Collin would be the sole purchaser at this time, I may have some interest in investing for future development of the property." Carolyn answered with confidence knowing she had her place at the table if she wanted it.

"But you're staying together in the same bungalow at the resort, no?" José was confused.

"Yes, we are involved. Is it difficult to imagine that two successful people find each other attractive?" Carolyn asked.

"No, but I've found it best if business and pleasure remained separate," José said.

"Too bad. I've found that business should be pleasurable, or it isn't worth conducting," Carolyn said with a self-delighted smile and got a good laugh out of the table.

Even Fabio looked up from swirling his scotch, to smile almost as though he didn't feel obligated to be there, chuckled, and said, "That was a good one."

"I apologize if I've offended either of you. It's very important to us to know the kind of people who would potentially become stewards of the land and the people who care for it. A couple with a family would be ideal. If you don't mind me saying, you would be a beautiful couple." José clarified his line of questioning.

Fabio returned to his obligations, swirling his scotch and staring out over the lake. He was probably daydreaming what it would be like if he could just do whatever he wanted to. I had more than a little experience feeling the same way.

José and Gabriel continued to ask lots of questions as we

enjoyed lunch and got to know one another. I had questions too, but they were all designed to help me negotiate the price. I didn't give a damn who I was buying from, but they certainly cared about who they were selling to. They asked about my business background in the United States, which I was happy to share, and I captivated them by discussing my current career trading the markets.

Strategically, I shared my plans to have Javier run the resort and Jennifer develop a medical clinic for the town's people. Carolyn informed them that was where she would come in, providing the funds for the clinic. They seemed impressed by the idea. After the staff cleared the table, Gabriel took the lead.

"I think I can safely speak for my father and brother and say we would be comfortable at least hearing an offer from you. As you know, we have not put any thought into selling the property and don't really have a price in mind. Tell us what you think is fair." Gabriel carefully solicited an offer, while his father nodded in agreement. His younger brother stared deep into his tedious, trite, and totally uninteresting future, in the center of the swirling scotch.

I'd brought a legal pad and pen with me prepared for this moment. I wrote, '$9 million USD CASH' on top of the page. Underneath it, I listed a rough draft of my terms: 60 days close from agreement, all staff to be retained and given 10% pay increases, all furnishings, fixtures, and inventory, all naming rights, internet property, and intellectual property of the resort to be transferred with sale. I signed and dated the page and slid the pad across the table. José took the pad, tore the top page off, folded it crisply without looking at it, and rose to shake our hands.

"Thank you kindly for your offer. We will consider it and let you know our response," the father said while shaking my hand, and the two sons took turns shaking Carolyn's.

Carolyn and I walked back across the resort to our bungalow.

"That was not at all how I pictured that going," Carolyn said.

"It was. Right up and to the point where he folded the offer up without looking. This is going to be a tough nut to crack."

"How much did you offer?"

"I started at nine. We'll see. In the meantime, let's enjoy the resort."

Carolyn agreed, and we changed into swimwear to go enjoy one of the floating cabana beds on the lake.

"I could really get used to this," Carolyn said with a contented smile, as we floated gently on the lake.

"You'd get bored."

"You're right. But no, I'm good decompressing for a bit. This is actually the perfect place for me to take some time to read the letters and figure out what I'm going to do about them," Carolyn said.

"Collin, can you entertain yourself for a while? I want to go back to the room and read through the letters and open the card that Abuelo Dan gave me with the box." Carolyn sat up.

"For sure, I'll be right here on this bed floating on the lake, worrying about whether or not that makes me a lazy person."

Carolyn went back to the room to open the two boxes of letters and the card Abuelo Dan gave her. I hoped that at least one would help her reconcile the truth of the past. One thing was for sure, her Abuela Rosa had sent her on a mission that had brought her to a crossroads. At the same time, I was crossing the road without looking both ways.

Whether it had been intentional or not on this journey to Perú, Carolyn had found the letters and the secret they contained. She'd found the jewelry box with its treasured locket. She'd found her estranged uncle—grandfather. And, despite all the odds, she'd found me. I think I'd finally found me too.

Anything could happen, if I was open to it. If I always did my best. That was the key. Action must be taken. The universe and its outcomes are probable by nature. Each moment in time is a new and separate event from the past or future. For the probabilities to work in my favor, I had to give 100% effort for the whole series of events to guarantee my desired outcome. By not taking action to go after what I wanted with the best effort, I guaranteed the outcome I didn't want.

With Carolyn, I thought back to all the other women I'd had interest in over the last 20 years, wondering if any of them could have been the one. Wondering if I'd really given my best effort and fully accepted the risk. I wasn't sure, which meant I hadn't.

I also hadn't ever had the same feelings for anyone else that I had for Carolyn. Was she the one? How would I know? What should I do about it?

CAROLYN FOUND me almost exactly where she'd left me floating on the lake and rejoined me as the sun was beginning to set.

"Collin, I think I figured it out."

"What did you figure out this time?"

"The difference between us."

"Ok! This will be good! And?"

"You're like a red wine bottle. Sturdy and opaque, so it's hard to see what's inside," Carolyn began.

"What wine looks like isn't nearly as important as what it tastes like," I interjected.

"True, but that's not where I was going with that. You're a sturdy bottle; you're not easy to knock over," Carolyn said.

"But when it spills, wow is it a mess to clean up," I said.

"Yep, it's going to leave stains," she said.

"And you?" I asked.

"I'm like a beer bottle. Easy to spill, but the mess fizzes away as fast as it bubbled up," she said.

"I've spent my whole life trying to figure out how not to get spilled," I said.

"And therein lies the difference between us!" Carolyn declared.

"So how do two people who are so different figure out how to get along?" I asked while laughing.

"I'm Phil Jackson, and you're Michael Jordan. I call the shots, you take the shots. Got it, Bubba?" She said while pushing me back with her index finger pressed into my chest.

"Got it, Coach," I said.

"In summation, there are basically two kinds of people in this world," she began.

"Those who put things into two categories, and those who don't," I concluded.

"Awww! We are finishing each other's sentences now." Carolyn pointed out how far we had come. "Collin, I've figured something else out too," Carolyn said.

"What's that?" I asked.

"I'm not bringing these letters back home to Chicago," Carolyn said, and I hated the way she said home. Like it was more than just a place she lived.

"Don't you think your mom would like to see them?" I asked.

"I'm sure she would, but I'm not going to tell her about Abuelo Dan," Carolyn said.

"I don't know what to say. I hadn't even thought of not telling your mom as a possibility," I responded.

"There are a few things I've thought about. First, unless my mom went to the estate, met her Tío Dan—who also actually happens to be her father—met her Tía Isabella on Lake Titicaca, and met her brother Daniel and his wife Carla, she would have no context to understand what I was trying to explain," Carolyn said.

"Definitely not," I said.

"Second, all those years we never went to Perú, because Abuelo Samuel said not to, was just an excuse. My mom certainly didn't always do what her father wanted. If she did, my dad would have been a different guy. She just didn't want to take the time, and she isn't that adventurous. Don't think for a second that she wasn't invited along both times I came," Carolyn continued.

"That seems so weird to me she wouldn't want to come," I said.

"Third, to that point, I don't think she wants to know. She knows enough to know there's something she should want to know, and you know what? She doesn't want to know it. That part is the hardest for me, but that is the part that also made up my mind. She likes her illusions," Carolyn explained.

"We all do," I said.

"I can't for the life of me figure out why Abuela Rosa kept this secret for all these years. It seems likely that she did it to protect my Abuelo Samuel's connection to my mom. He took a great deal of pride in providing everything any of us wanted. Whatever activities I had in high school, he attended nearly all of them. By the time I was at Northwestern playing basketball, he was the one at all my games—all my games—not just the home games," Carolyn said.

"Yeah, I don't know how you could take that away from someone," I said.

"One of my favorite memories, from my playing days, was hitting a game-winning shot at the last second. I celebrated like crazy with my teammates. Afterward, I looked in the stands and saw mi Abuelo Samuel, this short little Peruvian man with tears in his eyes. I think about that now, and I don't believe for a second he was cheering for his niece's daughter." A tear rolled down Carolyn's cheek.

"No, you were his granddaughter," I said as I put my arm around her.

"I also think he was so present by the time I came around, because he wasn't present at all for my mom when she was young, and he was trying to make up for it. When you're that young and become a parent, it's damn near impossible to commit to a high level of achievement as a professional, while also being present with your child. I know my mom appreciated his hard work and the life he provided for her, but she didn't know him at all and resented him for it. She didn't try and get to know him as they both got older. He should have done more to connect with her, but she could have done more too. I know she regretted it after he passed away." Carolyn shook her head from side to side.

"Maybe this will be good for your mom then?" I wondered out loud.

"Love your newfound optimism, Collin. But if she didn't want to get to know the man she thought was her father because he worked too much, how would she react to a father who wasn't in her life at all? She would hate him, she would hate her mother, and she would hate herself for not appreciating the father who raised her as his own." Carolyn had thought everything through.

"You're right," I said.

"I keep thinking about why my grandmother chose me. I couldn't figure it out, other than my own narcissistic inclination to believe I'm more responsible and qualified than my sister. There had to be more to it than that. It turns out, I think, she told me quite directly when she asked me to come to Lima for the jewelry box. She meant exactly what she said, 'Your sister can't keep her mouth shut.' She had two purposes. She wanted to give Abuelo Dan the chance to acknowledge a secret he'd been holding onto for nearly his whole life, and she wanted someone in the family to know so that the truth didn't die with her. The truth is my inheritance. I think it would be easier for me to tell my mom, but it wouldn't be better for her," Carolyn said.

"No, but—and don't get spilled like a beer bottle—doesn't she deserve to know the truth?" I asked.

"We all deserve to know the truth, but taking away someone's hope for the future is bad. Destroying their past is the most devastating thing you can do to the psyche. So I'll bear the truth by myself, without bearing it to my mother," Carolyn said.

"Nice job, you totally wine-bottled that one," I said while digesting all the ramifications of what Carolyn had just said. One of which was that Carolyn had no intention of pursuing a relationship with her family here.

"I'm going to give her the locket. That's what Abuela Rosa really wanted, was for her to have that. Then I'll tell her all about the time she almost had a grandchild," Carolyn said with a slow roll of her eyes pulling her head from shoulder to shoulder on a rainbow's arc.

"That's not going to be easy," I said.

"No, but she'll take me shopping or something fun. I don't know, she'll know what to do. There's a lot of things that could be said about my mother, but when you're in the middle of the desert, she is a cold bottle of water," Carolyn said with a smile.

"So anyway, that's my decision. I'm not taking these letters back with me to Chicago. They were sent here, and they belong here. They belong with Abuelo Dan. They belong to the next Rosa and Isabella. I want you to hang onto them for the time being, and when it's convenient, take them back to El Gran Sueño." Carolyn handed me the two boxes of letters with a card addressed to 'Tío Dan, Mi Abuelo Especial'.

"What do you plan to say to your mom, about the letters? She's going to ask," I asked.

"I'm not sure. Maybe I will tell her it was all a dream, and she can go back to sleep," Carolyn answered.

I wanted to tell Carolyn about her Tia Carla's dream. That it was her destiny to move to Perú, be the head of El Gran Sueño, and have a family. With me.

I didn't believe that was necessarily the case with a hundred percent of my heart, though. Just because it was revealed in an allegedly divinely inspired dream. Just because it made all the sense in the world to me now, as opposed to the first time I heard it. Just because I wanted it with every fiber of my being. Yet, I couldn't say the words. I rationalized if this was our destiny to be together that Carolyn would have it revealed to her somehow too.

For some reason it hadn't occurred to me, despite Carla's direct pronouncement, that maybe—just maybe—I was the vessel the universe had chosen to reveal Carolyn's destiny to her.

TWENTY-ONE
SUNSET

Lima

C arolyn and I spent the last two days of her trip back in Lima. We'd saved the grandest of all the Plazas de Armas, set beside el Río Rímac, to see last. The center of Lima, with its museos, grand palacios, and divinely inspired cathedrals, may be the finest example of an Old World city existing today. During our exploration of the soul-stirring natural wonders of Perú, I'd almost forgotten what life was like without the mind-numbing barrage of honking horns in constant bumper-to-bumper traffic. Afterward, we went to my place, took a trip up to the rooftop terrace, and wished upon the stars. With the whooshing of the waves and the smell of the Pacific Ocean, I knew I lived in a truly magical place. I've heard locals call it 'Lima Love.'

On our last night together, we enjoyed cena at La Rosa Náutica. El restaurante hovered over the ocean at the end of its own dedicated pier. It was the perfect place for us to watch the center of our solar system drift out of sight, together in Lima one last time. The orangish-red orb was so big and inviting it seemed almost as if we could reach out and take hold of it without getting burned.

After dinner we went back to my place, and I knew that would be the last time that would be happening for the foreseeable future. As I opened the door, Carolyn made a beeline through the living room to the terrace. "Just making sure!" she shouted back to me, as I casually came down the hall.

"Sure of what? That the sun has set?" I asked.

"No, that those terrible birds hadn't come back!" Carolyn said laughing.

"No, the serpent, who shall remain nameless, killed them all with their venomous bite, remember?" I reminded Carolyn.

"As soon as the serpent killed those damn birds in my dream, we should have known I was the serpent," Carolyn said while laughing.

"Namash told us the serpent represents wisdom. We should have known then."

I flipped the lights out, and we crawled into bed. I closed my eyes, but my heart was stuck open. Melancholy tears ran from the corners of my eyes. The future would be different, or it wouldn't. I would be different. That thought made me happy.

The next day, I would wake up and enjoy each moment as it came. Bewildered by each emotion, less sure of everything, while at the same time knowing everything I needed to. Thoughts and emotions would arise spontaneously, and I'd let them drift away like condors spiraling effortlessly to higher levels of understanding and enlightenment: to be fully awake and at peace enjoying each moment. That would be tomorrow. At the moment, I couldn't sleep a wink.

Neither could Carolyn, but we didn't talk either. We just laid there knowing the other one wasn't sleeping either, back to back, with our knees pulled up, not quite in the fetal position. We had become inseparable, except for the fact that tomorrow we would be separated. Carolyn had had enough, pushed herself up in bed, and turned the light on.

"Collin, you know what's missing in romance? No one writes love letters anymore. 'Wherefore art thou,' is replaced with a kissy heart face emoji these days. We've only known each other a few months, but we've gone through what couples normally take years to experience together. I've been drawn to you since the moment we met, and by the time we were walking along the malecón in

Huacachina, I've wanted some validation this was in fact more. That was impulsive, and it put too much pressure on you. I did it again the other night at the resort. You know, it's ok if we take more time to figure us out." Carolyn explained urgently that we didn't need to be so urgent.

"We still end up with the same problem. I'm here, and you will be there," I said.

"You say that like air travel doesn't exist between the two countries. We have the means. Can't we just keep seeing each other, and see how it goes? Time will tell us if we need to reconsider our geolocations to be together full time, or if this was just meant to be an amazing, once-in-a-lifetime, but short-lived experience together." Carolyn seemed to think we had a chance.

"You're right. My feelings for you are beyond anything I've ever experienced, and I'm trying to put our relationship into one box with the word 'all' written on it, or another box that says 'nothing' on it," I said.

"Why? Never mind. Let's make a deal. I get six weeks of vacation per year. We can take one week every two months and go somewhere together," Carolyn began.

"May I bring Tía Carla?" I interrupted.

"Collin, I'm being serious. Will you come to Chicago for one week during the in-between months? Let's see what happens." Carolyn had put together a pretty good plan, while I had been laying there sorting through my emotions.

"Deal. I'll even come the weekend before and stay the weekend after to maximize the time," I committed to the plan.

"Stalker." Carolyn raised her eyebrows.

We embraced and stared into each other's eyes with the brightest of smiles. I had hope that everything was going to be ok, maybe even better. Carolyn turned the light out again, and we fell asleep wrapped in each other's arms and legs, like kittens in a box or two pumas after a successful hunt. The sun was down, and it was time to dream.

JENNIFER WAS TIED up with work at the hospital, but Carolyn wanted to see Javi one last time before she flew back to Chicago, so we stopped by the bar at Tanta.

"Señorita! You have come to tell your good friend, Javier, goodbye!" Javier exuberantly greeted at least one of us as he came rushing around the bar to embrace Carolyn.

"See you later is more like it. I don't like goodbyes. I'm making Collin promise to drag you along on a visit to Chicago," Carolyn said.

"I would love to come to see your home." El Mago graciously accepted her invitation.

"Please tell Jennifer that I am eternally grateful to her," Carolyn said.

"I will," Javi replied.

"Javi, you know that she is beyond incredible and that you are lucky to have her right?" Carolyn asked.

"I do," Javi said.

Carolyn took both of Javi's hands into hers and said, "Then stop wasting time and act like it."

"Yes! Of course! Let's get you one last Pisco Sour!" Javi said as he pulled away from Carolyn and retreated behind the bar.

Carolyn had said what she needed to and let the mood lighten. She and Javi exchanged jokes about ghosts at bars and iconic, yet outdated, American TV shows. I was both joyful, and my heart ached all at once. I had a hold of the serpent's tail, but I had to let her go.

When it was time for us to head to the airport, Javi came from around the bar and gave Carolyn a huge hug. They were smiling brightly, and both of their eyes welled up with tears. It occurred to me I hadn't ever seen my close amigo cry. Then I flashed back to all the tears shed in recent days by Carolyn and me.

"I'll remember this day forever. The 9th of March, in the year 2020. The day Carolyn Grant broke Perú's heart." Javi was not making a joke.

I had a car pick us up at Larcomar to take us to the airport, so I could walk in with Carolyn. We could say goodbye inside the airport, instead of a hurried hug on the curbside getting screamed at by airport security officers to move the car along. There was a nice food court in the terminal before passengers went through airport security where we could spend a few more minutes together. At this point, I was cherishing every second, as though it would be the last, before Carolyn departed.

We climbed in the back seat, and as we pulled away, Carolyn said matter of factly, "You know what they say. When life gives you lemons, make lemonade with haste makes waste."

"You know what they say. Time flies when you're all fun and games until someone gets hurt. Albeit, just a manner of speaking," I rationalized.

"Be that as it may, only time will tell. It's just a matter in the nick of time, now and forever," Carolyn clarified.

"All's well that ends well if the cat's got your tongue with your tail between your legs writing on the wall without a care in the world looking a gift horse in the mouth," I said in a single breath.

"The cat caught the canary in the coal what's mine is yours is a strange kind of love thy neighbor as thy self-inflicted wounded duck with its pants down," Carolyn said triumphantly.

"And we have a winner!" I declared after she expertly wove eight cliches into one tapestry of linguistic genius.

"Takes one to know one." Carolyn took one last bow and rested her head on my shoulder as we rode to the airport.

"Like a snake in the grass," I said.

I had the same sick feeling in my stomach. Though not quite as bad as the first time Carolyn went back to Chicago, the nausea and heartache were wrenching nonetheless. I didn't despair this time. There wasn't the same uncertainty as before. This was only going to be a few weeks before I visited her in Chicago, and it would be hard. But not nearly as unbearable as the last time she left.

I pictured Carolyn walking through airport security, drifting little by little out of sight like the setting sun. I've always had an optimism watching the sun set. The intuition that tomorrow will bring a new day filled with infinite possibilities. Which reminded me that every challenge in my life had been an opportunity to grow and learn. A chance to seek a deeper understanding of the opportunity afforded by the universe in that moment. While the sun sets in one place, it is rising in another.

"Keep me posted when you book your flight to Chicago," Carolyn said as she took hold of my face through my beard with both hands.

"Text me when you land," I said.

"I will. Look me up if you're ever in Chicago. Ha! I've always wanted to say something like that! Down too. Look me down. Look me up and down. If ya know what I mean. Ha!" Carolyn worked in one last outburst as she slapped her thigh.

"Take care of yourself, Carolyn," I said, knowing she would.

"Collin!" Carolyn said as she wrapped her arms around my neck and pulled me in for one last embrace.

I leaned back my head with her hands clasping my neck, and my hands firmly holding the small of her back as our waists remained together.

"Collin…" Carolyn repeated as she started to say something and then paused.

"Yes?" I slowly asked, unsure I wanted to know what she was going to say.

Then Carolyn said everything and nothing at all, all at once, and for all, "Write me love letters from Lima."

POSTLUDE

The author would now like to play a few notes…

Throughout Perú in 2020, 2021, and 2022, I had countless life-changing experiences as I explored and interacted with the rich tapestry of human history set in the incredible natural wonders of Perú. The most important thing I learned is that happiness, fulfillment, or whatever word we ascribe to the feeling that our life is how we want it to be, is found inside each of us. There is not something we can search for, and find externally, that will provide meaning or lasting joy. We already have everything we need.

Lima, is a city that has preserved the architecture and culture of The Old World. Beneath that layer of Spanish Colonialism lie remnants of the Inkan empire. Miraculously, yet another layer has been uncovered by archeologists, the mysterious ancient world of the Lima culture indigenous tribes that existed before the Inkan Empire. In one place, you can witness the differences and similarities of four epochs of human history. It occurs to you that customs, lifestyles, and belief systems in a way similar to energy or matter, are neither created nor destroyed but rather morphed from one thing to another thing that will inevitably become something else. Just like people.

Larcomar is one of the most American places in Lima. It's hard to explain why. You will find high-end retail and over-priced, crowded restaurants. At Larcomar, you pay more just so you can say you had lunch at such-and-such restaurant in Larcomar, or you found a great new bag at such-and-such store in Larcomar. Luxury side by side with a line to get into Friday's, decked out with electric guitars, and posters of Elvis, Marilyn, Jimi Hendrix, and Jim Morrison, have something to do with feeling like you are in the United States.

Larcomar always reminds me that no matter where you are in the world, we all have hopes and dreams. In this place, modern indulgences are carved into the dark coastal bluffs of Lima's Costa Verde, perched just above the Pacific Ocean. There is beauty in human-created and crafted luxury, and when it is properly placed alongside the beauty of the pre-existing natural world, something really magical happens. Humans and our buildings, all of our entrapments, are nature too. Co-existence is simply just existence, with ourselves and this tiny spinning rock we call home.

One day I went to Larcomar to have coffee and write. The sound and smell of the ocean were strong that day. A steady breeze blew seagulls, salty air, and a surplus of potential over Lima's beachfront bluffs onto the sun-drenched sea foam of the ocean. The air and my soul had something alluring stirring in them, as I descended the stairs into Larcomar. When each step landed, I felt closer to destiny, that something or someone was waiting. Each submission to gravity gave me the feeling, though tempered, that anything could happen at any time if you are open to it. For most of my life, to that point, I had not been. I just didn't know any better.

The universe, with its quantum field of endless possibilities, has a funny way of working out for those willing to ask it to. As long as it knows what you expect from it. As long as you know that it will give you what you need before it gives you what you want. Happiness and contentment, like love and abundance, are elusive to those who work the hardest to acquire them. Lest the paradox be supplanted that everything you have ever wanted will be granted, once you realize that you already have everything you could ever want.

That day, while sorting through all the imaginary voices in my head, two new voices stood out: Carolyn Grant and Collin Allweather. We had all come from Chicago for different reasons, looking for different things.

Collin had weathered all kinds of storms, and this Hurricane Carolina should be no different.

SHAUN RANDALL

Puente de los Suspiros, Barranco, Lima, Perú, March, 2020

Shaun Randall is originally from San Diego, California and spent time as an adolescent in Portland, Oregon; Colorado Springs, Colorado; and South Florida. Growing up in those settings, on the coasts and in the mountains, instilled a wonder and love for our natural world. In 2008, Shaun moved to Chicago, Illinois which has left an indelible mark on his life and work. In early March of 2020, Shaun took a vacation to Lima, Perú where the next chapter of his life began when he met his fiancé Eliet. They currently make their home together in Barranco, Perú.

Shaun Randall's writing addresses the struggle to find inner peace and happiness amongst the trappings of modernity. Teaching and wisdom from ancient Latin American civilizations and eastern philosophies permeate his writing as he relates modern western experience with a dry sense of humor and zen master deadpan. Shaun uses an unorthodox approach to creating his phrases that challenge readers to think twice and sort through their emotions. To make sure they are deciding what to think and how to feel for themselves, in spite of the inundation of external influences on a minute-by-minute basis. Shaun Randall's purpose is to help people enjoy their lives to the fullest by choosing their own path in lieu of the many offered by others, in this miraculously unreal thing we call reality.

ALSO BY SHAUN RANDALL

Words Like Wine, 2020, poetry
A Peace of My Mind, 2021, poetry

coming soon…

The Manifestation Method, personal development philosophy
A Peace Within, poetry

The next installment of the Grant-All weather series, novel

If you loved this book and want more people to share in your experience, please help us spread the word by leaving a five-star review with the outlet you made your purchase. To receive Shaun's newsletter and learn more about the author and his work, please visit:

For podcast, television, radio, or live speaking appearances please email:
info@shaun-randall.com

Made in the USA
Columbia, SC
24 December 2022

74946031R00124